D0045519

THE CLOAK SOCIETY

FALL OF HEROES

Also by Jeramey Kraatz
The Cloak Society
Villains Rising

JERAMEY KRAATZ

HARPER

An Imprint of HarperCollins*Publishers*

The Cloak Society: Fall of Heroes
www.harpercollinschildrens.com

Library of Congress Cataloging-in-Publication Data
Kraatz, Jeramey.
        Fall of heroes / Jeramey Kraatz.
            pages   cm. — (The Cloak Society ; 3)
        Summary: Masquerading as a new group of superheroes, the evil
Cloak Society has taken over Sterling City—and ex-villain Alex Knight
must bring them to justice once and for all.
        ISBN 978-0-06-209553-4 (hardcover)
        [1. Superheroes—Fiction.   2. Supervillains—Fiction.]   I. Title.
PZ7.K8572Fal   2014   2013047952
[Fic]—dc23   CIP
                                                                          AC

Typography by Ray Shappell
14 15 16 17 18   CG/RRDH   10 9 8 7 6 5 4 3 2 1
❖
First Edition

For Meradith, my sister and original partner in crime.

CONTENTS

THE CLOAK SOCIETY

FALL OF HEROES

A TARNISHED
CITY

Alex Knight had never worn a mask. The High Council had always been against them.

"The Cloak Society has no need for such disguises," his mother once said when the subject came up. "At least, not *actual* masks. They cut off your peripheral vision and move around too much. Unless you glue one to your face, it's a liability. Masks are just gimmicks, like capes or sashes. If you really think a few inches of cloth or plastic are going to keep your identity a secret, you're an amateur."

Now, standing in an underground tunnel hidden below Victory Park, Alex hoped his mother was wrong. He placed a black bandit mask over his eyes, tying it tightly at the back of his head, careful not to get any of his brown, wavy hair stuck in the knot. As he adjusted the eyeholes in the front, he used his telekinetic powers to pull the hood of his dark trench coat up. It caused a shadow to fall over him, hiding his face completely except for two faint sparks of blue.

Beside him, another Cloak deserter, Mallory, super-heated one of her index fingers and expanded the eyeholes on a white, feathered mask that would cover the top half of her face. It looked as if the mask was crying runny plastic tears.

"These things are so tiny," she muttered. "No one has eyes this small."

"How did I end up with *this* one?" Kyle asked. His face was covered in a clear mask with painted-on, clownish features. It pushed up his blond hair and completely hid his identity. "I don't even know what I'm supposed to be."

"That's totally not my fault," Alex said. "This is all they had left at the costume store nearest to the lake house. Or at least, that's what Misty told me."

"But you just get to wear that domino mask? That's not even a costume."

"Yeah it is. I'm a bank robber."

"When I met you, you were robbing a bank," Kyle said. "That's *not* a costume."

"You're a Junior Ranger. People know your face too well. Besides, Kirbie's not complaining." Alex turned to look at Kirbie, Kyle's twin sister, whose face was hidden by a full vinyl werewolf mask.

"It smells super gross in here," she said. Her voice was slightly muffled. "But he's right. People are more likely to recognize us. Let's just get going before I start to get claustrophobic in this thing."

Mallory slipped her disguise on, pulling some of her chestnut hair out from under the elastic band. She gave Alex a thumbs-up, and they were off. The four of them made their way through a series of hidden locks and doors until they were finally passing out of a rusty old drain and into the midday sun. There was a metallic click as the drain locked back into place. Kyle motioned to a clump of vines. They grew over the metal grate as if by magic—though it was really just Kyle's power over plants—until it was completely hidden. Alex looked around, the autumn trees crackling with the blue layer of energy that had tinted his vision ever since he'd developed his telekinetic powers. They were far enough off the normal trails that no one had seen them. Perfect.

"All right," Alex said. "We've got a mission to complete."

Sterling City had been known as the birthplace of the twenty-first century, a metropolis that symbolized humanity's future. Some referred to it as paradise, a spring of progress and accomplishment. It had even been called a utopia—the safest and happiest place on earth. This city nestled in the center of Texas had prospered over the years thanks to the watchful eyes of a team of superheroes, the Rangers of Justice, but when Justice Tower had crumbled a little over a month before, it began to rot. Alex feared the people of the city would soon find out just how far it had fallen—unless he and his friends could do something to change things.

In the city's heart was Victory Park, a place where you could lose yourself, forgetting that you were in the middle of a sprawling concrete jungle. For Alex, it was where many of his problems had first begun. There, ten years ago, his family had fought against the Rangers and been defeated. At the southern edge of the park was the bank where he'd gone on his first mission—to steal a diamond. And it was where he'd started to question the motives of the Cloak Society. The rest of the world referred to the group as "supervillains," but Alex knew them as his family—the people he'd eventually turned against.

"It feels like I haven't been here in forever," Kyle said, taking a deep breath as they moved through the brush. "I basically lived here this summer. I know these trees better than I know most people."

Soon they came to an actual trail, one that Kirbie and Kyle recognized. From there they walked mostly in silence, and stopped only once, when they came to the statue garden erected as a memorial for all the Rangers lost in the battle against Cloak a decade before. Silvery sculptures of men and women forever stuck in heroic poses. Alex and the others stood silently for a few seconds before trekking on again.

They couldn't pause for too long. They had a job to do. Others were counting on them.

They made it through the park undetected. On the other side, the streets were swarming with people—sidewalks jammed with witches, goblins, and ghouls. A car honked as it sped past a mummy, almost knocking it over. A young ballerina paused and gave Kirbie a curtsy.

"We never got to go out in costumes on Halloween." Mallory sighed.

"People get weird when you can't tell who they really are," Kyle said flatly. As he spoke, his breath fogged up the inside of his mask. "Technically this is the Fall Festival. It's one thing I definitely wasn't looking forward to policing this year."

"Me neither," Kirbie said. "But I think I'd rather be doing that than what we're about to do."

"There." Kyle pointed to a street blocked off by traffic cones. In the distance, Alex could make out food trucks and street vendors. Somewhere, a band was playing. "That's the best way to the museum."

They started walking again. More importantly, they blended in. To anyone on the street, they were just four more kids in costumes, not two Junior Rangers and two former supervillain trainees. They were unrecognizable in the throng of citizens and tourists who'd shown up to partake in the city's annual festival. This was their cover—not the shadows and darkness that Alex had been taught to use to his advantage, but the simple anonymity of being one in a crowd of thousands. They had to play it safe. In the past few weeks, Cloak had made sure all their faces had been on the news. They were Sterling City's most wanted.

The area north of Victory Park—the arts district—was a maze of tall, darkly bricked buildings and glass storefronts touting expensive clothing and electronics. The city had strung lights in the trees for the festival, and fake spider webbing hung in stringy cotton-candy clumps. There were cameras on every major street corner, too, but those weren't decorations. They were part of the city's newly implemented "Ever Watchful" initiative. Alex frowned every time they passed one, resisting the urge to crush it with his thoughts. Instead, he suggested they avoid any big intersections and stick to the side streets. Eventually, they turned a corner, and Alex came face-to-face with his mother: Shade.

He froze.

She looked strange to Alex. It wasn't just that she wore a Rangers of Justice uniform instead of her usual Cloak getup, a golden starburst gleaming on her chest. There was something foreign about her expression. She was radiant. Alex had never seen her lips stretched so wide before, with so many teeth exposed. He could swear that there was a twinkle in her eye, but not the metallic silver flash that meant she was concentrating on using her telepathic powers.

Something else. He wondered if it was a trick of the light.

Or maybe just an effect added to the photo after it had been taken.

His mother's image was pasted on the side of a building. She was oversized, at least three times larger than she was in real life. Beside her was Volt, Alex's father. Photon stood next to the man, and in front of them was Titan—who Alex's parents now referred to as their son in interviews. Even on a poster, his smug smile got under Alex's skin. All of them wore Ranger uniforms that matched Shade's. Above them, in shining gold letters, was RANGERS OF JUSTICE: THE PROTECTORS OF STERLING CITY.

It had been almost a week since Photon—*Dr.* Photon, technically—had appeared at a press conference and paraded Alex's parents and Titan in front of news cameras, calling them his saviors and the city's only hope against the Cloak Society, who had recently gone public. Everyone started calling Photon and his teammates the "New Rangers," since it was the first time the Rangers' roster had changed so drastically in a decade. Part of Alex took delight that this nickname stuck, as he'd previously heard the term used only to describe weak, virtually powerless amateurs wanting to be known as heroes. The city all but turned itself over to the New Rangers, desperate for heroes to fight against the underground supervillain menace they hardly dared speak about. Those who were skeptical of the new team were quickly won over as their exploits began to surface. There were news reports of a Cloak hideout discovered in an old Gothic mansion on the outskirts of town. Photos of the New Rangers standing beneath a crushed silver skull in the entryway of the base popped up in every newspaper and website imaginable. They were on the news every night for vanquishing some great threat to the city. Crime rings were exposed. High-profile robberies were foiled. The cameras were always rolling, and the New Rangers were always there to save the day.

All of it was an act.

Shade, Volt, and Titan were members of the Cloak Society. Everything was orchestrated by Cloak's High Council. Photon had been brainwashed by Alex's mother, who, to keep the public in the dark about her telepathic abilities, positioned herself as the New Rangers' weapons expert without any *real* superpowers. It had been Alex and his teammates—Junior Rangers and ex-Cloak members—who'd stormed the old mansion on the outskirts of Sterling City, taking out a group of Cloak's elite warriors, the Omegas. But the New Rangers took credit for the event, spinning the news in their favor, turning Alex and his team's victory into their own.

While half of the Cloak Society's most powerful members served as the New Rangers, the others popped up every so often to remind the city that they were still there, plotting its downfall. The grinning silver skulls they wore on their chests became symbols of terror. As the heroes and the villains of Sterling City, the Cloak Society could do whatever they wanted, playing off one another to keep everyone under their control, until the public one day woke up and realized that their city wasn't theirs anymore. And by then it would be too late to do anything about it.

Unless someone stopped them. Soon.

Alex stared at Titan in the photo. His mouth was dry. He couldn't help but think that in a way, his parents had finally gotten exactly what they'd always wanted: a son who wholeheartedly believed in the glory of Cloak. Shade, Volt, and Titan looked like a model family. It was impossible to tell from the outside what evil lurked behind their smiles.

Alex gritted his teeth.

"They changed the uniform," Kirbie said, stepping up beside him. "It's a darker blue. The star is smaller and metallic. Everything looks more . . . I don't know. Textured, I guess."

"Probably ballistic fibers woven in, like our Cloak uniforms had," Mallory said. She batted a big white feather on her mask back, trying to keep it out of her face. "I'd bet these new metal chest emblems are bulletproof."

"There aren't any capes," Kirbie said. "Lone Star *always* wore a cape."

Alex smiled a little. "My mother *never* would."

"The way the city's fallen in love with the New Rangers," Kyle said softly, "it's like they're the only ones who ever existed. Like *we* weren't the ones protecting them just a few weeks ago."

"Shade should have changed her code name," Kirbie said as they continued down the street. Her voice had a hollow sound to it as it echoed out of her mask. "It just *sounds* villainous. At least Titan and Volt could go either way."

"I think they're trying to tie it in to the fact that she's always got on sunglasses." Alex shrugged. "That it's, like, her trademark or something."

"Back in the day there was a Ranger who had the power to basically scream really loudly," Kyle said. "She called herself 'Aria.' Anyway, she was always carrying these opera glasses around with her and posing with them for pictures. The photographers loved it. Apparently when the Rangers started wearing matching uniforms, they tried to make her get rid of them. She fought them on it for weeks."

"Yeah, it's the same kind of thing. Only with my mother, it gives her a way to hide her silver eyes when she's controlling Photon. That way no one knows her real power."

"Plus, those silver eyes are super creepy-looking," Kirbie added.

"You kind of get used to them after a while," Mallory said.

"Same with Phantom's paleness and tendency to walk

out of shadows," Alex said. "And did you know that Barrage always, *always* smells like a barbecue? It's some weird side effect of his explosive powers."

Kirbie let out a short laugh, and then they walked on in silence. Alex kept thinking about the picture of his mother. With every step he took, he was marching toward a confrontation with her. Not just her, but his father, too, and the rest of the team he'd been raised to think of as his family. Facing them was inevitable. Still, thinking about actually having to fight against his parents made his stomach churn. He'd come to realize that they really *were* villains, but he didn't want to hurt them. They were his parents, after all.

They'd looked so happy in the poster. Would they be happy to see him, even if it was on the battlefield?

"Deputies at two o'clock," Kyle whispered.

Alex turned to see two figures standing on a street corner not far ahead. One female, older, and a boy who looked to Alex as if he couldn't have been out of high school. Both wore matching black pants and dark blue shirts with silver starbursts on the chests.

The Deputies had begun to show up after Justice Tower fell, keeping a constant vigil for the Rangers. To some degree or another they all had minor superpowers. From what Alex could tell, their abilities ranged from levitating a few inches off the ground to shooting harmless fireworks from their fingertips. At first Alex and the others had referred to them as "Powers." They were hardly anything to worry about until the New Rangers showed up and deputized them as their personal task force, doling out uniforms with silver starbursts on them instead of gold ones. Now they patrolled Sterling City, armed with Cloak weaponry they barely knew how to use and nearly unlimited authority—a dangerous combination.

There were Deputies everywhere. Alex and his companions crossed to opposite sidewalks as casually as possible whenever they popped up. The Deputies were always stopping someone, frisking them, asking them questions about who they were and where they were going. Alex tried to make some sort of sense out of who they chose to interrogate, but it seemed completely random. Around them, the rest of the crowd seemed blissfully ignorant of what was going on. Alex even heard some passersby thanking the Deputies. They welcomed the added sense of security.

"The Deputies think they're doing the right thing," Mallory said. "They think they're Rangers."

"They're acting like thugs," Kyle said.

"Come on." Kirbie nodded her werewolf head forward. "We're almost there."

The buildings were getting shorter the farther they walked from the center of the city, until they were only a few stories tall. Still, the streets were scattered with handfuls of people in costumes. After a few more blocks, they finally reached their destination: the Sterling City Museum of Art and History. The museum was open to the public for the festival, but they had no time to stop and admire the ancient stone columns or suits of armor as they hurried through the inside—though Alex made a mental note of all the daggers and swords they passed, just in case they might come in handy. Soon they were on a back lawn surrounded by a tall stone fence. In the center of the space was a sandstone replica of Stonehenge, one of the museum's most well-known exhibits.

"Well," Alex said, turning to the others. "This is it."

They nodded to him.

"Let's make a scene," Kirbie said.

Alex wrapped his thoughts around Mallory and lifted her up onto one of the tallest stones in the exhibit. She slipped off her mask and flung her jacket to the grass, revealing her old Beta uniform top. The silver skull of Cloak gleamed in the sun. Alex, Kirbie, and Kyle stood on the ground below her.

"Citizens of Sterling City," Mallory shouted in her most authoritative voice. "My teammates and I demand to speak to the New Rangers. Call for them. Send them here. And then leave this place before you find yourself in harm's way."

There was a restless movement through the crowd. One man spoke up.

"What, are we supposed to be afraid of a bunch of kids?"

"Is this some kind of prank?" someone else asked.

"Don't make us ask you again," Alex said.

With that Kirbie transformed. The vinyl werewolf mask split and fell apart, revealing a very real blond she-wolf. She leaned back, her toothy snout pointing into the air, and let out a monstrous howl. The bystanders screamed, panicked, and rushed back into the museum.

The site had been Kyle's idea. Public enough that they could get the New Rangers' attention, but small enough that any bystanders could evacuate safely and efficiently. The lawn was surrounded by huge, solid walls. The only way in or out was through the doors at the back of the museum—doors that Mallory was already melting together, rendering them practically impenetrable.

Kyle took a few seed pouches from his pocket, but replaced them when he noticed an old shade tree planted near a few benches and tables. He hurried over to it and rubbed a hand on its trunk, coaxing its branches to grow and thicken, feeling out its root systems.

"I've got a good tree here," Kyle said. "This'll definitely come in handy."

"Good," Alex said. "Let's see if we can lure a few of the New Rangers over there. Yeah?"

Kyle murmured something, and the still-expanding tree slammed a branch down onto the ground.

"Yeah," Kyle said as the tree straightened itself once more. "Do that."

Alex and Kirbie stood back to back, their eyes darting all around, looking for movement.

"We're as ready as we can be," Kirbie said, stepping beside Alex with her eyes to the sky. "Just try to keep Shade's attention so she's not digging around in any of our heads."

"Right," Alex said.

There was a sound cutting through the air above them—a helicopter flying low.

"Newspeople?" Kirbie asked.

"No," Alex said. "I don't think so."

"That didn't take long," Mallory murmured.

"Get ready, everyone. They're here."

Something fell from the helicopter, plummeting through the air at an incredible speed. Something blond and human shaped. Titan. He landed in a crouch, one fist slamming into the ground, the other reared back, ready to strike. The earth trembled beneath him.

Alex smiled to himself. The New Rangers had come. But they had no idea that the real action was taking place miles away, where two of Alex's friends were getting ready to enter the Gloom and rescue Lone Star and Lux—the *actual* Rangers of Justice.

Alex and his teammates were just decoys.

INTO THE
GLOOM

The Rook was the tallest structure in Sterling City, a glass-and-stone tower of offices, fancy shops, and luxury apartments piercing the sky above the eastern side of Victory Park. Misty stood on her tiptoes at the very edge of the building's roof, nothing but open air and a thousand-foot drop in front of her. The breeze ruffled her red curls as she peered across the city with wide eyes.

"Sooooo high," she whispered.

"Uhhh," Bug said. He started toward her, but stopped a few feet away. "I know you could just break apart and float back up here if you fell, but you're kind of freaking me out standing so close to the side like that."

She turned her head to him, flashing a grin. "Don't

worry. I was always really good at balance and stuff like that. I could *probably* even do a handstand right here and never have to use my powers once."

"Please don't." Bug gulped. A huge green-and-blue dragonfly circled around his head—Zip. Thanks to Bug's ability to control insects and see through their eyes, Zip was about to become a key member of the Gloom expedition team.

Near the center of the roof, Gage was carefully setting up the device he'd created using part of the Umbra Gun that had banished many Rangers to the Gloom in the past. The invention, which he called the Gloom Key, looked simple enough—just a metal box with a giant diamond attached to the top of it—but it held a concentration of shadow energy from Phantom, one of the four members of Cloak's High Council. Only recently had they managed to obtain that piece of the gun, thanks to an incredibly risky infiltration of Cloak's underground base. The Gloom Key enabled them to enter the Gloom and rescue the Rangers. Lone Star and Lux were the powerhouses they needed if they were going to expose the New Rangers as frauds and bring Cloak to justice once and for all.

The problem was how to *find* the lost Rangers in the Gloom. Gage hypothesized that the place acted as a sort of dark mirror to the normal world, meaning the smartest thing to do was go into the Gloom as close to where Lone

Star and Lux had been sucked into it as possible—somewhere near where Justice Tower had stood. That meant finding a place where they could camp out in secret in the heart of Sterling City during one of the most crowded times of the year. The Rook was their choice, a rooftop Kirbie and Lux had used as a meeting and scouting place back before everything had gone wrong. There were only two ways of accessing the roof: the stairway coming from inside the building and the sky. Amp was busy making sure no one came through the door by jamming the lock shut, using his ability to absorb and channel sound to make sure no one on the floors below heard him.

Their only real threats were Photon and Phantom. Photon, the only flier in Cloak's ranks, could be seen approaching in plenty of time for Misty to give them a quick exit.

As for Phantom, she was a threat no matter where they were. Since her powers gave her the ability to travel through the Gloom and walk out of a shadow in the real world at practically any moment, they would never find a place out of her reach. All they could do was hope that she wouldn't discover their location, and try not to let the fear that she could appear at any time distract them.

"All right," Gage said, standing. "We're ready."

Misty stepped back from the roof's edge. There was no sound but the wind and distant noise of traffic floating up from the street as the four teammates looked at one another.

"What are we waiting for?" Misty finally asked.

Gage tapped on an electronic screen. Inky energy shot from the Gloom Key, and a dark diamond formed on the wall beside the now-barricaded door. A low roaring sound emanated from it.

Gage and Amp put on their goggles, which Gage had specially designed for the mission. Bug's eyes glowed a golden metallic color. Then Zip did a diving loop and shot through the portal and into another world. They'd discovered that radio waves couldn't cross planes. Amp, Gage, and Zip would travel to the Gloom, and Bug would stay behind with Misty, following along via the dragonfly.

"So far I don't see anything strange," Bug said, scouting out the Gloom through Zip's eyes. His voice was low and soft, as if he were in some sort of trance. Keeping up with Zip in the Gloom was a strain on his powers. "I mean, other than what looks like miles and miles of shadowy wasteland."

"Misty," Amp said, "you stay by Bug's side no matter what. Keep your eyes open. The slightest hint of trouble and you two take the Gloom Key and get out of here. Don't worry about us."

"Got it," she said, clicking her heels together with a smile. "I'm the only line of defense. No big deal."

Amp walked to the portal, standing beside Gage as they

peered into the roiling darkness. They were both dressed for the extreme cold of the Gloom, in puffy coats and gloves and scarves.

"You ready?" Amp asked.

"As I'll ever be," said Gage.

"You guys don't let anything happen to Zip, okay?" Misty said. "Or yourselves."

"Don't worry. Just a quick trip through a nightmare," Gage said flatly. "What could go wrong?"

Misty didn't laugh.

Amp held his arm out, ushering Gage to go in front of him.

"How chivalrous," the inventor said, and then he was gone.

"See you guys in a bit," Amp said, as he followed Gage into the void.

For a few seconds, the world was nothing but shadows and freezing air, and then the two boys were standing together in near-complete darkness. There was a whirring sound as their goggles automatically adjusted to the dim light, allowing them a slightly clearer view of the world. A glimpse of the Rook's rooftop was visible in a diamond shape. Zip hovered in front of Amp, who gave her a thumbs-up. She made one circle in the air, signaling that Bug understood. They couldn't afford to leave the portal open for fear that it would attract Phantom's attention. It closed in on itself. The normal world disappeared.

Gage and Amp were alone together in the Gloom.

They found themselves near the top of a dark cliff that appeared to be composed of some sort of solid shadow— a substance now familiar to both Amp and Gage after spending hours of time in the Gloom while preparing for this rescue operation. Amp squeezed the side of his electronic watch, starting a timer. Thirty minutes. That's all they had. Through their training, they'd discovered that after that amount of time they both felt drained and tired. Gage had feared what would happen to them should they stay longer than that.

Besides, the faster they were out of the Gloom, the sooner Alex and his distraction team could stop fighting.

Above them, where the sun should have been blazing gold, a dark orb caused the sky to pulse with a strange, dull glow. It was as if the plane existed as a photo negative of the normal world, except that none of the darkness had bothered to become the light.

The ground they stood on sloped until it gave way to rolling hills on one side, and what looked like a black-sand desert on the other. Amp took a look over the edge of the cliff. There was nothing but darkness, an inky sea, though points of half-formed structures poked out of the murk here and there. In the real world he would have been able to see for miles, but everything in the Gloom was hazy. Shapes in the distance became nebulous, or turned out to be nothing but mirages if he stared at them for too long. The only thing he could make out clearly was the silhouette of something that resembled the building sketched out in the blueprints Kirbie had found in Cloak's War Room—the structure that was to be built on the ruins of Justice Tower. It was a craggy, imposing building that looked as if it had grown from the ground itself, rising high into the air in a sharp pointed spire.

"What is this place?" Amp asked. "Everything else I've seen of the Gloom was miles of nothing. This area looks like someone glued pieces of different maps together."

Gage was quiet for a moment, as if he was doing some difficult calculation in his mind. His head darted about, though his eyes were hidden behind the tinted lenses of his goggles. When he spoke, there was a hint of wonder in his voice.

"We're in the heart of the city. I doubt Phantom ever spent much time in the part of the Gloom near the lake house, but she would have been here often. There's no way of knowing how much of her life Phantom spent in the Gloom. I've heard she used to disappear here for days when she was younger. I imagine we're looking at the kingdom that Phantom built for herself over the past few decades. A place to rule. She *did* once go by 'the Phantom Queen.'"

"And that," Amp said, gesturing to the castle of shadows. "I guess that's her palace."

"It's like something out of an old fairy tale," Gage said as he tapped away at an electronic device. "I half expect that if we get closer to it, we'll find it surrounded by brambles. Perhaps she and Shade built it together."

"Shade was here, too? I thought the others only passed through the Gloom when Phantom was transporting them."

"That's true now, but when they were younger— younger than us, I think—Phantom used to bring Shade here sometimes. She was the first person Phantom ever marked with her energy."

"So what happened?" Amp asked. "Why'd Shade stop coming? Did they have an argument or something?"

"Oh, no. They're still practically sisters. It's just that the Gloom got too draining for Shade. Phantom's powers work with the Gloom. She feeds off its energy, but it's the opposite for everyone else. That's why we should only be in here for a half hour, tops."

"How do you know all this?"

"I used to play a weekly chess game with the Tutor, who taught the High Council when they were young. He was quite a talker when he thought he was winning."

There was a blip on Gage's screen. He smiled.

"Ah. Fortunately, it looks like we'll be heading in the direction opposite of the big scary castle."

"You've got a lock on Lone Star?" Amp asked, his voice growing louder.

Gage shushed him, glancing around. "I do. But it's faint. More of a general area than a pinpoint."

"Lead the way. We need to get moving." Amp wrapped his scarf tighter around his neck. He waved his hand in front of Zip, then drew an arrow in the air with his finger, knowing that somewhere only steps away but in a completely different world, Bug was watching.

"Scout ahead," Amp said.

Gage placed a tiny black cube on the ground—a beacon they would use to find their way back to this place and the portal home. Then they began to walk.

The landscape changed erratically. Everything was constructed out of the same dark elements, but there were hints of the normal world as well. Gage led them over the rolling hills and past a half-formed building that contained several glass windows. A handful of trees dotted a lane in front of it, their branches bare and trunks curved over, as if stooping to greet the two boys.

"She must have taken whatever she liked from the real world and brought it here," Amp said quietly, his eyes lingering on a decades-old phone booth that sat in the middle of the nothingness.

"The metal and glass seems to be doing better than the organic matter. Things just decay into nothing here," Gage whispered, gesturing to a grove of skeletal trees that looked as though they would crumble under the slightest touch.

"Right," Amp said quietly.

"Oh, I apologize," Gage said a bit awkwardly. "I didn't mean—"

"It's all right. I gave up any hope of ever seeing my parents again a long time ago."

Amp walked on. His parents had been among the Rangers who had been lost to the Gloom a decade before. And while Gage had surmised that Lone Star and Lux could definitely have survived their month in the dark plane, he'd admitted that doing so for ten years was rather unlikely.

They passed between two craggy cliffs. Their footsteps made soft pads on the ground. Amp took in each echo, storing the noise inside himself as ammo. He'd found that being inside the Gloom for extended periods of time temporarily dampened his powers, and so he made it a point to actively absorb any stray sounds. Zip flew several yards ahead of them. Amp kept one eye on the dragonfly at all times. The last thing he wanted was to miss a message, or have the insect disappear in some shadowy crevice, never to be seen again.

"I keep thinking I see movement just out of the corner of my eye," Amp said.

"I know," Gage said. He touched the side of his goggles, and the lenses changed from black to a dark green.

"Something about this part of the Gloom feels like it's much more alive than where we've been training. But I'm registering nothing as far as heat vision goes."

"That doesn't exactly make me feel better." Amp pulled the strings of his hood, tightening it around his face. He shivered. "If we run into anything in this pass, we're done for. We'll be stuck."

"If you have a map of the Gloom, I would happily lead you a different way," Gage said calmly.

They carried on, communicating only with nods and gestures as the space between the cliffs got smaller, the darkness closing in above them as their goggles whirred, adjusting to the lack of light. Until finally the tops of the shadows began to recede and they could make out an opening at the end of the pass that promised at least a little more breathing room.

It was at about that time they realized they were being followed.

There was a sound from behind them, like silverware scraping against a dinner plate. It echoed off the walls of the cliffs so that they were unable to tell exactly where it was coming from.

And then there was a rasping laugh, deep and menacing.

The boys didn't wait to see what had made the noise. They sprinted for the exit to the cavern, Zip rushing overhead. Then they were in open air again, surrounded by hills and boulders and mounds of craggy shadows jutting up into the sky.

"We're getting closer," Gage said, staring down at his screen, and then taking a moment to look over his shoulder. Nothing came out of the pass between the cliffs. Nothing had followed them. At least, nothing they had seen. But the shadows around them were moving of their own accord, roiling and bubbling and yawning and stretching. The two strangers in the Gloom continued to run, Gage leading them around ponds full of impossibly dark pools and black columns that rose from the ground with seemingly no purpose.

"I hear something behind us," Amp said through heavy breaths. "It's faint. I don't know what it is. But it's definitely getting closer. I can hear it breathing."

It was as if by admitting this, the thing behind them allowed itself to make noise, and they could both hear something scrambling to catch up with them, and again a sound like screeching metal.

And then another noise, right in front of them. *Bang.* Gage and Amp stopped dead in their tracks. Amp shot his hand forward, concentrating all the sound energy the Gloom hadn't sucked out of him, readying for attack. Gage froze, his tracking device in hand, a yellow blip pinging on the screen.

The new sound had come from a long piece of wood

brought down against the top of a craggy shadow above them. It was sharpened on one end, like a spear. A man was holding it, staring down at them. He had a square jaw with a dimpled chin set beneath a straight nose. The skin around his eyes was dark and creased and stood out against his pallid skin. His hair was greasy and askew, slanting off to the right like a ramp.

His blue-and-white uniform was full of rips and tears, the entire right sleeve missing. Hanging from one shoulder was the smallest scrap of gold, which complemented the starburst on his chest perfectly.

"Who are you?" he asked, his voice a cracked baritone. "Where did you come from?"

Amp slowly lowered his hand.

"Lone Star," he whispered.

The man's expression contorted in confusion. Amp ripped off his goggles and took off his hood, exposing his face. Lone Star stood completely still, stunned for several moments, before dropping to his knees. He looked as though he might be sick, or burst into tears. Or both.

"Amp," he said, his voice now soft and fragile. "Not you, too."

"You misunderstand, sir," Gage said, stepping forward. "We're here to rescue you."

Lone Star stared back at him, shaking his head slightly.

"We have a way out." Amp's voice practically boomed

with excitement as he climbed the craggy shadow to be at his mentor's side. "We're here to take you back home."

Lone Star seemed unable to process anything that was happening.

"But how? How did you get here? Are the others safe?"

"Where's Lux?" Gage asked, looking over his shoulder. "We need to get out of here. Fast. We think we've picked up a tail."

"Amp, I . . . ," Lone Star started, and then trailed off. His eyes stared into Amp's, but there was something distant about them, as if he wasn't sure he was seeing the boy at all. "How long have we been in here?"

Amp crouched down beside the Ranger. He spoke softly.

"About a month. But we can get you out. You and Lux. She's here, too, right? We just need to return to the portal, and we'll bring you back into the real world. Everything will be back to normal."

"My powers. I haven't been able to use them in I don't know how long. Lux's too. We can't figure out what to do."

"It's okay," Amp said. "We just have to get you out of here. As soon as you're back in the real world, you'll feel like yourself again. You'll burst with energy. You *have* to. We need Lone Star back. The *city* needs you."

Lone Star didn't move at first. Then his face began to harden, and he nodded. Suddenly he was on his feet, his chest puffed out. He looked at Amp with a faint smile.

"I never hoped you would do something so reckless as to try to rescue us." His voice was bolder now, more theatrically heroic. "But now that you're here, I couldn't be prouder of you."

Somewhere behind them came a sound like that of falling rocks, only like everything else in the Gloom, it seemed murky and ill-defined. Lone Star's eyes widened.

"It's not safe out here," he said. "A monster lurks in the shadows. Follow me. We need to get back to our shelter. We can collect Lux and the others and get out of here."

"Others?" Amp asked.

But Gage and Lone Star were already hurrying away.

3

FAMILY
REUNION

Titan cracked his knuckles. The metallic sound echoed through the outdoor area. Alex shuddered slightly. The noise was a reminder of Titan's strength and near invulnerability thanks to a layer of metal beneath his skin, and was something Alex had grown to hate in the past when the two had still been living in the underground base together as teammates.

Titan stood a few yards away from Alex and the others—the decoy team. Surrounded by high fences, the Stonehenge lawn felt like a boxing ring.

"Well, well, well," Titan sneered. "Looks like somebody finally stopped being chicken and came out to play. Hey, Mallory. Long time no see. I can feel your chill from all the way over here."

"Maybe you're just getting flashbacks of when I froze you solid the last time I saw you," Mallory said, shrugging.

"Don't be like that." Titan pretended to be hurt. "It wasn't long ago we were breaking through vault doors together, Temptress."

Mallory didn't respond, but Alex could feel the heat radiating off her at the mention of the code name Titan had tried to give her countless times in the past. Titan smirked. He was already gloating. *Good,* Alex thought. The longer they talked, the less time they'd need to spend fighting. He silently hoped that everything was going well for Gage and the others.

As the helicopter overhead descended, a black rope uncoiled from its open door. Volt slid down it, jumping off at the end and landing beside Titan. Both of them were dressed in the new Ranger uniforms.

It was the first time Alex had seen his father since the man had been sucked into the Gloom the night that Justice Tower had fallen. In his Ranger uniform, the man looked heroic. Even regal. Alex's mouth parted slightly as he stared at Volt. He tried to pretend that there wasn't part of him that was happy to see his father in person after so long.

"Hello, son," Volt said. He let the last word hang in the air for a few moments. He looked down over the tip of his nose at his child, but his eyebrows were scrunched together. Alex recognized the expression. It was the look Volt used to give in training sessions when he questioned if Shade was pushing their son just a little too hard. "I see you've brought quite a party with you."

"Father," Alex said, his voice cracking slightly. He steeled himself, curling his fingers into fists at his sides. "I see you brought your metal ape."

Titan started forward. A crackle of Volt's purple electricity landed at his feet, holding him back.

"Patience," Volt said. "You know my wife would hate to miss anything."

Above them, Shade and Photon descended from the sky. Alex had never seen the true Ranger up close. His skin was a deep olive, his hair dark and wavy. And his eyes, which stared straight ahead, were a curious mix of amber and green.

He carried Shade. Or, Alex thought, it would have been more accurate to say that his mother was lounging in Photon's arms, as if he were a very comfortable piece of furniture. Her legs draped lazily over one of his forearms, while the other supported her back. She smiled beneath her oversized black sunglasses and leaped gracefully off her transportation once they were close to the ground. The helicopter, which must have been waiting for them to land, flew away.

Alex's family was reunited. Father and mother and son. His pulse thumped in his head. He felt like years had passed since he'd seen his parents, but at the same time, like it had been yesterday.

"My, my," Shade said, smiling. "If I'd known that all we had to do was become Rangers to get you to come out of hiding, I would have arranged it sooner."

"You are *not* Rangers," Kyle spat.

There was a flippancy to his mother that Alex had never seen before, even with all of them standing there facing her, ready to fight her. She acted as though she didn't have a care in the world—that she had everything figured out.

It made Alex nervous, as her happiness tended to do. He grimaced.

"My darling boy," she said, ignoring Kyle. "Why do you look so sad? Could it be that you're not as glad to see me as I am to see you?"

Shade smiled. It was an altogether different smile from the one he'd seen in the poster of her not fifteen minutes earlier. There was something scary about this one. Alex had seen a few movies and read a few books about families who were reunited after long periods apart. They were always sobbing and hugging, professing their love and happiness to one another. Months ago, he might have thought such displays were signs of weakness, but now he felt angry that this wasn't the case for him and his family. Angry, and sad.

"The last time I saw you," Alex said slowly, "you left me and my friends in a crumbling building to die."

"But you *didn't*," Shade said. "And in my defense, it

was *your* telekinetic blast that brought down Justice Tower. What I can't figure out is what you're doing here now. If you're hoping to have some sort of revelation for the media about what's *really* going on around here, I'm afraid we've got all that covered. You're all wanted criminals, after all. As we speak, half of our Deputies are surrounding the front of the building."

"Aren't those untrained idiots the kind of people you always told us we should never think twice about?" Mallory asked.

"Everyone serves a purpose," Shade said. "Everyone can be used for—"

"For the glory," Alex said, finishing her sentence. "Yeah, we've all heard it."

"Photon," Kyle shouted. The man turned to stare at Kyle. There was a brief moment of confusion on his face, and then Shade's eyes went silver and the man stood upright, ready for her command.

"Oh, I see," Shade said. "You thought that if he saw you, he might turn against me. I can assure you that's not how this works. Photon's my little magnetic puppet for the foreseeable future. Until we don't need him anymore." She shifted her gaze between Kyle and Kirbie, and lowered her voice. "Just between you and me, I can see the allure of this hero stuff. All the fawning and worship. But then, we'll have plenty of that once Cloak takes over as well."

"They only follow you because they don't know who you really are," Kirbie said.

"That's the trick to all celebrity, isn't it? That's *power*, little girl." Shade narrowed her eyes. "And that's all that matters."

"Take them alive," Volt said flatly.

Everyone moved at once.

Titan barreled toward Alex, but the roots of the nearby tree shot up from the ground, tripping him. Before the metal boy could pick himself back up, the tree was growing and bending, and its branches wrapped around him and held him high in the air. Titan thrashed, but off the ground he had no leverage, and every snapped piece of wood was replaced by two sturdier branches, like some sort of Hydra. At Kyle's command, the tree slammed Titan back and forth from the ground to the nearby brick wall.

Mallory ran and began firing off icy blasts at Volt. Kirbie leaped from stone to stone, taking swipes at Photon. It was a tricky situation—they needed to fight the man, to keep him busy, but they didn't really want to *injure* him. He was a Ranger, and his actions were not his own. Using his control over magnetic and electromagnetic waves, Photon darted through the air. With a wave of his hand, a metal bench flew toward Mallory, wrapping itself around her and trapping her near Stonehenge. She grunted, pouring subzero temperatures into the restraints, then rammed herself into one of the stones that made up the exhibit. The metal fell to the ground.

The extent of Alex and his new teammates' training in the prior weeks was unmistakable. Alex wondered if his mother noticed this, and if so, if she was proud despite the situation.

His target was his mother. After all, he was the only one who knew how to fight off her attacks. He kept his mind wrapped in telekinetic energy. There were flashes of silver behind Shade's sunglasses as her thoughts pushed against his shield. She looked at him with a mixture of disappointment and curiosity, as if she couldn't quite figure out how to approach him.

Without warning, Shade pulled a pistol from her belt holster and fired. The bolt of energy that shot out came within a few inches of Alex's chest before his thoughts batted it away. It landed on the ground, scorching a small bit of grass. With a single sharp thought the gun flew from her hands, slamming against one of the sandstone slabs.

"Just checking," his mother said casually. "I'm happy to see you've been honing all the skills I taught you."

Technically things were going well: if his mother was focused on him *and* keeping Photon on the field, she would learn none of their secrets. He was suddenly thankful for her powers. Telepathy was an incredibly useful and dangerous skill to have, but Alex had perfected his defense against it.

Shade could fire all the weapons she wanted at him, but she had trained him too well against such attacks. If she wanted to fight him, she'd have to use someone else or get in close. As long as he could keep her at a distance, he would be fine. He could use his own powers to keep her at bay.

He wouldn't have to worry about actually attacking his mother.

"I've thought of this moment many times, Alexander." She walked slowly, circling him. "Have dreamed of it, even. Though I have to admit that in my dreams you're usually on your knees, begging me to allow you back into our ranks."

"That's never going to happen," Alex said. He thought about when he'd met Novo in the alleyway. She had taken his mother's form, offering him a place back with Cloak that he had rejected. In a strange way, it had prepared him for this moment. He wondered if his mother knew about that incident. If she had been changed by knowing what his response had been that day.

"So, why are you here, then?" Shade asked. She stopped circling. Alex's back was to the museum building. He could see the others fighting, doing an admirable job of keeping Photon and Titan and Volt in check. Titan shouted in the tree. Kirbie leaped from one of the taller stones and dragged Volt to the ground, catching him by surprise.

Shade continued. "Do you want to bargain for the city?

Or is it just a fight you want? To see if you're really ready to take on dear old Mom and Dad?"

"The way I see it, I've already won." He had to keep her talking, to keep her focused on him.

"Oh? Please explain that to me."

"I beat you," Alex said. "I was supposed to be your biggest victory, and look at me now. I got away from you. I didn't turn into your weapon. And you know how strong my powers are. I could crush you. Right here. Right now."

"But you won't, will you?" Shade asked, shaking her head. "All that power is trumped by your weaknesses. Don't you see, Alex? The very reason you *think* you've beaten me is why I will continue to prevail."

"You're telling me that *not* killing you is a weakness."

"I'm saying that you're only prolonging this little conflict by not taking out your enemy. Look around you. You could use my own weapon against me or silence me with one giant stone from this idiotic exhibit. You could take care of me right here and now, but you won't, will you? Because of some moral code you've adopted. I'd rather have a victorious traitor for a son than an incompetent coward."

"Stop playing mind games with me, Mother," Alex said. He knew what she was doing. These were the kinds of things she'd whispered into his head in power training sessions anytime he felt like giving up or failed to meet her expectations. She was pushing his buttons. It made his blood boil.

"And what are you going to do to stop me?" she asked.

His thoughts shot out, pushing her to the ground. He immediately started forward, to attack, and then stopped, unsure of how to continue.

Shade began to laugh, low and quiet.

"Poor Alexander. Is that all? Another test failed." Her eyes turned a cold silver behind her sunglasses. "Oh, well. Let's get this over with, then."

Behind her, Photon suddenly snapped into action, using his powers to pull a lamppost from the ground. It sparked as it flew through the air, slamming into Kirbie's wolf form and sending her flying. She collapsed in a heap at Alex's feet. Before Alex could react, Photon focused on Titan—in particular, the boy's metal under-skin. He ripped the Beta out of the tree and sent him hurtling through the sandstone blocks where Kyle and Mallory stood, shattering some and knocking others over, sending up a cloud of dust.

Then, as if someone had turned him off, Photon floated silently over Shade's head. In a matter of seconds she'd used him to turn the course of battle.

Kirbie slowly got to her feet.

"You—" Alex didn't know where to begin. "You just used your own teammate as a human wrecking ball."

"Like I said, everyone serves a purpose." Shade pulled a black spike from her belt and tossed it toward them as she walked away. It landed at their feet, embedded in the grass.

"Titan will be fine. He will be *happy* to have been of use. You two, on the other hand—well, I can't say for sure how things will end up. I'm a telepath, not a fortune-teller."

She smiled a shark-like smile.

"Well," she said. "A telepath, *and* a weapons expert."

She slid behind one of the remaining rocks that made up the Stonehenge replica just as the spike let out a beep.

"Get dow—," Alex started.

Then there was nothing but the sound of an explosion.

GHOSTS OF THE
PAST

Gage and Amp followed Lone Star through dark paths in the Gloom. The boys explained to him all they knew of the place, which didn't take very long and raised many questions that they couldn't answer. Lone Star shook his head.

"It's a relief to hear that this is just some other world, or whatever you called it. We'd had our suspicions. Photon was the first to connect the Umbra Gun to Phantom after seeing her powers at work. He'd studied the weapon, of course." The Ranger lowered his voice. "Honestly, I thought we were dead until Phantom showed up. And even after that, I wasn't certain we were alive."

"She came to collect Photon?" Gage asked.

"Yes. I don't know how long after everything at Justice

Tower that was—a few days, maybe? Time doesn't mean much here. There are no days or nights. We'd lost our powers by then. It was like her every thought shaped this place. The ground and air and shadows moved at her whim. We didn't stand a chance. She forced some sort of energy into him and then they were gone."

"She marked him," Gage said, nodding. "So she could carry him in and out of the Gloom."

"Why Photon?" Amp asked. "Why not Lux, or you, our leader?"

"Strategic purposes, for one," Lone Star said. "Lux and I are strong and can fly and control light in different ways, but Photon's powers are much more versatile."

"It's not just a matter of controlling metal," Gage added. "With his powers he has sway over electronics, communications—I'd even go so far as to say he could endanger Earth itself if he was strong enough to alter the planet's magnetic fields."

"You're a smart one, aren't you?"

"He's more than that," Amp said. "He got us in here and figured out a way to home in on your energy and track you."

They continued in silence for a while as Lone Star led them deeper into the Gloom. Gage didn't bother explaining that the reason he had notes on the Ranger's energy signature to begin with was because he'd been helping with Cloak's attack on Justice Tower. Gage had hoped that their current mission might balance that fact out in some way.

"It's so cold here," Amp said. "How can you stand it?"

"I guess you get used to it," Lone Star said. "After a while, you forget you're supposed to feel cold."

They came upon a clearly defined road that led between two huge, gate-like structures of darkness crafted to look like wrought iron. Inside was something of a ghost town—rows of half-built structures made of shadows, and occasionally doors and glass from the real world. A little village Phantom had created at some time or another and then abandoned.

"When we first got here, we stayed in a cave for a while, until Phantom came," Lone Star said. "After that, we started exploring. We made for the big castle you probably saw, but it's only accessible by a crumbling bridge that's covered in strange, thorny tendrils. We didn't even bother trying to cross it. We happened upon this place by chance."

He led them to the sturdiest-looking building. It was a simple two-story design, symmetrical with four shuttered windows and a real, wooden front door. The walls were made up of the same oily shadows that Phantom controlled, only these had been carved to resemble bricks.

"Another playground from when Phantom was a kid?" Amp asked.

"Possibly," Lone Star said. "But she hasn't been back in at least a decade."

"How do you know?"

Lone Star hesitated at the door. He turned to the two boys.

"Wait here for a minute," he said. When Amp looked anxious, the man's ears moved back slightly, giving his face a commanding appearance. "I'll only be a moment."

Amp nodded, stepping back. Lone Star disappeared into the house.

There was noise from inside, but it was muffled. Gage looked at Amp, trying to decode his expression.

Amp's eyebrows knit together. "I can hear them. Lone Star. Lux. But there's something else. There are other people in there, but their voices are . . . strange. I can't make out their words." He glanced at his watch. "We're fifteen minutes in."

"We need to head back," Gage said. "By the time we reach the portal again we'll have been in here for half an hour. I don't want to risk staying in longer than that if we don't have to."

Lone Star appeared again, but closed the door behind him.

"We have to go," Gage insisted.

"Just one moment," the man said. "Amp, there's something you should know. There's something about this place—"

"They're here, aren't they?" Amp asked. "The others. The ones who fell to the gun at Victory Park."

"It's not—"

"My parents are in there," Amp said.

Lone Star lowered his eyes. He paused before speaking again.

"In a way, yes."

Amp pushed past the Ranger and swung open the door.

The inside was one big, dark room. Fortunately, Phantom had built a huge fireplace into one wall, where tall flames burned pale silver, casting a flickering light across the house. Lux stood near the fire, her mouth hanging open and eyes wide with happiness.

"Amp!" Lux shouted, running to him. She wore a uniform similar to Lone Star's, but without a cape and with a gold sash around her waist. Her light green eyes were encased in the same dark circles Lone Star had developed since his time in the Gloom. Her once-shimmering hair was now a dull, whitish blond that fell just below her shoulders. Amp gave her a half embrace. His eyes were focused elsewhere, and Lux turned to follow his gaze.

Sitting around the room on strange benches and stumps made of shadows were four things that Amp might not have registered as being human were it not for the outdated Rangers of Justice uniforms that they wore—and even those were mostly in tatters. They were little more than skeletons, their skin gray and stretched thin over the bones, eyes sunken in and dark. A man was missing his right hand and had a bandage tied across his face, obscuring one eye. A woman had what looked to be opera glasses hanging from her neck and a swath of cloth tied around her mouth. Based on the way the fabric hung, her jaw must have been missing.

The other two figures stood close together. The shorter of the pair was a woman who stared at Amp with as expressive a look as her face could muster. The man was taller, with a sturdy frame. He stared at Amp, and then lowered his eyes to the floor. He looked embarrassed, or ashamed. Under the circumstances, it was difficult to tell which, exactly.

"Mom?" Amp whispered, stepping toward them. "Dad?"

He started to say more, but his words caught in his throat. His knees shook.

The Sentry and the Guardian. His mother and father.

"They can't speak," Lux said quietly. "They can make sounds but not form words. There's something about this place. It drains the life out of you slowly, but at the same time keeps you preserved. It's a sort of living . . ." She struggled for the right word.

"Purgatory," Gage said from the doorway. The word fell out of his mouth before he could stop it.

"Like I said," Lone Star murmured grimly. "I thought we were dead."

"I never dreamed you'd still be alive," Amp said quietly, moving toward the two skeletal figures.

"They're so *proud* of you, Amp," Lux said. "We've told them all about the leader you've become."

"It's been ten years," Amp said quietly, his eyes shifting between his parents. "I was only four the last time I saw you. I know your faces more from pictures and statues than I do my memories."

Amp's mother stared back at him. She held out a hand. For a moment, Amp stood there, staring down at it, the only movement in the room the soft licking of the flames against the shadowy walls. Then he was on both of them, his arms wrapped around their fragile frames, face buried in what remained of his mother's dark hair.

Lone Star turned to Lux, trying his best to give Amp and his family some privacy. "Lux, this is Gage. He's the one who figured out how to get in here."

Gage held out his hand.

"Is it true?" Lux asked. "You can get us back to the real world?"

"Yes. But we have to hurry. In fact, we should really be—"

She cut him off with a quick hug. Gage stood motionless, finally using one hand to pat her on the back.

"Of course," she said. "But we have to give them a moment. What about our powers? Will they come back? Do you know?"

"I don't have powers myself, but Amp and I have spent

some time in this realm. His powers always seem to bounce back once we're in the real world."

"Gage, this is Storm Lad and Aria," Lone Star said, gesturing to the two seated figures. They nodded to him but made no movement to stand.

"There were others who fell to the Umbra Gun that day," Gage said. "Are they here, too?"

"They were," Lone Star said. "But it became too much for them. This place *took* too much of them, and they just became husks. By the time we got here, almost everyone was gone."

"I'm sure you're feeling it already," Lux said, picking up on Lone Star's thought. She ran her fingers through her hair. "This place sucks the energy out of you. If you stop fighting it, you're done for."

"And there's something else, too," Lone Star said. "A monster in the shadows. Something like the old Rangers here have never seen. When we first found this house, there wasn't any danger aside from giving up on life or Phantom showing up to take you away. But now something's hunting us. It killed Ms. Light. And, well, you can see that Storm Lad and Aria have had run-ins with it as well."

"A monster?" Gage asked. "What *kind* of monster?"

"I don't know. It seems to be hunting purely for sport, though, not for food. None of us have seen it well enough.

It sticks to the shadows. I was trying to track it when you stumbled upon me."

"We're leaving," Amp said, taking a step back from his parents. His voice was wobbly. "We're going back to the real world. All of us."

"I . . . don't know if that's wise," Gage said.

Amp whipped his head around, staring at the young inventor.

"Excuse me?"

"In this state, I don't think it would be . . . safe . . . to bring the old Rangers back into the normal world," Gage said, choosing his words very carefully. "Their bodies have been through quite a bit of trauma. After ten years, I—I don't know that they would survive the transition, Amp."

Amp started to take a few steps toward Gage but was stopped by a hand that grabbed his forearm. The fingers were thin and bony, but the grip was strong. His father's. The Guardian looked down at his son long and hard before shaking his head.

"No," Amp said. "I won't leave you here alone. You can't ask me to do that."

Amp's father made a few signs to Lux, then wrapped one thin arm around Amp's mother.

"Not alone," Lux spoke softly. "He says he's not alone."

Amp's body began to shake, as if he was holding in a great sonic blast that he was ready to loose. Instead, tears began to stream down his cheeks. He took a deep breath and wiped his face.

The Guardian stepped forward and made a few gestures to Storm Lad and Aria. There seemed to be some sort of disagreement among them. A strange bellow escaped from somewhere within the Guardian's throat, like the sound of a rusted machine trying to start. He pounded his fist on the right side of his chest, over his heart, where there was a golden starburst on the old Ranger uniforms. Slowly, the two seated Rangers stood, their bones creaking.

"We should go now," Lux said. "They'll travel with us to this portal you have. They'll make sure we get there safely."

They made their way back through the gates, over the shadowy hills and dark wasteland of the Gloom, with relative ease. Once Amp's parents and the older Rangers were out of the house, they moved with surprising agility and speed. Gage led the way, his device locked on to the beacon they'd left when they arrived. When they got to the narrow path carved between cliffs, the inventor paused. The road ahead looked like an impossibly black scar on an already terrifying landscape—the kind of route people took and never returned from.

"Is there another way?" Gage asked. "We went through here earlier and it didn't feel like the safest route."

"I understand your concern," Lone Star said. "But it's

the fastest. We could travel around and over the mountains, but that'll triple our time."

"We'll hurry through," Amp said, glancing at his watch. They'd be lucky if they made it back on time already. Even if they didn't tire out, Alex's team was counting on them to be as fast as possible. "We can't afford to take any longer. Who knows what's going on with the others at the museum?" He took a moment to glance at Zip, who flitted her wings on his shoulder. If something had gone wrong, Bug had given them no sign about it.

In the narrow crevice between the mountains, they had to walk single file half the time. Again, the darkness seemed to close in on them. Amp and Gage lowered their goggles, but even they had trouble finding light in the pass. In the worst moments, there was nothing but shadow, and they bumped into one another and the sides of the cliffs. No one spoke. The only sounds were their shuffling and the ragged whistle that wheezed from the mouths of the decrepit old Rangers.

Soon they were almost to the end, where their way home waited at the top of a cliff. Amp took his mother's hand. She squeezed his in return.

"Wait," Lux said, stopping the others. She was toward the end of the line. "Where's Aria? She was right behind me."

They turned to look for her, but there was only the black void of the pass. Then a metallic noise—the same one Gage and Amp had heard earlier—and something flying through the air, shiny and trailing a chain. The object landed on the ground at Amp's feet. A pair of broken opera glasses.

Somewhere in the darkness there was laughter.

"Run!" Lone Star shouted.

They barreled through the crevice, half tripping over one another on the way out. Once in the clearing, they ran across the wastelands and up a sloping mound of shadow that ended in a steep cliff, dropping off into a sea of darkness. And at the very top of the cliff, a light began to shine. Just a pinprick at first, and then suddenly a diamond portal looking out onto the roof of the Rook. Bug was there, as was Misty, their silhouettes distorted, like they were being seen through a veil of water.

Behind them, there came more laughter. Gage and Amp turned to see a figure running out of the shadows of the mountain path. They recognized him immediately.

Ghost.

"Oh no," Amp whispered.

"He's with Cloak," Gage shouted. "Everyone, get through the portal. Now!"

Ghost moved with a quickness that shouldn't have been possible. His skin was even paler than the last time Gage had faced off against him—when the inventor had turned Ghost's powers against the Omega and banished him to the Gloom. His silver, clawed glove shone as it caught the light from the portal. The metallic sound they'd heard earlier suddenly made sense. Lone Star swung his spear at Ghost, who caught it, and with one squeeze splintered the wood into hundreds of pieces. He kicked the Ranger, sending him soaring backward. Lone Star would have tumbled off the edge of the cliff and into the abyss had Amp not managed to stop him.

Ghost locked eyes with Gage.

"*You*," he seethed. "You're the reason I'm here. That weapon you had put me in this prison."

"I guess it hasn't been Phantom's top priority to break you out of here," Gage said. He kept one eye on the others, trying to distract Ghost long enough for them to make their exit.

"The darkness of the Gloom has made me so much stronger." His gray lips spread over sharp white teeth. "You've only made me more powerful."

Ghost lunged at Gage, his clawed hand outstretched. Storm Lad intercepted the attack at the last moment, pushing the young inventor up and back, toward the portal. In a flash, Amp's father was there, too, trying to restrain the Omega.

Lux started after them, but Gage grabbed her arm.

"Come on," he shouted. "Now's our chance. We have to go while he's occupied."

Lux hesitated, but nodded, and the two of them ran through the portal.

"Stop!" Lone Star shouted, taking a step toward Ghost. "We've done nothing to you."

"You idiots," Ghost said, laughing. He sent the Guardian tumbling backward with an elbow to the chest. In one swift move, Ghost was holding Storm Lad over the edge of the cliff by his neck. "You think I care what happens to any of you? I just want *out*. Why do you think I let you get this far? Phantom's kept me in here long enough. I've learned my lesson. I'm ready to take on the real world."

Ghost released his grip. Storm Lad plummeted into the darkness far below, a terrifying howl escaping his lips.

"No!" Amp shouted.

Amp's father tackled Ghost. Amp started toward them, but his mother blocked his path. She gave him a long look, and then raised one hand to the starburst on her chest. After a pause, she moved her fingers to her son, pressing down on the space above his heart.

"Amp!" Lone Star started toward the portal as the Guardian wrestled with Ghost. "Go. Now. That's an order."

"Good-bye," Amp said softly, afraid that any hint of power in his voice might force his mother away from him.

The Sentry mouthed a few words to her son. Then she pushed him with a surprising amount of strength, sending him falling through the portal.

The sun was blinding as Amp spilled out onto the roof of the Rook. His mind was spinning. Someone was at his side, pulling him to his feet. He tried to get his bearings, but everyone was yelling at once. He finally focused enough to see Bug tapping away at the electronic screen. Zip flew in quick, frantic-looking circles above his head.

Lone Star tumbled out of the portal.

"Close it," he choked. "He's right behind me."

They watched in horror as Ghost's clawed hand emerged from the rift between worlds.

"Finally," Ghost said as his head came into view, his voice a rasp. He was halfway out of the gateway as it began to close around him, one foot on the ground. Amp focused and tried to loose a sonic blast at the Omega, but it was no use. His powers hadn't fully returned yet.

And then, just before Ghost's body was completely in the real world, he stopped and jerked back. A thin gray hand latched on to one of his biceps, then another on his neck, and an entire arm around his waist.

"NO!" Ghost screamed as his body was pulled back into the Gloom. "I won't—"

But whatever he shouted was cut off as the portal melted away, leaving nothing but bricks in its place. Amp ran forward, but his hand met with solid wall. He leaned his head against it. His breathing was fast and deep.

"Was that Ghost?" Misty asked. Bug was on his feet beside her. The light from his eyes faded as Zip alighted on his shoulder.

"Yes," Gage said, staring at Amp.

"So, whose arms were those that pulled him back in?"

"Heroes from another time," Gage said as he shoved the Gloom Key into a small bag.

Lone Star stared into the sun, his arms out, palms up, as if absorbing its energy. Lux stood near him, in a similar pose.

"The sun," she said quietly. "I never thought I'd feel it on my skin again."

"How are you?" Gage asked.

"Tired," Lone Star said.

"Your powers, though. What about them?"

"I . . . I can't feel them," Lone Star said. He stared down at his hands.

He looked over to Lux. Before they'd been in the Gloom, her hair had always shone as if it were made of moonlight, silvery strands of pure brilliance. Now it was simply a dull, near-white color. She shook her head.

"Don't you feel them returning?" Amp asked, stepping away from the wall. "I mean, I'm already absorbing sounds and feel stronger. It usually only takes me a few minutes to get back to full power. Aren't you recharging? We can go fight Cloak right *now*. This can all be over in minutes."

Lux and Lone Star said nothing. They didn't have to.

"Your powers will come back," Amp said, though more to himself than to them. His voice was verging on panic.

His eyes were bleary. He pounded a fist against the wall. "We rescued you. They *have* to come back."

"Until then," Gage said, "Misty, if you'll—"

Misty stared at Lux and Lone Star for a beat before giving them both a slight curtsy.

"Mr. Lone Star, Ms. Lux—I'm the Mist. Take my hand and I'll get you off the roof. Then I have to go save the rest of our teammates."

Reluctantly, the two adults put their hands in hers, as the rest of them touched her shoulders and arms.

"I hope the others are safe," Bug said.

"We'll know soon enough," Gage replied as they all began to break apart.

TRAPPED IN A
BUBBLE

Alex tried to orient himself as he flew backward, but the air was full of smoke and debris. Somewhere near him, Kirbie was screaming, but he couldn't find her. He couldn't even tell which direction was up. He curled himself into a ball like he'd been trained to do in situations like this, surrounding his body with a telekinetic shield. The next thing he knew, stone was breaking against his back as he smashed through one of the few pieces of the Stonehenge replica that were still standing. His body slammed against the grass on the other side of the display. Kirbie rolled to a stop beside him. The blast had caused her to change back into her human form.

"You okay?" Alex asked, scrambling to stand and

looking for cuts on himself. Kirbie did the same.

"I think so," she said. "What *was* that?"

Alex's ears were ringing, making Kirbie sound muffled and far away. His eyes scanned the cloud of dirt and debris in front of them, looking for his mother. She was nowhere to be found.

"Concussion grenade."

"Your cheek," she said, looking worried. "You're bleeding."

How sweet. Shade's disembodied voice rang clear in his head. *I'm glad to see someone's been looking after my son in my absence.*

From somewhere across the lawn, Alex could hear the sound of a fight continuing: the cracking of thick wooden limbs and pings of metal alongside shouting that was just distorted enough by the ringing in his ears that Alex couldn't distinguish who was yelling.

There was a pounding noise behind him, low and resonant. Someone was trying to get through the sealed-off museum exit. Deputies.

You probably think that was a clever move, what you did with the doors, Shade's voice came again. *But I control the one who has mastery over metal. You're not keeping anyone out. You're trapping yourselves in.*

"Make sure the others are okay," Alex whispered to Kirbie, who nodded and disappeared into the wall of dust.

There was a glint of silver amid all the debris, and the

outline of his mother's head. Alex wrapped his thoughts around a Gasser in his back pocket—one of Gage's inventions that emitted a nearly invisible cloud of knockout gas—and sent it flying toward Shade. But there was a small burst of light and a high electronic sound and then the Gasser was in pieces, shot out of the air by one of his mother's laser pistols.

"Still relying on that Uniband's inventions, I see," Shade said, stepping into view. She aimed her gun at him. "Is that the best you can do?"

"You're one to talk," Alex said, nodding at his mother's weapon.

Shade looked puzzled for a moment, and then realized what he meant. She looked down at the laser pistol and chuckled, holstering it.

"You've got a point." Her eyes went silver. "But you have to admit I've been making the most of my abilities lately."

Alex noticed the movement beside him too late, and suddenly he was in the air. Photon held him by the coat. Alex started to focus a telekinetic blast, when the brainwashed Ranger smacked the back of his head, causing his thoughts to go fuzzy.

"Ow," Alex yelped.

"You must be very desperate if this is your sad attempt at a last stand," Shade said, grinning. "I expected more from you, Alexander."

"The story of my life," Alex muttered.

Static crackled out of a walkie-talkie on Alex's belt, followed by Bug's voice.

"Everyone's out of the Gloom. We've got the Rangers. Retreat to the Rook."

Everyone froze, even Titan and Volt, who battled the other members of Alex's team on the other side of the now-demolished area. They'd heard. Shade could probably feel the joy now surging through Alex's mind. The mission was a success. They'd rescued the Rangers. Everything was going to be okay.

Alex's grin threatened to take over his entire face as he used the moment of surprise to wriggle out of his coat. He landed gracefully on the ground, in a crouch, and then stood tall, beaming.

"Well," Alex said, "I guess I wasn't as much of a disappointment as you thought."

Shade's lips peeled back, her teeth clenched so tightly Alex thought they might break.

"You're decoys," she spat.

"Impossible," Volt shouted from behind her.

Shade's eyes went silver. Photon rushed to her side and picked her up. Titan let out a sharp cry of surprise as his body flew off the ground under Photon's powers.

"What about—," Volt started.

"I can't carry all of us," Shade said. And then they were

gone as Photon flew at incredible speed in the direction of the Rook.

Volt turned to his son, a stunned and confused expression on his face. Alex held out one palm as he walked toward his father and poured all his excitement and relief into constructing a bubble of blue energy around Volt. The first time he'd ever created such a force field had been only a few weeks before, when his mother and father had shot rubber bullets at him in the name of power training. His father's electricity had been unable to pass through Alex's telekinetic powers—something Alex had not forgotten. Inside the sphere, Volt shot off a crackling arc of energy, but it bounced off the invisible bubble, lighting it up in sparkling blue as it ricocheted around. Finally Volt absorbed the electricity again.

"Nicely constructed, son," Volt said.

"Looks like she abandoned you," Alex said, ignoring the compliment.

The crashing against the museum doors grew louder. It was only a matter of time before the Deputies made it through, or scaled the walls with hooks and ladders. Alex didn't worry. It wouldn't be long now before Misty got there.

"So what are you going to do now?" Volt asked. "Kill your father? The public already thinks you're in some way responsible for the disappearance of Lone Star and

Lux—which isn't *exactly* a lie. Do you really want to add the death of one of their New Rangers on top of that?"

As his father spoke, his voice grew slightly more panicked, as if he actually thought that Alex might execute him then and there. Alex's eyebrows knit together.

"I'm not a killer," Alex said firmly. "That's not who I am. That's who you *wanted* me to be."

"Besides, didn't you hear?" Kirbie asked, barely able to contain herself. "We've rescued the Rangers."

Volt was laughing now. A soft, quiet laugh.

"Your mother's on her way to the Rook with two powerhouses," Volt said. He tapped on the communicator around his ear. "Phantom and the others have been alerted and are probably there already. It was a good plan, Alex, but not good enough. Your friends are done for."

"They would be," Alex said as he narrowed his eyes in concentration. Inside the bubble, his father's communicator floated from his ear, sparked with blue energy, and then broke apart. Alex smiled. "If they were actually still *at* the Rook."

"But—," Volt started.

"'Retreat to the Rook' is just code. For *you* to hear. It means they're long gone by now."

"We figured anything radioed in would be intercepted or overheard," Mallory said. "We're not stupid."

"Another deception," Volt said.

"Our Cloak training's paid off."

Alex picked his coat up from the ground and shook a few bits of rock and dust off it.

"It's over now," Alex said, taking a few steps toward the bubble, until he was only a foot away from his father. "Why not tell us what else Cloak has been doing? I'm sure there's a lot we haven't uncovered yet."

Volt began to laugh once more.

"Even if that's true, do you think that pulling them out of the Gloom really changes anything?" he asked. "You think we haven't factored that remote possibility into our plans?"

"It changes *everything*," Kyle said, taking a step forward.

"You're all so naive," Volt spat. "Your mother may like to talk and play games, but I'm a much more straightforward parent, Alex. Trust me when I tell you that there's no defeating us. Let me out of this bubble and come back to the base with me. It's only going to get worse from here, and when the time comes that we see each other again, I can't promise that you'll survive. You've had your fun, your little act of rebellion. But this isn't training. There are no more practice rounds. Come back, and we'll fix all of this."

Alex had rarely heard his father sound so sincere. The man had never been much for words. He was reminded of the day after his last birthday, when Volt had stopped him in the hallway of the underground base and given him a family photo from when Alex had been just a few months old. His parents were younger and smiling as they held a baby up. As they held *him* up. It was one of the few things he'd taken with him when he'd left Cloak's underground base to warn Kirbie about the impending attack on Justice Tower. Everything else he'd brought that night was pinned to a wall at the lake house, but he had the family photo with him now in the inside pocket of his coat. He could almost feel it there. It was something he'd kept to himself, had hidden away. He didn't know why, really. Only that he wanted to keep it private. Some small memory that couldn't be touched by Cloak or the Rangers or anyone else.

"Is he . . . frozen?" Misty asked. She'd materialized off to the side of the others, and now stood staring at Volt, who stood completely still, resting his forehead against the telekinetic prison and looking at his son. Waiting.

"I've got him trapped in a bubble," Alex said quietly.

"You're here fast," Mallory said.

"The wind was good," Misty said. "Once they got out of the Gloom—"

"Whoa, whoa. Save it for when we're alone."

"You know we'll come after you," Volt said to Alex. "You were just a small threat. A low-priority capture. And now you're prime targets."

Alex stared at Volt, unsure of what to say. He knew he

didn't want to go back to the base, but part of him wanted to trust in his father and make him proud. Or try to talk sense into him and get him to see things from Alex's point of view. From Kirbie and the Rangers' points of view. Volt stared back at him, his eyes almost pleading.

Alex turned away.

"Let's go," he said. Across the city, the others—the *Rangers*—were waiting on them.

"Alex!" Volt shouted, slamming a fist against the force field. "You should have stayed hidden away. You've brought all this down on yourself."

"Good-bye, Father," Alex said quietly.

Volt sneered. His fingers were twitching, sparks falling from them. The bubble filled with brilliant electricity. Alex could feel it knocking against the walls of his telekinetic sphere.

And then they were gone, flying across the city in a mess of particles with Misty as their pilot.

It was an odd feeling for Alex, having his body and mind taken apart and dragged through space. Thoughts got distorted and were hard to put together. But this time he was happy for the fuzz that came with being pulled around by Misty. He didn't want to have to think about the fact that he'd just faced his parents.

The decoy team rematerialized beneath the runoff drain in the underground tunnel, where a short platform led to a metal transport booth that would shoot them across the city. Everyone spoke at once. Bug kept Zip patrolling the park above them. Kyle and Kirbie practically knocked Alex over to get to Lone Star and Lux, who were slumped against each other in the transport, apparently sleeping. Amp sat watching the two Rangers. Misty looked tired and leaned on Mallory.

A wave of relief washed over Alex as his eyes settled on Lone Star and Lux. Then his heart jumped as he realized that the Rangers were unresponsive to all of Kyle and Kirbie's embraces.

"The Rangers—are they . . ." He wasn't sure how to even begin to finish the sentence.

"Just unconscious. Sleeping," Gage said, stepping up to him. "There's a cut on the side of your face, Alex. You're bleeding."

"I don't feel it," Alex murmured. He looked at the two adult Rangers in the metal booth. They were both so pale, the space around their eyes so dark. Amp stared at them and yet somehow through them. He made no motion to celebrate with Kyle and Kirbie.

"That's them," Alex said. "We really did it."

They'd rescued the Rangers, pulled them from the Gloom. Somewhere inside Alex, a weight was lifted. The night that Justice Tower had fallen, when he'd woken up in the middle of a field with a handful of people he'd been raised to think of as his enemies, he'd promised that he would make sure the Rangers were all right. Even when he had no idea if that was even possible. And now, they were here in front of him.

Mallory and Misty crowded into the booth with the others, leaving Alex and Gage alone.

"Everything went okay?" Gage asked.

"I kept my mother's attention," Alex said. "And she was controlling Photon the whole time. The lake house is still a secret. We should be safe for now. Besides, we have them." He nodded to the Rangers. "Everything's about to change."

"About that . . . ," Gage started. Alex turned to him, but Gage wouldn't meet his eyes.

"What is it?"

"Lone Star and Lux don't have their powers anymore. For now, at least. If they *don't* return . . ." He raised his eyes to Alex's. "What should we do?"

Across the platform, Lone Star began to snore. It was only then that Alex realized how fragile he looked among the others. Alex took a deep breath and felt like everything was going to fall apart around him. They'd fought so hard to rescue Lone Star and Lux, but what if they weren't actually useful?

Then he shook his head. They'd done the impossible. They could fix this.

"We'll figure out what to do at the lake house," he said. "Let's go home."

SKI
CHAIR

Lone Star and Lux slept as they were jettisoned underground across the city. The others grinned at one another, trying to talk over the roar of the air shooting past them but settling for giddy shouts and screams. Amp sat silent the whole way. He just closed his eyes and leaned his head back. Whether he was pretending to be asleep or actually tired, Alex wasn't sure. It seemed like *something* was wrong, but as they flew through the tunnel, it was impossible to really communicate.

Once they finally got to the secret lake house base, they could hardly get the sleeping Rangers to open their eyes, much less climb the ladder and stairs to the basement. In the end, Misty had to take the two heroes up, placing them on one of the first-floor beds.

There was a lot of ruckus as everyone tried to figure out what to do while they waited for the Rangers to wake. Amp refused to leave Lone Star's side. Misty wanted to throw some kind of party. Alex found himself dragged into Gage's garage, where the young inventor swabbed his cheek with antiseptic and filled him in on everything that had happened inside the Gloom.

"This cut is much better-looking cleaned up," Gage said when he was done with Alex's wound. "I thought we were going to have to give you stitches. It may scar a little."

"Thanks," Alex said. "How are you doing? I mean, after the Gloom and all."

"A little tired. But that's never stopped me from getting work done before."

"And Amp? How's he? I mean, he didn't really say anything the entire way home."

"Can you blame him?" Gage asked. As he spoke, he began unloading his pockets with the various gadgets and equipment he'd taken into the Gloom. "He just lost his parents for the second time, and his *other* guardians are both so drained they can't even stay conscious. If you're wondering how he'll deal with all this, I can't really say. Besides, strange family relationships are more your department than mine. No offense intended."

"None taken," Alex said. "I just left my dad in a telekinetic bubble behind the museum."

"Your power would have faded away as soon as you were gone. I wouldn't worry about it."

But this did nothing to make Alex feel any better. He'd never been concerned about his father getting out of the force field—he was worried what he might do *after* he was free. What everyone might do. The ragtag team at the lake house was probably easy to overlook or underestimate, even if they *had* managed to defeat the Omegas. But now . . . Alex shuddered as he wondered what form Cloak's vengeance might take.

"As for Amp," Gage continued, "I'm guessing he needs time to figure out exactly how he feels."

"Amp will be okay," Kirbie said from the doorway. "Bug told us what happened. Before he led the Junior Rangers, Amp was like Lone Star's sidekick. They have a pretty long history together. I think he just needs to see Lone Star and Lux up and planning and back to their rightful places so he knows that everything that happened in the Gloom was worth it."

"Right," Alex said. "And Gage, you did say that you don't know what happened after the portal closed. Amp's parents could have defeated Ghost. We could maybe find them again once the real Rangers are back in power."

"Anything is possible," Gage said. He tapped on the electronic screen of the device he'd used to track down Lone Star in the Gloom. "That's what makes not knowing so terrible."

"Don't be such a downer, Gage," Kirbie said. She smiled as she flicked her blond ponytail to one side. Behind her, Alex caught sight of Misty and Bug running down toward the dock, excitement practically radiating off them. "We got the Rangers back. We've won."

But Alex could detect an uncertainty in Gage's eyes as the inventor stared at the screen. Gage might have been the expert at reading other people, but Alex had known him long enough to see when something was not right.

"What is it?" Alex asked.

"Hmmm? Oh, I'm sure it's nothing," Gage said. "I'm probably just fatigued from having been in the Gloom for so long today."

Alex wasn't convinced. As he wondered if he should press this issue, Misty appeared on the other side of the garage, beside the boat they'd used during their attack on the Omegas. She didn't say anything—or even acknowledge that there were other people in the room. Instead she kept her eyes high on the walls and ceiling, searching for something. Alex was just about to ask her what, exactly, she was doing, when her face lit up and she disintegrated. She reappeared again near the top of the garage, where a pair of old water skis hung across two ceiling beams. Her hands shot out and grabbed the equipment, and she was gone again, this time filtering out through the open door.

Alex turned to Kirbie.

"What are they doing out there?"

"Your guess is as good as mine," Kirbie said, turning to the door. "Everyone's so excited that the Rangers are back. I don't blame them for . . ." She trailed off as she stepped outside, staring down toward the dock. "Wait, what?"

Alex hurried outside, where he found that the water in the small, private cove was completely still. Frozen. Mallory lay at the end of the dock, half her body over the side and palms flat against the newly formed ice.

"Uhh . . . ," Alex started, unsure of what question to ask, when Kyle darted past him, holding a lawn chair above his head.

"Here!" the blond boy shouted. "We can use this!"

In a flash he was at the edge of the ice, where Misty and Bug were huddled over the skis. Alex and Kirbie met the others on the shore. Gage followed behind, more hesitantly.

"Perfect!" Misty squealed.

Kyle wiggled his fingers. Vines twisted and grew from a seed packet, securing the skis to the aluminum legs of the chair. When he was done, he picked up the new ski chair and shook it, smiling at the firm attachment.

"Milady," he said, setting it down in front of Misty. "Your throne."

"Mal?" Misty called.

"You're good to go." Mallory stood up on the dock,

stretching. "It's a foot thick, at least. Just don't go flying out of the cove or anything."

"You've got to be kidding me," Alex said, but he couldn't hide his grin.

"This is very important training," Misty huffed as she took a seat. "What if we have to sneak up on someone who's hiding out on a frozen lake?"

"We live in Texas," Gage stated flatly.

"We do *now*. What if we end up teleported to Russia or something? You're going to thank me."

"Actually, Russia does have a history of using its cold climate as a strategic advantage in wartime."

"All right, let's go," Misty said to Bug and Kyle. "He's starting to sound like the Tutor."

The two boys lifted the chair and set it carefully on the edge of the ice. On the count of three, they pushed, sending the chair-on-skis flying across the lake. Misty screamed at first, which quickly devolved into a fit of laughter as she spun around on the frozen water. When the chair finally came to a stop, Misty floated it back over to the edge of the beach.

"Who's next?" she asked, catching her breath and grinning from ear to ear.

"I'll go," Mallory said, running across the dock.

Alex stood at the edge of the ice, staring down at it.

"You look scared," Kirbie said.

"I've never actually been on ice before, I don't think."

He stuck a foot out and tapped.

"At that rate you'll never learn how to walk on it," Kirbie said. She pushed him.

Alex took a few awkward steps forward before he stopped moving anywhere. Instead his feet just continued to slide without traction every time he tried to move, like he was running in place. Finally his legs went one way and his body went another, and he found himself sitting on the frozen lake water.

"OW!" he said loudly, exaggerating for Kirbie.

"Graceful." She grinned.

Alex started to retort, when something yellow caught his eye, half-hidden behind the garage. He smiled and wrapped his thoughts around it. Suddenly a huge inflatable raft was sailing toward him through the air—the raft that Kirbie had tried to carry several of them in when they were first planning on storming Cloak's base, when everything had felt so hopeless. Kirbie recognized the mischievous look in Alex's eyes a second too late. The raft hit her, sweeping her legs out from under her as she fell backward into the cushiony yellow plastic with a small scream. Alex could hear her shout the word "jerk" as the raft sailed out to the middle of the cove, Misty chasing after it.

Gage started back up to his garage, but something caught his leg. A vine shot out of the earth, thick and strong, and pulled him a few feet off the ground.

"No way," Kyle said from the ice. His hands were held out in front of him. "You're not having enough fun. You just spent half an hour in the Gloom. Take a break."

Smaller vines started poking around in Gage's pockets, pulling out any tools and electronics.

"I've got all sorts of tests I should be running and—Hey, be careful with that."

"What do you say, Alex? I think he needs to take a little ride on the ski chair."

"Yeah," Alex said, grinning wide as he carefully stood up on the ice. "He's right, Gage. Live a little."

"Alex Knight," Gage said, a bit flustered, "if you think my idea of fun is jettisoning across a hastily frozen lake in a contraption—"

The vines tossed him toward the cove, where Alex intercepted him with his thoughts. Gage flew through the air wide-eyed, until he was planted firmly in the chair. He yelped as a telekinetic push sent him flying across the frozen cove. Alex watched a smile take over his friend's face as Kyle slid over the ice after him.

There was a flash of silver out on the ice that caused Alex to immediately go on guard, but it was only Mallory. She hadn't bothered to change out of her Beta uniform. The grinning Cloak skull gleamed in the fading sunlight, and as she laughed and conspired with Misty and Kirbie on the lake, Alex's father's words crashed down on him. What would his parents be doing right now? Plotting at the underground base in the War Room? How long before they focused all their resources on finding Alex and the newly rescued Rangers?

He scanned the ice. Everyone was so excited, so *happy*. But their downtime would be short. After this—when Lone Star and Lux woke up—they would return to fighting. Now they were in it more than ever. This was probably the last time they'd get to just play around and be kids until it was all over—and who knew what *that* meant.

His thoughts were interrupted as he watched Bug step carefully onto the ice, placing one foot in front of the other and moving so slowly that for a moment Alex thought he, too, had been frozen. He had a death grip on the dock. He'd pulled his long, dark hair into a short ponytail that stuck out of the back of his head. Alex cautiously took a few steps, found his composure, and was able to move without too much trouble.

"I shouldn't have come out this far," Bug said warily. "Please tell me you had extensive ice-walking training or something so I don't feel like a total loser."

"Actually, it's our first time. Well, the Betas', at least. I don't know about Kyle and Kirbie. But I'm sure all our other agility trials and stuff over the years make it a lot easier for us."

Bug smiled a little, clinging closer to one of the dock posts. Alex smiled, too. It hadn't been long ago that he would have used this as an opportunity to point out how much Bug might weigh the team down or what an amateur he was. But they were well past that now. Bug had more than proved himself. There was no way they would have made it this far without him.

Bug's eyes fell on something between two of the posts on the dock, a glimmer in the breeze. A dragonfly—much smaller than Zip—struggled against the sticky silk of a web. In one corner, a large gray spider looked on.

"Oh, man," Alex said. He suddenly found himself in a situation that he'd never imagined he'd be in. In the past, he wouldn't have given a second thought to the insect, but he wasn't sure if Bug was going to freak out over the drag-onfly's impending doom. "Are you going to help it?"

"Who, the dragonfly?" Bug asked.

"Well, yeah."

"I could probably get it free," Bug said, turning to Alex. "But I'd have to take down the whole web. Then the spider might starve. I'd just be punishing it for doing what it was born to do."

"But Zip . . ." Alex was finding it hard to articulate what he was trying to say.

"Zip actually eats these small dragonflies, too. Different species, though. She's a carnivore, not a cannibal."

"But you'd rescue her if she was in the web, though, right?"

"Of course," Bug said, looking puzzled as to why Alex would have to ask such a thing. "She's my friend. I'd destroy every web for her." Zip alighted on his shoulder. Bug turned to look at her. "But she's too smart to get caught in something like that. Go on, girl. Go find something to eat. You must be starved from the Gloom."

Misty materialized beside Alex and grabbed his arm.

"This is from Kirbie," she said with a wicked grin.

Before he could reply, they were swirling dust on the breeze. He was nothing but a consciousness and tiny bits of matter, and then suddenly he was whole again and falling through the air. He landed on the big yellow raft in the center of the frozen cove. Mallory and Kirbie pushed it hard, sending Alex spinning across the ice.

"Hey!" he shouted, wrapping his blue energy around the raft to stop it. He got to his feet, eyes flickering blue as he focused on the two girls a few yards away from him. With his thoughts, he scooped up some of the melting ice that had been dislodged from the surface of the lake by all the skiing and rafting, until two small balls of slush orbited his head. He smirked.

"Uh-uh, Alex," Mallory said. She held a hand out, heat radiating from it. "I know what you're thinking. If those things come anywhere near me, you'll find out how fast I can melt a foot of ice under you."

"That's assuming I'm on the water," Alex said. As he

spoke, he raised the raft—and himself—until he was floating several feet above the surface of the cove on his own personal flying carpet.

"Are you forgetting?" Kirbie asked, taking off her jacket. Her face was hinting at transformation, lips and nose jutting forward, beakish. "You're not safe from us in the air, either."

Somewhere inside Alex a voice was telling him to enjoy himself. *Have fun while you have the chance. Forget that you're now targets, just for this one hour.*

Alex grinned. The raft started forward. Mallory reared back, ready to strike. Kirbie jumped into the air.

And then a voice from the patio stopped them all.

"They're awake!" Amp's words boomed.

There was a pause on the ice, and then all at once they scrambled across the lake as fast as they could. The time to play was over.

LEADER OF THE
RANGERS

Despite his sunken eyes and pale skin, Lone Star had an imposing presence, tall and barrel-chested. He stood in the Rec Room, staring at the wall covered in note cards and lists and yarn that mapped out the Cloak Society's reach and resources. Lux sat on the arm of a chair beside him, looking run-down but with a dignified posture. As the Junior Rangers introduced the other residents of the lake house, Lone Star took an interest in Alex. The man towered over him, looking down at the boy with his chin jutting out. For a moment, Alex thought that the great Ranger might hit him, or yell at him—after all, it had been his fault that Justice Tower had fallen so quickly, and that Lone Star had been trapped in the Gloom for the last month.

"Alex Knight," he said. "I know your parents."

Alex stared up at him and nodded slowly.

"Well, we have much to discuss," the Ranger said, turning his attention to the rest of the group.

The others methodically spelled out everything that had happened in the heroes' absence—the crumbling of Justice Tower, infiltrating Cloak's underground base, the ordeal with the Omegas, the sudden rise of the New Rangers. Amp spoke the most, the words spilling out of his mouth so fast that they were at times half-garbled, and Lone Star or Lux would have to ask him to repeat things. He didn't seem to mind. There was something about the way that Amp interacted with the adult Rangers that brought out a side of the boy Alex had never seen. He wanted to impress them. He wanted to make sure they knew he'd been fighting for them.

"This is incredible," Lone Star said. He finished the last of a granola bar and pulled another from a box on the billiard table. Both he and Lux had hardly stopped eating since they'd woken up. It seemed like the Gloom had drained them of so much. "It's remarkable you've been able to put all this together and make so many jabs at Cloak's plan without our help."

"The plans we *knew* about," Kyle said. "Ever since they appeared as the New Rangers, I keep thinking we have no idea what their next move might be. So we've really just been focusing on getting you two out of the Gloom."

"What are these?" Lux asked, picking up a set of sketched blueprints from a side table. "This looks like . . ." She trailed off.

"We found them at the underground base," Kirbie said. "We think they're plans for Cloak's new headquarters. For the New Rangers."

"On the ruins of Justice Tower," Lux said. "It certainly makes a statement."

"Let's go over the safety of *this* base," Lone Star said, walking over to a map focusing on Silver Lake and the area around the lake house. "I want to know everything. What kind of security do we have?"

"Motion, infrared, a veritable truckload of cameras set up around the premises," Gage said. "Access to the cove is protected, which should take care of any boats wandering in." He held up an electronic screen. "There are alarms in here and in my garage, and everything can be adjusted and controlled from here or one of the laptops."

"I've got scouts out every hour on the hour when I'm awake," Bug said. "Which is more often than I should be, probably."

"It's been years since we sanctioned this place as a safe house, but if I remember correctly, there's a long path from the yard that leads to a gate somewhere off a dirt road," Lone Star said.

"There *was*," Kyle said with a hint of pride in his voice. "But I've overgrown the old path to the point that no one would be able to find it, much less drive anything down here. If we're attacked, it'll probably be from Phantom's transportation or the air."

"Oh yeah," Kirbie chimed in. "Cloak's got a helicopter now, too. It's what brought the New Rangers to the museum."

"We haven't come across the resources to install any antiaircraft measures," Gage said. Alex couldn't tell whether he was joking or not.

"As soon as I can fly again, the helicopter will be no problem," Lone Star assured them.

There was a cockiness in the man's voice that—combined with his hulking body and brassy blond hair—couldn't help but make Alex think of Titan.

"And you're sure your mother didn't figure out where we are while she was in your head?" Lux asked.

"Positive," Alex said.

"But that brings up a good question," Mallory said, twisting a few strands of her brown hair between two fingers. "Why *haven't* we been attacked yet? Photon must know about this place, right? Amp said you guys went through psychic training or something, but it doesn't seem to be doing him much good against Shade."

"After Victory Park, we didn't know who had survived

on Cloak's side, but we were pretty certain Shade was still alive," Lux said. "We'd heard her shouting after the explosion. Knowing there was an enemy with such powers on the loose, we sought out other telepaths across the world, who taught us how to protect ourselves in the event of psychic attacks. We hadn't thought the Junior Rangers were in danger of needing such training yet." She took a glance at Kirbie. "Obviously we were wrong."

"So why isn't Photon fighting back against my mother's powers?" Alex asked.

"He *is*," Lone Star said. "From what you've told me, it sounds like Shade has to be near him at all times to keep him in line. A lesser mind would just be her drone and follow her blindly. Don't doubt the power of a Ranger for a second. There are levels to these kinds of things. Up against her powers, he may give his body over to her control, but that's just so that he can focus on keeping important things locked away inside his mind."

This made sense to Alex. It wasn't unlike what he did with his telekinesis.

"He's still in there," Kyle said, his hazel eyes looking soft. "When I yelled at him today, there was a moment where I could tell he recognized me. I could see it in his eyes. Then Shade touched him and he was a zombie again."

"My mother once told me it was difficult for her to control strong minds," Alex said quietly. "Even if it's within her power to break down every barrier in Photon's head, with everything going on she must not have had a chance to interrogate him and completely rewrite his brain. That's good news, at least."

"We haven't gotten to the important thing yet," Amp said, finally speaking up. "We've been waiting for you two to be back in this world for a month now. How soon can we take down Cloak?"

"This isn't the sort of thing we should rush," Alex said. "Now that you're out of the Gloom, we should—"

"We'll go public as soon as we can," Lone Star said.

"But we need to talk about—"

"We don't have time to argue about how almost a dozen people think we should be doing things. The longer we wait, the more time it gives Cloak to plan. This is our city. It always has been. The people love us." He turned to Gage. "Now, what can you tell us about our powers?"

Gage frowned. He rolled a pen back and forth between his palms.

"Not much, I'm afraid. I'd thought the homing device I built to zero in on your powers was just not effective long-range, but it appears that's not the case. Even in the same room with you, I'm getting a fuzzy reading when I should be getting a strong signal. I think . . ." He hesitated a beat before continuing. "I think the Gloom has drained you of most of your powers. Both of you."

"But they'll come back, right?" Kyle asked.

"Amp," Kirbie said, "when you were training in the Gloom, how long did it take your powers to come back all the way?"

"Usually just a few minutes," Amp said. He moved his hands to the back of his head, digging them into his short black hair. "I guess it took a little longer if we spent a lot of time inside. This last time in, it took me half the ride back to the lake house before I started feeling up to full strength."

"There's where our answer lies, I think," Gage said. "The longer inside, the longer it takes for your powers to return."

"So, how long, then?" Kyle asked.

"That's the thing. We have no way of knowing. It's not a standard amount of time, obviously, since Amp's back to full power. If it normally takes, say, half the time spent in the Gloom back in the real world—which would correlate with Amp's experience—we're looking at maybe three weeks."

"But it could be anything," Lux said. "The time needed to recover could be exponential when compared to the time spent inside."

"That's correct," Gage said.

"But Photon's powers are fine," Kyle said. His voice was getting higher. Alex could almost see his already fair skin paling as he tried to figure out a way to prove that the Rangers would return to full power.

"Yes, but he seems to have spent much less time away from the normal world. Lone Star and Lux might never get their powers back at all. Or at least not to the full extent that they had them."

Alex closed his eyes and took a deep breath. The entire point of the mission—the thing they'd worked toward since Justice Tower—was to bring the Rangers out of the Gloom so that they could defeat Cloak. And now, all he was hearing was that they had taken yet another small step forward when they needed to be sprinting in leaps and bounds in order to stop whatever Cloak had planned for Sterling City—and them.

"I want to make it clear to everyone that this is nothing more than a guess," Gage said, his eyes staring at a spot on the floor. "This is science that's so far beyond my area of knowledge that everything I say could be wrong. I'm simply going off what we know, which at this point is very little."

"We don't need powers," Lone Star said. "We just need the people of Sterling City on our side. Cloak is strong, but they can't win if we have the entire city behind us. When the public realizes that Lux and I are back, and the so-called heroes they're looking up to are actually supervillains, most of their power is gone."

"Cloak . . . I can't imagine what they'll do after today,"

Mallory said. "We can expect some sort of retaliation."

"Right now they're figuring out all our possible moves," Alex said. "Will we go to the police? Will we try to get Lone Star and Lux on TV? Will we stage some sort of attack? And they're figuring out ways to block us at every turn. We have to assume they're going to expect anything we do and have some sort of counter ready."

"What could counter Lone Star and Lux?" Amp asked. "Even without their powers."

"Alex is right," Mallory said. "The New Rangers—"

"Would you all stop calling them that?" Lone Star asked, his voice growing louder. "They're *not* Rangers."

"We know that," Misty spoke up from one of the sofas. "We're not *dumb*."

"This city has lost its mind if it thinks these people are anything like us," Lone Star said, motioning widely to the wall of cards and yarn.

"Star, the people of the city are just scared," Lux said softly, trying to calm her teammate down a bit.

Alex turned to her. "They should be."

There was a brief silence, finally broken by the lake house computer beeping across the room. Kyle rushed over to it and tapped on the keyboard.

"Oh no."

"What is it?" Kirbie asked.

Kyle clicked on a video and spun the computer around

to the others. Photon stood at a podium onscreen, Shade and Volt on either side of him. A huge crowd of onlookers quietly waited for him to speak.

"After a ruthless attack on innocent citizens during the city's Fall Festival, the Rangers of Justice have unanimously decided to implement a city-approved curfew from sundown to sunrise until the Cloak menace has been eradicated. Only authorized parties will be allowed on the streets during the curfew period. All others will be charged with violating a direct mandate from the Rangers of Justice and Sterling City, and will be prosecuted as criminals."

"What?" Lux asked, jumping out of her chair. "The people won't stand for this. It'll be met with revolts. Riots."

"We can do this," Photon continued on the video. "Together, we can defeat the villains known as the Cloak Society and usher in a golden age for Sterling City."

He stepped away from the microphone. All around him, the crowds cheered. Alex noticed something off about his mother. At first he couldn't place it, but then it dawned on him. Something was odd about her posture. It was rigid. He could see her left fist at her side, clenched and shaking slightly. Her knuckles were white.

The video ended.

"I know we can't trust the media here," Kyle said quietly, "but all reports say that the people are happy about this. They support the New Rangers. They want the city to be safe."

Lone Star took a long look at Kyle, then turned to Gage.

"You seem to be the authority on electronics around here. Do you have a burner phone I can use, or do I need to find a pay phone to keep things anonymous?"

Gage grinned and dug through a duffel bag he'd brought in from the garage. After a little rummaging, he pulled out a small black device.

"It's a modified satellite phone," he said, handing it over. "It'll bounce your signal halfway across the country before it connects."

"Who are you calling?" Kirbie asked.

"A friend in the city."

Lone Star walked to the other side of the room, standing in a corner near the unused billiard cues and a dusty stack of old board games. He dialed slowly, as if he had to talk himself into pressing each number. Finally he raised the phone to his ear.

The others watched in a mixture of confusion and anticipation. Alex glanced around the room, making eye contact with the Junior Rangers, but they all looked as puzzled as he felt. He took a step forward, ready to point out that the last thing Lone Star should have been doing was acting without their knowledge, but Kirbie shot him a concerned look.

"It's okay," she mouthed. Alex grimaced, but nodded.

"Hi," Lone Star said into the receiver. "It's me." He

paused for a few seconds before whispering, "It's Victor."

There was a voice on the other end of the phone, but Alex couldn't make out any of the words.

"Yeah, I'm okay. It's a long story. No, no, the phone is secure. Listen, I know this is a lot to take in and short notice, but I need you to do me a favor."

He finished his conversation in whispers, Alex only able to pick out a few words. Then the leader of the Rangers of Justice turned back to them.

"There's going to be a press conference tomorrow afternoon," he said solemnly. "The . . . *impostors* are breaking ground on their new headquarters. Where Justice Tower stood. It's not public knowledge yet, but it's happening."

"That was fast," Bug said quietly. Zip twitched on his shoulder.

"This is perfect," Lone Star said. "There'll be cameras, a crowd—all we have to do is show up. The citizens of Sterling City may be under the spell of these tyrants, but we're Lone Star and Lux. If we show up and explain what's happened, the people will listen."

Something didn't sit well with Alex. His mother knew the Rangers were out but was carrying on with the press conference anyway. What did she know that they didn't? What was her plan?

"Gage and I have been working on exploring new uses for my powers," Amp said eagerly. "I can do more than just shoot bolts of sound now. I can be one big speaker for you. Broadcast your voice to the crowd."

"He's really very good at it," Gage said.

"Excellent," Lone Star said. "There's no need for us to engage in any sort of combat. If Shade and Volt make a move, our priority will be to protect any bystanders, then to subdue the enemy."

"Don't you think they'll be expecting us?" Mallory asked.

"It'll take more than cunning to keep their charade going when we're standing in front of everyone in the flesh," Lone Star said, his voice resonating throughout the room. "This *isn't* up for discussion."

"That's a lot of civilians," Kirbie said. "I mean, if fighting breaks out, and I assume it will . . ."

"We do this peacefully," Lone Star said. "When the public sees us—when we *explain* what's happened—they'll be cheering us on. I know how the people of this city work. They're *good* people. This is our plan. It's what we're going to do. If you don't like it, you can stay here. Otherwise, rest up for the next few hours."

"Who was that on the phone?" Kyle asked. "Where's the info coming from?"

"That's classified. The fewer people who know, the less likely it is that the information leaks should we run into Shade along the way. All I can tell you is that it's from a trusted source."

"You won't tell us where this intel is coming from?" Alex asked, trying to restrain his growing annoyance. "We've been planning things together up here for a month now and—"

"And we're very grateful," Lone Star said. "But now we're back. Trust me. I'm the leader of the Rangers of Justice. This is what I do."

Alex started to argue but kept his mouth shut. He could see that he wasn't going to change the man's mind.

"One more thing," Lone Star said, his voice calmer now. "I don't want you to take this the wrong way, but when it comes time to talk to the crowd, I think it would be best for you and the other former Cloak members to stay back. It will be quite a shock to the public to see us, I'm sure, and the less we have to explain the better."

"Lone Star," Kirbie said, her voice hesitant. Alex could tell she wasn't used to disagreeing with him. "We're a team now."

"It's only for tomorrow. I'm sure they understand. Don't you, Alex?"

"Of course," Alex said obediently. He bit the insides of his cheek in frustration. It felt like he was being fed the same kind of unquestionable orders the High Council used to force on the Betas.

Lone Star yawned, glancing out the window where the sun was setting in the distance.

"Everyone get some sleep. We'll regroup in the morning.

Kyle, you've studied this area thoroughly. I want you to walk me through all possible routes and methods of transportation from here to the south side of the city. Downstairs. I'm going to try to find coffee somewhere in this place."

"Of course, sir," Kyle said, jumping to his feet. He followed Lux and Lone Star downstairs, leaving Alex and the others alone in the Rec Room.

"Well, *he* definitely took over quickly," Misty said.

"I can see why he became the leader after everything happened in Victory Park," Gage said.

"I guess we can get used to taking orders again." Misty's face scrunched up a little.

"I don't like this." Mallory's usually stoic expression was twisted. "I feel like we're walking into a trap."

"Lone Star and Lux are idols to this city," Amp said, rising to his feet. "You just have to put your faith in them. Trust them. Everything is going to be fine now that they're here. Everything will be okay."

"Amp . . . ," Kirbie said. She seemed unsure of how to continue. "Do you want to talk about anything? I mean, what happened—"

"You heard what Lone Star said. We should get some sleep."

And then he was gone, up into the little finished attic room that his father had once claimed as his own a long time ago when the safe house had just been Amp's family's lake house. Alex listened for footsteps or pacing, but there was no noise filtering down through the ceiling.

Everyone turned to look at Kirbie. Her eyes darted away from theirs.

"I guess we've gotten used to running things ourselves," she said. "In chaos. This will be good. It'll get things back in order." The more she spoke, the less she sounded like she believed it. Her eyes met with Alex's. "He'll warm up. I mean, he's been stuck in the Gloom for a month. He's just a little . . ."

She struggled to find the right word.

"Cranky?" Misty asked.

"Full of himself?" Alex suggested.

"Of *course* his real name is Victor," Gage said flatly.

"You guys—" Kirbie sighed. "—this isn't going to work if you don't *try*."

Alex shrugged. She was right. Powers or not, this might be their only shot. This *could* work. And he had to admit Lone Star definitely seemed like the kind of person who could get things done. Besides, Alex had bigger things to worry about. After weeks of trying to stay off Cloak's radar, he was about to confront them head on for the second day in a row. Tomorrow, he'd be facing his parents again.

8

GROUNDBREAKING

Alex stood in the center of the Rec Room alone. It was morning, but not yet light outside. He assumed the rest of the house was still in bed, exhausted from the previous day, but he'd awoken early and couldn't go back to sleep. There was a nagging thought in the back of his mind— they were missing something. Cloak was going to subvert them in some way. He just didn't know how. And so he'd returned to the place where all their information was noted and filed and sketched out in the hopes that something would suddenly make sense to him. He focused. Around the room, maps and blueprints floated in the air above the tables they'd been sitting on.

He let one newspaper clipping drift in front of his face.

The New Rangers smiled back at him from thin, ink-smudged paper.

What is it, Mother? he asked himself. *What trick are you going to spring on us? I'm your son. I should be able to figure it out.*

Of course, he knew deep down that this wasn't actually true. He'd spent almost his entire life trying to guess what his parents wanted from him—what would make them proud. And then he'd gone and done the exact opposite. He didn't know what his parents might be up to now because he'd failed to become like them, to live up to the family's standards.

A photo drifted in front of his face. The Beta Team, one of the other pictures he's taken with him from the underground base. He took it in his hands, staring at it as he'd done countless times in the past few weeks. He wondered if he'd end up seeing Julie today. If so, it meant that they'd be fighting the entire Cloak Society. He hoped it didn't come to that. He wanted to trust in Lone Star's plan. "Subdue the enemy," were the Ranger's instructions if a fight broke out, which Alex could only assume was inevitable. Even if fighting led to Cloak's defeat and somehow Phantom was unable to whisk them away, what would "subduing" his parents look like? How was that even possible? What would his father say to him from behind bars? How would his mother's face look as she was dragged away by the Rangers?

"You beat me to it," Amp said from behind him. Alex jumped, lost in his thoughts, and the hovering notes and blueprints trembled in the air. "Sorry. I didn't mean to scare you. I was just coming in to stare at all this stuff until everyone woke up."

"Couldn't sleep?"

"Bad dreams."

Amp's tone was smooth and quiet, which was unusual for the boy who had to focus on keeping his voice from rising half the time on account of his powers. There was something else different about him, too—something vacant in his brown eyes. His mind was obviously somewhere else. Alex couldn't imagine what Amp must have been going through, and he didn't know the words to even begin to ask him. Suddenly his own thoughts about his parents seemed selfish, though he wasn't sure what was worse: a mother and father wasting away in a dark world or parents actively trying to destroy you in the real one.

"Yeah," Alex said, "I'm sure the Gloom will do that to you." He stood there, very aware of how awkward he felt.

"You're looking at me like I'm an alien," Amp said, sitting on the couch near Alex.

"Sorry. You all right?"

"Kind of tired of people asking me that, but yeah."

"Sorry."

"Quit saying that, too." Amp gave him a small smile. "I

mean, you're fighting against your family and stuff all the time now. For us. The last thing I should be doing is feeling bad about mine."

"Well, it's kind of a really different situation," Alex said.

"Maybe. But you still lost them." He frowned. "I didn't mean for that to sound like it did. I'm just trying to say . . . you know."

"We've all got some serious parent problems." Alex nodded.

"It's weird. I barely remember mine. Even the memories I do have of them are so hazy that they might not be real. I used to imagine everything I'd say and ask if I ever got the chance to see them. But that's not how it was in the Gloom. I don't think I actually believed they were really my parents until the very end, when they were dragging Ghost back into the portal. And then it clicked. Of course they were my parents. They were the Guardian and the Sentry, Rangers of Justice. They were heroes until the end."

Alex listened and bobbed his head in agreement while Amp spoke. The Junior Ranger never looked at him, just stared ahead at nothing. Alex didn't know what to say, but Amp seemed just fine with that.

"I'm back to where I started before we ever went into the Gloom. Not knowing for sure if they're alive or dead in there. Except now I know what that place is like."

"When all this is over—when we've defeated Cloak and

Lone Star and Lux are back to full strength and the Rangers of Justice are *the Rangers of Justice* again—we'll figure out what we can do for your parents. I mean, Gage basically punched a hole in reality. You were standing in another plane of existence yesterday. Figuring out a way for your parents to come back into our world should be a piece of cake, right?"

"Yeah," Amp said quietly. "I guess so."

"Say it like you mean it," Alex said. "You're the one who has always told me that if we're going to do something, we have to *believe* it can be done."

Amp let out a small laugh.

"You're right," he said. "Lone Star will get us out of this. We're smooth sailing now."

Alex forced a smile and walked away, putting all the floating notes and newspaper clippings back in their proper place. He was back in his room before he realized he was still holding the photo of the Beta Team. Instead of taking it back, he slipped it into his inner coat pocket, with the picture of his family. It was one of the few mementos he had of his past, and there was a possibility that he might not be back to the lake house after this afternoon.

We're going to do this, he thought. *Lone Star is going to lead us against Cloak. This is what we've been working toward. This is the end.*

* * *

Alex had worried that blending into the crowd would be easier said than done, even with hoodies and sunglasses and beanies obscuring their faces. Once they got near the former site of Justice Tower from the underground exit in Victory Park, all those fears vanished. He hadn't been prepared for such a mass of people, and from the shocked expressions of his teammates, he guessed they hadn't been expecting them either. Crowds littered the wide street for over a block, getting more congested the closer they got to the stage set up in front of a chain-link fence surrounding the leveled ground that had once been the Rangers' headquarters.

"How do we get through all these people?" Kyle asked as they reached the back of the crowd.

"We'll force our way forward," Lone Star said. "Once people realize who we are, everyone will part."

Long, dark-blue flags with golden starbursts hung all around from the tops of buildings and lampposts, the metallic symbols gleaming in the sunlight. Dozens of them, everywhere Alex looked. People carried signs, homemade posters, and banners singing the praises of the Rangers. At several stations, volunteers were painting golden starbursts on the cheeks of children.

Not far from them, a Deputy and a policeman argued about something near the officer's motorcycle, which was stopped at a traffic barrier. Alex strained to hear their conversation over all the other noise. Amp noticed.

"They're fighting about who's in charge of managing the crowd," Amp said, using his powers to isolate their voices. "It sounds like the Rangers wanted to use their own Deputies for this, not actual cops. The cop's not happy about it. He says they're obstructing law and order."

From somewhere in the crowd, another Deputy appeared, joining the argument. It took only a few words before the two figures with silver starbursts on their chests were accosting the officer, brandishing weapons. They used his own handcuffs to secure him before pushing him down the street, toward some unknown location. Amp stepped forward, but Alex reached out and grabbed his shoulder with his thoughts.

"We've got bigger problems right now," he said as he nodded to the front of the crowds.

The New Rangers began to climb onto the stage, accompanied by the whoops and joyous shouts of everyone in the audience except for Alex and his group. For a single moment, Lone Star looked taken aback by the crowd's reaction, but he recovered quickly.

"Thank you, good citizens," Shade said into the microphone. As usual, oversized black sunglasses hid her eyes. Titan, Volt, and Photon stood smiling at her sides. "It means so much to us that you've come to support the Rangers of Justice as we break ground on the site of our future headquarters . . ."

"This is it," Lone Star said.

Lone Star and the other Rangers weaved their way toward the stage, leaving Bug and the Cloak defects behind. Gage lowered his goggles, tapping on the sides to zoom in.

"Anything goes wrong and we send Misty to pull them out of there," Alex said.

"Lone Star won't be too happy about that." Mallory squinted at the stage.

"He's no good to us dead. Or under my mother's control."

". . . a place Sterling City can look to and know that we are watching." Shade continued to speak to the crowd.

When Lone Star got to the line of Deputies in Ranger-inspired fatigues, there was a small commotion. And then Lone Star's hood fell back. Even pale and weathered, there was no mistaking that it was him. Lux followed suit, as did the Junior Rangers. The crowds around them erupted and backed away.

"We will build our new stronghold atop a place of tragedy and—" Shade stopped midsentence and stared down at the five people gathered at the bottom of the stage. There was a beat before anyone spoke, and in the moment, Alex's mother simply cocked her head slightly to one side. She gave no hint of emotion, be it surprise or anger.

"Not good," Alex murmured.

"You are no Ranger," Lone Star said, thrusting a finger

forward and pointing it at Shade. When he spoke, his baritone voice was a bellow of sound projected through Amp's body. Kirbie's features were hinting at transformation. A tree growing from a sidewalk planter near them began to sway as Kyle held his hands out.

Lone Star turned back to the crowd. "I am Lone Star, leader of the Rangers of Justice. These are my teammates, Lux and the Junior Rangers. The woman who stands before you is no hero. Neither is Volt nor Titan. They are villainous members of the Cloak Society who have brainwashed Dr. Photon and are using him to gain power over this city." He turned his attention back to Shade, who regarded him with what Alex could only describe as a look of boredom. "In the name of justice, I demand that you surrender and turn yourselves in."

There was a snapping of photos as the crowd began to murmur. Shade let a long sigh out into the microphone. No one else on the stage moved, which worried Alex. In fact, he was surprised that they'd even let the Ranger talk for so long. What game were they playing?

His mother leaned in to the microphone.

"Citizens of Sterling City, this is not the first false Ranger to come forward claiming to be Lone Star, or Lux—though these appear to be in the company of the Junior Rangers, who, as recent investigations have confirmed, were working in league with the Cloak Society to plot the terrible attack on Justice Tower."

"Photon," Lux said, stepping forward. "I know you're in there somewhere. Help us. We're here now. Break free."

Photon took a few steps forward, staring down at his former teammates on the ground below. He clenched his teeth, and his body began to shake. While everyone's attention was on Photon, Alex watched his mother, whose eyes were shining silver so brightly that her sunglasses did little to hide the effect. She turned away from the podium. Photon walked rigidly to the microphone.

"We were going to wait until the end of the ceremony to share the good news," he said, "but I guess now is as good a time as any. Ladies and gentlemen, I apologize for the actions of these delusional impostors. What they're saying is simply impossible."

"No," Amp said, stepping forward, his voice echoing through the crowd. "Look! This is Lone Star and Lux! These are your protectors. Your *heroes!*"

"But how can that be when Lux is right here?" Photon asked.

It took a moment for Alex to figure out what Photon was talking about, but then he couldn't miss her. Floating down from the roof of a nearby building was Lux. Or at least, it was someone who looked exactly like every photo of Lux Alex had ever seen. Her hair was splayed about around her head, beautiful and luminous, as if producing a light of its own. Her eyes were bright and vibrant. On the ground in front of the stage, the other Lux reached out and gripped

Lone Star's arm. She already looked tired and weary from the Gloom, but all the blood had now drained from her face. It wasn't that the two women looked drastically different, but there was no denying that the woman slowly drifting to the stage and waving to the shouting crowds *looked* more like a superhero.

"What's going on?" Alex asked. "Wait, we do have the real Lux, right?"

"Look," Gage said, as his goggles whirred. "Did you see that? A slight ripple across the new one's face."

"Novo," Mallory spat.

"She's put herself back together," Bug whispered, his eyes glinting metallic.

Dread sent Alex's heart plummeting into his stomach.

"But how is she flying? And her hair . . . those aren't her powers."

"The hair's a trick of the lighting," Gage said. "If she can fake any material with her powers, she can produce highly reflective strands of hair. And she's not flying. Photon's doing it. Look at the belts and emblems on the new Ranger uniforms. They're all metal. He's using his powers to create the illusion that she's flying."

Novo alighted on the stage and walked to the podium. She smiled and waved as if she were in some sort of pageant. The crowd cheered and backed farther away from the five intruders at the foot of the stage.

"You have no idea how happy I am to be back, my friends," she said into the microphone, her voice a lilting singsong. "The New Rangers have rescued me from a terrible fate. In the coming days, I'll be sharing the story of how Shade, Photon, Volt, and Titan faced great evil to save me. But for now, I'd just like to thank them, publicly, and to say to the *real* Lone Star, wherever he is: we will find you, and you'll rejoin our ranks." She turned her head down to the Gloom-weathered man at the foot of the stage. "Soon."

"No!" Lone Star shouted. "You are *not* Lux. Lux is *here*."

"If that's true," Shade said, leaning over the microphone, "why doesn't she show us some of her powers? Why don't both of you fly up here and prove to the good people of this city that you are who you say you are?"

Lone Star and Lux stared back at her.

"I thought not," Shade said.

There was a gasp somewhere off to the right side of the stage, which morphed into screams. A pillar of darkness had grown out of the earth, and out of it walked three figures clad in black, hooded trench coats. Phantom. Barrage. Julie.

Alex's hand went icy as the mark of Cloak surfaced on his palm. A grinning, inky-black skull.

"Oh crap," Misty said.

"Villains!" Photon took the microphone. "You would

try to trick the public with henchmen made up to look like the heroes of this city?"

Phantom stepped forward. Even far away, Alex could see the glee on her face. They'd expected this, had turned it into an act for their benefit. A farce. In a single move, they'd taken all credit away from Alex and his team.

"Just a little joke, Rangers," she hissed. "But now comes the real fun."

Beside her, Julie's fingers stretched out into long, diamondlike talons. Razor-sharp spikes ripped through the upper arms of her coat.

"Deputies, take these agents of the Cloak Society into custody," Photon commanded. "That's a direct order."

"Move in," Alex shouted. He started forward, but someone grabbed his arm. Before he could cry out, several people in the crowd nearby turned to stare at him. All of them had the same face and body, with brown hair slanted off to one side. Beneath their hooded sweatshirts, they wore Deputy uniforms.

"Going somewhere, Knight?" they spoke in unison.

"Legion," Alex muttered.

And then, chaos.

9

A DEATH IN THE
FAMILY

Alex unleashed a telekinetic wave, pushing Legion and his clones back, giving him and his teammates some space. At the front of the crowd, Deputies swarmed Lone Star and the other Rangers as civilians darted in every direction, panicked, trying to fight through one another to get out of the way of what was fast becoming a war zone.

"I hope you've been working on your aim," Gage said, pulling two laser pistols from his pockets and handing one to Bug.

"Go," Mallory said to Alex as she incinerated one of Legion's clones. "Misty, take him to the front. We'll handle the others here."

Misty nodded and grabbed Alex's sleeve, and then they

were tumbling over the yelling crowd, molecules veering and swerving through the air, until they were put back together again between Kirbie and Amp, who were dodging stray punches from the Deputies trying to arrest them.

Two beams of light shot from a female Deputy's eyes, landing on Kirbie's shoulder. She looked down at the marks. A faint wisp of smoke drifted up from her hoodie. She took a single step toward the woman, transforming to her wolf form and loosing a terrifying roar. The Deputy retreated.

An explosion shook the ground near them. Thick black smoke billowed across the crowd. Barrage wasn't pulling any punches—he was using his power to create explosive balls of energy right beside hordes of civilians.

"We've got to take him down," Alex said.

"I'm on it," Misty said.

"Wait, don't—" But she was gone before Alex could finish his sentence. His gaze shot to Barrage. Suddenly Misty was beside the man, and then they were both gone.

"In the name of justice, I demand you—," one of the Deputies began, but Amp silenced him with a sonic blast.

A few yards away, Lux fought several opponents hand to hand while Kyle roused a few plants from Justice Tower's trampled garden back to life, sweeping them back and forth and knocking down Deputies while at the same time attempting to keep Julie from rampaging into the battlefield. Volt and Phantom pretended to fight, putting on a good show for any cameras that were still rolling.

Onstage, Shade stood between Titan and Novo, the Lux impostor, surveying the scene with what looked to be deep satisfaction. Photon floated above them, blank-faced. From the corner of the stage, Lone Star approached.

"You sadistic people," he said. "Don't think for a second that this means—"

In a flash, Shade drew a Taser gun from her belt and fired. An electronic charge sailed through the air, striking Lone Star in the chest. He hit the stage, convulsing.

"We've heard enough out of you for one day," Shade said, holstering her weapon.

"Lone Star!" Kyle shouted from the ground. He started toward the stage. A crackle of purple electricity snaked over his body, taking him down. Volt stood grinning behind him.

Alex leaped onto the stage, boosted by a telekinetic blast. With a nudge of his thoughts, he knocked Lone Star's body to the ground below, where Amp fought off wave after wave of Deputies. Shade reached into the podium and pulled the cord of the microphone out. She smiled at Alex, then her arm and the Taser shot out to her side, pointing at the crowd.

"No! You villain!" she shouted. "No! Don't make me fire!"

Electricity shot out of the gun. It hit one of the

Deputies—the woman with the failed laser eyes—in the shoulder. The woman was knocked back, screaming, and fell to the ground.

Oops, Shade's voice rang in Alex's head. He tried to pull the gun from her hands, but there was an impossibly strong resistance. And then he realized what was happening: Photon was making sure the weapon stayed right where it was. She was using Photon's powers to combat his telekinesis.

Settle down, or it will be your fault when half the crowd ends up collateral damage. His mother was in his head again. *I'd hate to lose that many loyal followers.*

"Titan!" she yelled, more to the crowd than her teammate. "Quickly, son. Grab him. He's using his telekinetic powers to make me fire on my own Deputies."

Titan grinned and walked around Alex, taking him by the shoulders and lifting him off the ground.

"Guess this didn't go like you wanted it to, huh?" Titan sneered into Alex's ear.

Alex focused his thoughts on his mother. She sparked a bright blue under his gaze and flinched.

"There you go again," she said. "What exactly is your plan here, Alexander?"

And in that moment, Alex didn't know what to do. He had his mother wrapped in his crackling telekinesis, but he didn't know how to proceed. She gestured out to the fighting on the ground at her feet. Several dozen Deputies were swarming Lux and Amp. Kyle had regained consciousness and now had Volt wrapped up in a mass of vines, while Kirbie slashed away at tendrils of shadow conjured up by Phantom. Farther back, Mallory, Gage, and Bug took on swarm after swarm of replicating Legions.

He could put an end to it right there. He had the power to do so. All it would take was a squeeze of the energy around his mother. It would release Photon and cripple all of Cloak's plans. One squeeze. That's all it would take. . . .

What was he thinking? He shook his head, frustration boiling in his brain. How was he supposed to protect his teammates and the city *and* his enemies? He felt helpless.

Shade smirked.

"Novo. Go untangle my husband from that overgrown shrub. Titan, help Legion."

"But—," Titan started, dropping Alex.

"Go," Shade commanded. Her eyes flashed behind her sunglasses. Photon's arm shot forward. Titan flew through the air, over the crowd, landing somewhere in the back near Legion and the others.

Novo hissed at Alex as she passed by, slamming one fist into the back of his head, causing his vision to blur and spark. He stumbled forward. Shade looked at him with consideration.

"You know," she said, "if we really wanted to, we could have gotten rid of you at any time. Found out all your secrets. Had you killed. Imprisoned. I could've locked you all away and made you live out every nightmare you've ever had in your head over and over again. Or slowly rewritten each of your minds like I'm doing to Photon. It would have taken a lot of time and a lot of work, sure, but we'd have had your powers on our side in the end. So I've taken it *easy* on you for the past month, treated you as a potential resource. If you were smart, you would have laid low. I might even have overlooked you. But then you had to go and *complicate* things."

Alex almost laughed at the idea that his mother might ever "overlook" him and his teammates.

"You can't keep this up forever, acting as both hero and villain."

"Of course not," Shade said. "Though I'd say you're hardly one to talk. To be perfectly honest with you, I still haven't figured out which way things will end. Becoming the Rangers had never been the plan—not until we realized what *potential* there was in having one of them on our side. At first I thought we'd just expose ourselves as being Cloak once we were in complete control, when it was too late to do anything about it. But it's so much easier to get what you want when the people think you've got their best interests in mind. Maybe we'll just absorb Cloak into the Rangers. Barrage and Julie will have changes of heart and pledge themselves to us. The public does love a reformed criminal."

"You always told us we would rule out of fear," Alex said. He knew there was no talking sense into his mother, but he could still keep her attention on him, off the others. Besides, he had to admit to himself that he was curious about what she was saying. He couldn't fit it all into the long speeches and manifestos about Cloak's superiority he'd grown up listening to. "The Cloak Society is better than normal people, right? Why care about what they think?"

"I thought the Tutor made you read Machiavelli. To be feared is to have power over someone, true, but it's always better to be feared *and* loved. *That's* real control. Besides, look how easily they accepted us. They can't be trusted on their own. The people need us to tell them what they should do."

"You won't get away with this. Even if you stop us, someone else will oppose you. Some other force."

"Other force?" Shade asked. "Look at Lone Star and Lux, Alex. They're the heroes. They're supposed to be the most powerful beings on earth. And what are they doing? Fighting for their lives. They're powerless. Nothing."

"You're insane," Alex said, his mouth hanging open.

His mother's face grew dark as she clenched her jaw.

"That's not a very nice thing to call your mother."

Her eyes flashed silver behind her sunglasses and she took a few steps back. Above her in the air, Photon's face strained, the veins on his neck popping out. At first Alex couldn't figure out what the man was trying to do, and hoped that maybe he was waging a war in his head and about to break free from Shade's control. Then Alex turned and saw the police motorcycle from down the street flying through the air, sailing right toward him. Its speed shocked him so much that for a second he didn't move. And then it was upon him, closing in, faster and heavier than he could have any chance of stopping with his powers.

He ducked and weaved at the last possible moment. The back wheel of the motorcycle—still spinning—came within an inch of his nose. It splintered the wooden podium before rolling several times and exploding somewhere atop the ruins of Justice Tower.

Shade didn't let up. As Alex tried to make sense of the fact that his mother had just hurled a motorcycle at him, Photon shot straight down, all fists. Alex barely had time to catch him and hold him in midair. Suddenly Julie was on him, too, charging at him from behind. Alex thrust his right hand up, wrapping her with his thoughts, keeping her trapped in the air. She let out a howl and slashed at the empty space in front of her. Spikes jutted out from her shoulders and elbows.

"Let me down and fight me, you idiot!" she shouted.

"Tell me, Julie," Alex said as he poured everything he had into his powers, "how mad are you that your brother got picked to be on the Ranger team while you're still stuck underground?"

Julie's lips drew back in an angry sneer. "My role in all this is very important."

Alex started to sweat. His breathing grew labored. He slowly turned his head back to his mother.

"Is this it, then?" Alex asked through gritted teeth. "Are you going to make an example of me here on the stage?"

Shade shook her head slowly.

"For a while I wasn't sure what to do with you," she said. "If it came down to it, how would I end my only son? Could I? But the answer was simple. I *don't* destroy you. I make you watch as we triumph, knowing that you can't stop us. We're gathering arms, Alex. Gathering comrades. While you were breaking into the underground base to help rescue your useless Rangers, we were visiting the Guild of Daggers in New York. In exchange for leaving the Northeast to their control, they're making all sorts of fun things for us." She raised a hand, as if to stop him from speaking. "Don't worry. The Guild will eventually kneel to us once they've served their purpose. With Gage's notes and drawings and Photon's brilliant mind, you can't imagine the surprises we've designed."

Alex's head spun.

"You mean *weapons*," he said.

Shade shrugged. "We'll really only need to make an example of one or two major cities before the rest of the country does whatever we ask of them. Scare them into trusting us or scare them into fearing us."

"The rest of the country?" Alex asked. His mind raced. Photon was inching closer to him. He couldn't think straight. "What are you talking about?"

Shade's face lit up with laughter, as if this were the silliest question she'd ever been asked.

"My dear Alexander. You didn't think we were going to stop with Sterling City, did you? This is just the first step. And look how easy it was."

"Impossible. You'll never be able to—"

"But you're going to see it, Alexander! All of it! And when you break, I'll know your thoughts. I'll know all your secrets. And then I'll rewrite you. I'll rewrite all of you. And in the end you'll look at me with nothing but unshakable love and respect."

Suddenly his mind was clear. Her threats had struck a nerve. For the first time Alex understood that Shade was a villain first and a mother second. She had always told him that Cloak was to be put before everything in life—that it was priority above all else. Up until recently, that had included Alex. He realized that somewhere deep down he'd been hoping that her love for the Society would carry over to him even if he wasn't a part of it. But it didn't. He was a means to an end. And that *hurt*.

Alex began to tremble. His hair and clothing started to billow, as if he were underwater. Power welled up inside him like he hadn't felt in weeks—since he'd faced off against the Cloak Society in that very spot. He started to rise up off the stage, until he floated several yards in the air. There were flashes where he was sure that the others could see his energy, like crackling light wrapped around Julie and Photon. A radiant blue poured out of his eyes as he stared down at his mother. Shade took a few steps back. There was the slightest twitch of worry on her face.

I have to do something, Alex thought. *I have the power. I'm in control. I have to do something and then get us all out of here.*

"That's it," Shade whispered. "Burn out. Put on your big show and then end up cowering on the floor. I'm going to lock you down in the depths of the underground base and make you watch as I reprogram every one of your new friends."

Alex's eyes shot across the street in front of him. Kirbie was pinned down by Phantom's energy. He couldn't find Misty or Mallory anywhere among the panicked crowds of Deputies and onlookers. Amp held out against combatants but looked exhausted.

And then there was Gage. Titan held him up in the air by his throat. The inventor's hands shot to his white lab-coat pockets, where Alex was sure he had a stash of Gassers or some kind of weapon. But Titan caught his arm—he'd fallen for that once already, when they'd stolen the Umbra

Gun from the underground base. Titan grinned, and his eyes turned to Alex, onstage. He let go of Gage's neck and swung him out to one side, holding the boy in the air.

Then Titan squeezed his fist tight around Gage's forearm.

Gage's face twisted in anguish. Even over the commotion, Alex could hear the inventor's scream, primal and filled with pain. Titan dropped the boy to the ground, kicking him out of the way like trash. Gage's arm swung loosely, awkwardly in the air. Broken.

Instinct took over for Alex. His friends. They were being hurt. They would *continue* to be hurt. Unless he acted. Somewhere in the back of his mind, his mother's voice was shouting. Not telepathically this time—it was the memory of something she'd once taught him. *Don't be afraid to strike. Protect yourself and your team, for you are one and the same. Show your enemy how powerful you are. Make them fear you.*

And so he did.

All the energy that burned up inside him burst outward in an explosion of blue light. Waves of Deputies fell to the ground as the stage pitched and collapsed beneath him. His mother flew back, tumbling into the chain-link fence behind them. Photon's body was pushed to the ground, where he landed in the crowd, taking out a handful of opponents swarming Amp. And with a little guidance from

Alex, Julie slammed into Phantom, freeing Kirbie.

Alex hovered in the air for a few seconds and then dropped straight to the ground, landing hard on his knees. He struggled to catch his breath. His powers had knocked the wind out of him.

"No, no, no!" Julie shouted. "Somebody, help. Dad! Shade! Anybody. Somebody do something."

Beside the girl, Phantom was on her knees. There was a look of disbelief on her face, her dark lips forming a loose O. She slipped one hand underneath her trench, over her heart. Alex could see her pale white skin through a hole in the coat. When she brought her fingers back out, they were stained a deep red.

"My spikes." Julie was nearing hysterics now. "I didn't know. I didn't know she was in the way."

"No . . . ," Shade whispered as she climbed to her feet.

Phantom fell onto her back. Shade was by her side in an instant. Phantom sputtered, but Shade shook her head, her eyes shining silver. Everyone stood frozen, unsure of what to do. Except for Julie.

"It's Alex's fault!" She was shouting now. "Alex did this."

Before Alex could begin to process what was happening, Phantom took a ragged gasp and then went very still. He'd never imagined her skin could go any paler than it already was, but somehow that was happening right before his eyes. Then, slowly, her body began to melt away. There was no portal, no inky tendril pulling her into the Gloom like when she used her powers. Her body simply turned into darkness, until it was only a shadow, and finally, nothing at all.

There was a sudden burn in Alex's right palm. He looked down at it, the mark of Cloak staring back at him. The oily black skull began to dissipate. Phantom's energy left Alex's hand, floating up into the air in front of him before fading away completely.

"No," Alex started. "I didn't mean to—I mean, I never wanted her to . . ."

Shade raised her head and stared at her son, her eyes normal, human, so that he could see every ounce of anger and hate in them. Without opening her mouth, she let out a psychic scream unlike anything Alex had ever felt before, an animal wail that echoed through his thoughts. All around her, people fell to their knees, clutching their heads.

The next few moments were a blur. Alex's brain felt fried from the energy it had taken to fight off his opponents and from his mother's scream. Someone—Amp—was dragging him off the stage, past Titan, who sprinted by them and toward Shade. Amp was asking him something, but Alex's head was ringing so loud he couldn't understand what Amp was saying. And then Misty was there, and he was no longer whole, just floating over the wall and through the city and the park. It was hard to piece thoughts together when he was like this, under Misty's power. Hard to make the right connections. Everything was a haze of thoughts and memories blending into one another. He saw his mother at the dinner table, eyes wet and severe, telling him and the other Betas what it was like to survive Victory Park and the horror of hearing her teammates' last thoughts shouting in her mind. Another memory, this time both of his parents, calling him the greatest weapon Cloak would ever know.

And finally, something almost completely forgotten. A Thursday outing from before his powers had ever developed. Misty was there, five or six years old. Phantom was in charge of them. They were at a carnival, or fair—he couldn't remember the details. Only that he was very happy. Misty had her hand in her aunt Phantom's. And when Alex had wanted to get his fortune read, Phantom had simply smiled at him and told him that he was destined for great things.

Alex and Misty reassembled outside a long white van with blocked-out windows. They were somewhere a few streets away from the groundbreaking catastrophe. Before he could ask questions, Lux pulled him inside the van, where his other teammates were waiting. Gage was in the seat beside him, his teeth gritted together, clutching his useless right arm as Mallory waved a cold palm over it.

"That's the last of us," Misty said, almost collapsing into the backseat.

"Get in already!" someone shouted from the driver's seat

as Amp climbed into the back and slid the door shut.

"Who . . . ?" Alex mumbled, unable to finish his thought. He felt so tired all of a sudden.

The woman in the driver's seat looked at Alex in the rearview mirror, and then nodded toward Lone Star, who sat in the passenger seat.

"I'm the cavalry," she said.

"It can't be like this," Lone Star murmured to himself. "How could the people of Sterling City turn on us like that? This can't be right. This can't be right."

As they sped through the streets, he continued to chant these words over and over again, as if by saying them enough times, he could convince himself and everyone else in the van that they were true. Alex fought to keep his eyes open, to figure out what was going on, but the world faded to black around him.

10

PAPER ANIMALS

When Alex woke up, he was on an unfamiliar couch in a room he'd never been in before. His forehead was freezing. The first thing he saw was a framed poster of Lone Star hanging over him. It was old, and torn in the corners—the kind of decoration that had probably moved around from wall to wall and room to room until someone finally put it behind glass to protect it. Lone Star was younger in it, his suit slightly different—a gold starburst over his heart. Alex stared at the poster, blinking, trying to make any sense of where he was or how he'd gotten there.

Phantom. The image of Shade cradling her and screaming into the sky flashed through his mind, the memories of the botched mission flooding in. His head throbbed.

Around him, the couch and side table and lamp trembled.

"You're awake," Mallory exclaimed, rushing over to him. Behind her Misty was lying unconscious on a bed. Gage watched over the girl. His right arm was in a sling.

Words started to pour out of Alex's mouth, a gush of half-formed questions and worries and confusion. When he sat up, a cold, damp towel fell from his head, landing on his lap.

"You were sweaty and gross," Mallory said. "Gage thinks you overheated or something. I was trying to cool you down a little." She nodded to the towel.

"Misty?" Alex asked.

"Just sleeping," Gage said. "You both exerted an enormous amount of power today. It makes sense that you're both exhausted. You've been out for half a day."

"Gage . . . your arm."

"Broken, I'm afraid," Gage said. "Carla managed to get me in a cast before Deputies were sent out to hospitals or anything like that. But I can still type and fire a weapon with my other one."

Alex's eyes darted around as more questions tumbled from his lips. They were in a bedroom somewhere. But where? And who was Carla?

"Lone Star's sister," Mallory said, recognizing his confusion. "This is her house. She's his secret contact in the city. Really secret. I don't even think Lux knew she existed until

Lone Star was directing us to the van. He was afraid that Phantom or someone might be able to track us if we went to the tunnel. . . ."

The mention of Phantom's name derailed the sentence, and Mallory trailed off, unsure of what to say. Alex's breath got heavy and fast.

"Where's everyone else?" he asked.

"Downstairs," Gage said.

"Is anyone else hurt?"

"Not physically. But I think Lone Star's ego is more than a little bruised."

"We're on the far east side of the city," Mallory said. "Suburbia. We managed to slip out unnoticed. With all the chaos, no one was able to follow us."

"The cut on your face opened up again," Gage said. "We'll need to clean it."

Alex raised a hand to his cheek. "I don't feel it."

"You're in shock, Alex."

The word "shock" only made Alex think of his father's purple electricity, then the High Council, then the now-vacant seat at the head of the table where Phantom always liked to sit in the War Room of the underground base. He shivered as a chill ran up and down his body.

"Phantom is dead," Alex said. His voice had no emotion attached to it. He didn't even know what he was supposed to be feeling.

Gage and Mallory stared at him, both silent. Finally Mallory spoke.

"Then that feeling in my palm—our marks are really gone."

"She's dead because of me," Alex said, staring past them. "It's my fault." Even as he spoke the words, he wasn't sure he was saying them loud enough for anyone to hear. Everything felt fuzzy. All he could think was that he'd finally lived up to his potential as a killer, as a weapon. What must his parents have been thinking at that moment? Was his mother proud?

"It was an accident," Mallory said. "You can't blame yourself."

"Their response to this will be brutal. They'll go insane."

"We can't go back to the lake house." Mallory shook her head slowly. "Shade's going to rip apart Photon's head trying to find us."

"I can't even check in on the cameras and alarms," Gage said. "My electronic tablet was damaged while I was fighting against Legion and his clones."

"Gage, what about the Gloom Key?" Alex asked. "It's still there, right?"

"Hidden in a cooler in the rafters of the garage. But honestly, if your Cloak marks disappeared, I don't even know if it's functioning now. It ran on Phantom's energy."

"All our notes," Alex said. "All our stuff."

"I guess we can officially say that rescuing the Rangers was not the answer to any of our problems," Mallory murmured. "Everything's gone wrong."

"It's going to get worse. What do we know about the Guild of Daggers?"

Gage and Mallory both looked puzzled.

"The who?" Mallory asked. "Wait, aren't they—"

"The group that Cloak was visiting when we snuck into the underground base to steal the components to the Gloom Key," Gage said, picking up on her thought. "They're some sort of organized crime syndicate in New York. Not as old or powerful as Cloak, but just as secretive. I think there are a few superpowers between them, but they're mostly mob and Mafia families. I only know that because of information I picked up here and there at the base. Why?"

"Cloak is working with them on something."

"On what?" Mallory asked.

"I don't know," Alex said, rubbing his temples. "Weapons and plans. Once they have the city, they're going to take over the rest of the country. We were talking right at the end, right before everything went terrible and I . . ."

He couldn't finish the sentence.

"Phantom's death has severely hindered Cloak's ability to move around," Gage offered. "Not to mention it's severed their connection to the Gloom. Really, this is a key strategic victory."

Gage stopped talking when he realized that nothing he was saying was helping.

Alex felt sick.

"Bathroom?" he asked, getting to his feet.

Mallory pointed to the door. "Take a right. It's the first door on the left."

He rushed out, a little wobbly on his feet, and found himself in an open den with a staircase leading down on one side. A few steps later he was in the bathroom, where he fumbled with the light switch. He didn't throw up, but his body and head hurt. Before he knew what he was doing, he had his face underneath the faucet, letting cold water run over it.

When he finally calmed down a little, he wiped his face with his sleeve and stared into the mirror. His fingers traced the red cut that started on his cheek, just below his right eye, and disappeared into his wavy brown hair. His head was reeling. Scenes from the day kept flashing in his mind. He wanted to hit reset. He needed a do-over. And more than anything, he needed someone to tell him what to do. That things would be okay. That they had a plan.

For the first time since leaving Cloak, he unquestionably missed his parents. Not the ones who had trained him and had fought against him earlier that day, but the parents who smiled when he'd made them proud. The ones in the picture his father had given him on his twelfth birthday.

That Volt and Shade were all grins. They were the parents who'd sat on the end of his bed at night and told him stories about the glory of his destiny and his ancestors. His thoughts went back to when he'd first developed his powers. He'd woken up—still just a Gamma, one of the unpowered children of Cloak—and discovered that his vision had been tinted blue. Freaking out, he'd made his way down to the bottom floor of the underground base where his parents lived, a place that normally he'd need to be escorted to or from. His mother had been unhappy that he'd broken the rules but had let him into their apartment. As he stammered, trying to explain to her that something was wrong with him, she'd tapped her fingernail against the side of her coffee mug, a sign of annoyance. Alex had stared at the mug, hating it as he spoke. And then suddenly, it sparked a bright blue and flew across the room, shattering against one of the walls.

Shade had looked shocked for only a few breaths before a smile spread wide across her face. She'd run to Alex, scooping him up in her arms and holding him tightly.

"My darling son," she'd whispered into his hair. "You've finally gotten your powers. You're one of us."

Alex had felt so safe and happy and proud.

In the bathroom, he tried to hold on to that feeling, that one good memory, but his thoughts insisted on straying. Kirbie pinned to the ground by Phantom's powers. Photon,

Julie, and his mother all attacking at the same time. Gage's arm, snapped. An explosion of telekinetic power, and the slightest nudge of his thoughts to ensure that Julie rammed into Phantom. It was this last detail that caused his chest to tighten and clench. In the heat of battle, he'd directed the girl with all the spikes sticking out of her into his enemy to free his teammate.

He told himself over and over again as he stared into the mirror that Phantom's death had been an accident. He'd only meant to free Kirbie and hopefully escape with their lives. But there was a voice of doubt in the back of his head that kept asking questions he didn't have answers to. Had he thought that Julie would transform back to flesh and blood before hitting Phantom? Or maybe that Phantom would disappear or dodge? Or had he known in some horrible place within himself that sending Julie careening toward Phantom would result in injury, even death? It was only logical. It was an *obvious* risk. But he'd done it anyway.

He worried that he had not escaped the darkest parts of his past. That killing ran in his blood. He'd done what his mother had taunted him about not being able to do. Even if he blamed the attack on instinct, all that meant was that he couldn't trust his own nature. He couldn't trust *himself*.

He felt helpless.

There was a knock on the bathroom door.

"Alex," Gage said softly. "Is everything all right?"

"Yeah," Alex lied.

"Misty's up. I think it would help if she saw you. I'm . . . I don't think I was helping when I talked to her."

"Sure. I'll be out in just a second."

Alex tried to compose himself as best he could. Misty needed him. The *team* needed him. Now more than ever. He had to put on a brave face for them. Things would only get worse from here. The Cloak Society would become vengeance incarnate.

The sound of sobbing could be heard from outside the bedroom door. Alex stopped. His heart sank. He knocked on the door. From inside there was shuffling, followed by some sniffles, then Misty's voice.

"Come in."

Alex found Misty and Mallory sitting side by side on the end of the bed together. Mallory gave him a small smile as he entered, but Misty turned her face away. Even without a clear view of her, he could tell that she'd been crying. Her cheeks were all puffy and red.

Alex pulled a chair over and sat across from the two girls.

"Uh, so . . . ," he began, "are you okay?" He felt stupid asking. Of course she wasn't.

Tears immediately began to fall from Misty's eyes. She pretended they weren't there, looking away from Alex. Her chin quivered a little.

"Misty . . . ," Alex said, but the sound of his voice was apparently a trigger for her, and she fell back on the bed, burying her face into a pillow.

"She was a bad person." Her voice was muffled. "But she was my aunt. I saw her all the time and now she's dead."

Alex looked at Mallory, who shrugged back at him, not knowing what to do. Misty started crying harder. He thought about finding Kirbie, but he doubted that anything anyone could say to Misty would make her feel better at that moment. How was he supposed to know how to comfort her when he was barely able to comfort himself? They had never trained for this.

He looked around the room, exasperated, trying to find something, anything to console her with. His eyes landed on a stack of multicolored construction paper on a desk in the corner of the room. He used his powers to drift it over to them, until it was in his hands.

"Misty," he said, "what kind of animal do you want?"

She sat up, confused at first. Then she understood.

"I don't care. Just something pretty."

Alex stared down at the paper, pulling a few sheets into the air with his thoughts. Simultaneously, they all began to fold, and then suddenly there was a swan, and a crane, and a butterfly floating around Misty's head. But Alex didn't stop. Sheet after sheet flew into the air, creasing and folding and tucking. He racked his brain for every pattern he'd ever seen or used in his precision training with his mother. When he ran out of dragonflies and birds and pterodactyls, he switched to things that couldn't fly—frogs, giraffes, flowers, and stars. He kept folding and folding until there was no more paper. Only then did he really look up. All around the room origami shapes hung in the air. Dozens of them, floating and bobbing on little clouds of telekinetic power.

Misty smiled a little bit. She reached over to put her hand on Mallory's, then jumped.

"Mal, you're freezing."

Mallory looked confused for a moment. Her eyes had been drifting among the paper designs.

"Oh, sorry," Mallory said, little white puffs of breath accompanying her words. "I just got a little caught up in everything."

There were tiny crystals of ice around her eyelashes, perfect frost flakes shimmering in the light. As she concentrated, they melted.

STARLA

They regrouped downstairs. Bug and the Junior Rangers lounged around in the living room, a big area with cream-colored carpet and brown, overstuffed leather furniture. Through a window, Alex could see Lone Star in a chair on the back porch, huddled in the corner, as far out of sight as possible. He looked defeated.

When Alex walked in, he felt as though all the sound had been sucked out of the room. Everyone stared at him, and he looked down at the floor uncomfortably, trying to figure out if he should say a few words to address what he was sure everyone was thinking about. Luckily, a rising argument from down the hallway started to drift into the living room, capturing everyone's attention. He didn't recognize the voice that spoke.

"This city's about one disaster away from crowning the New Rangers as absolute rulers, and it seems like every local government body is onboard with them. Whatever's happened since you've been gone happened by design, and I'm guessing you know more about it than I do."

"That's Carla, Lone Star's sister," Mallory whispered to Alex. "Apparently she works with the district attorney in the city."

"You should ask Amp and Alex to walk you through it." Lux's voice filtered out from the hallway. "They know the information inside and out. They probably have a better idea of what Cloak's going to do now than we ever could."

"I am *not* trusting the fate of the city to the imaginations of a handful of kid superheroes and possibly reformed supervillains," Carla spat.

The door in the hallway flew open, and Carla stepped out. It was the first time Alex had gotten a good look at her. She was in her midthirties, he guessed. She wore a dark-navy suit, her strawberry-blond hair cropped short around her head—maybe even shorter than his own unkempt hair. She didn't look much like her brother, exactly, but there was something similar about the way they presented themselves. She might not have had Lone Star's height or stature, but she stood in front of Alex with a look of determination and self-assurance.

Carla locked eyes with Alex and his fellow former Cloak

members. Her frown deepened as she shook her head.

"I apologize if you heard me say a few harsh things just now," she said, stepping forward. "You can imagine that emotions are running a little high. I never meant to question how much any of you have contributed to this city. And from the brief rundown I got from Lux, it sounds like I owe you for saving my brother. I'm Carla, by the way. As you probably already know, my relationship with Victor—I'm sorry, with Lone Star—is highly classified information."

"I didn't even know about her," Lux said quietly. "It was a matter of protection. The last thing Lone Star wanted was for one of our enemies to hurt our loved ones to get to us."

"The rest of my family is on an emergency trip to the in-laws until everything blows over," Carla said. "I have a lot of explaining to do once they get back."

"Do you have powers?" Alex asked. A glimmer of hope welled up in him that they might have stumbled across a new Lone Star.

"Only in the sense that I've managed to figure out how to convict all the criminals dropped off on our doorstep by flying men and women in tights and spandex over the last few years. Some of us have to keep our feet planted in the real world." She cocked her head toward the window. "He wanted to call me 'Starla' and market us as a brother-sister crime-fighting duo when we were kids."

One by one they introduced themselves. When Misty spoke, Carla's eyes narrowed.

"I've seen you on the news. There's a *billboard* with your face on it near my office. I know the woman claiming to be your mother. Is she?"

"She's my mom," Misty said quietly. "I haven't seen her for a long time, though. She always lived in the city, and I always lived underground. She's a part of Cloak, but she doesn't have any superpowers." Her voice got quiet. "A billboard?"

"I never did like her," Carla muttered.

Misty stared down at the floor.

"I'm sorry," Carla said. "I didn't mean—You all must be hungry. I'll order—No, we probably don't want people coming around. I'll see what I can find in the kitchen. You can make yourselves at home. My children's rooms are upstairs, but some of you will have to sleep on the couches down here. I can't say I was prepared for anything quite like this."

She seemed happy to excuse herself, leaving Lux to face her younger teammates. She looked weary. Haggard.

"You're not feeling any . . . stronger?" Bug asked.

She shook her head, glancing out at Lone Star. She moved toward the back door but then stopped, sinking instead into an oversized chair. The room was quiet again.

"Listen," Lux said. "I don't want you to take anything

Carla said to heart. No one's questioning your loyalty or anything."

She spoke as if she was talking to everyone, but her eyes were on Alex.

"I guess if I were in her shoes, I probably wouldn't trust us either," he said.

"It's almost funny," Lux said. "You're probably more like the founding Rangers than any of us."

Everyone looked to her in confusion. At first she seemed a little worried, opening her mouth to speak but not actually saying anything. Then, she got a curious expression on her face and turned to Alex and his fellow ex-Cloak members.

"How much do you all *know* about the history of Cloak and the Rangers?"

It was just one question, but at the same time, every question. It was something he'd never really had to think about before. He'd grown up in the shadow of Victory Park—the Rangers of Justice had always been their ultimate enemies. They were the force that stood in the way of Cloak's rule, perhaps the only people who had the power to do so. That's all he'd ever *needed* to know. Beyond that, he knew that the Rangers had first banded together before he'd been born. They'd cleaned up Sterling City, and their presence had helped to turn it into the metropolis it was today. Or it least that it *had* been.

"The Cloak Society is made up of people unafraid of breaking laws to get what they want," Gage said. "The world calls them supervillains. The Rangers of Justice are the law enforcers called heroes. It's only logical that two such forces would clash. Philosophically speaking, I'm not even sure one could exist without the other."

"How does that make sense?" Kyle asked. "I mean, if we stop Cloak, we'll still be Rangers."

"You can't have heroes without villains. And there will always be someone else," Gage said, glancing at Alex. "We'll need to brief them on the Guild of Daggers when you're feeling up to it."

"Then they didn't tell you," Lux said. "I can understand why. I mean, we hadn't told the Junior Rangers yet."

"Told us what?" Kirbie asked.

Lux paused. She took another look at Lone Star outside, then a deep breath.

"How did the Rangers of Justice form?" she asked.

"Bastion," Amp said. "He was the first Ranger almost three decades ago. When he saw that crime in America was on the rise and that villains with dangerous powers were becoming more and more common, he gathered together forces of good from across the country. In the name of truth and peace, they formed the Rangers of Justice. Eventually, they settled in Sterling City. Bastion died fairly young. He was sick. Leadership was passed down over the years to my father, the Guardian, and after Victory Park, to Lone Star."

Alex could tell that this was something Amp had probably heard a million times. When he spoke, it was like he was reading from a teleprompter.

"That's exactly what Bastion wanted the public to believe," Lux said. "That people with astounding powers banded together in the name of justice. Who wouldn't read that story and champion their cause?"

"But it's not true?" Kyle asked warily.

"Only partly," Lux said. "The myth of the Rangers leaves out an important detail: Bastion had grown up in the Cloak Society. He was a deserter. The Rangers weren't going all over the place just to rid the country of crime. They were recruiting. Bastion knew if Cloak ever took action, he'd need other superpowers to fight against them. He founded the Rangers to protect the world against Cloak, or any other force like them."

Alex's eyes went blank. His lips started to form a series of words all starting with *W*, but his brain couldn't figure out which question to ask first. Around him, the others looked dumbfounded. Everyone except for Gage, who narrowed his eyes in contemplation.

"Who knows about this?" Amp asked.

"Only us, now," Lux said quietly. "Actually, I'm assuming the higher-ups in Cloak know as well. It's a closely guarded secret. We were just waiting for the right time to tell you."

"I can see why the High Council would want to keep this from us," Gage said, nodding. "It doesn't really bode well for their ideology if their greatest enemies came from their own ranks."

"It would have been the generation between my mother and grandfather," Alex said. "No wonder my mother and the others were so eager to go into battle against the Rangers at Victory Park. They were fighting against someone who'd betrayed them."

As he spoke the words, he realized immediately how well they described him, too. He shuddered.

"It also explains why they moved from the old mansion to the underground base so quickly," Mallory said, smoothing down her chestnut hair.

"Wait," Misty said, joining the conversation. "So we're basically just like the original Rangers, right?"

"Exactly," Lux said.

"Most people who made a difference in history were rebels or deserters of some kind," Gage added.

"It's a good story," Amp said, "but it doesn't really change what's happening *now*."

"What do you think they're doing?" Lux asked.

Alex explained to the others the only updated information they had—who the Guild of Daggers was and that the group was somehow involved. Cloak would be expanding as soon as they'd secured Sterling City. Their retaliation for Phantom's death would no doubt be swift and extreme.

"I don't even know where they'd be right now." Alex sighed. "But the way my mother talked today . . . I think there's something big coming. Something that threatens everyone, not just the people of Sterling City." He glanced at Gage. "I just don't want anyone else to get hurt."

The back door swung open. Lone Star stood there, grim.

"It's time for the news," he said, staring at the television. "I want to know what they say about us."

Alex and his teammates gathered around the television in Carla's living room. The news coverage from the groundbreaking played out just as they'd expected. Newscasters praised the return of Lux while condemning the Junior Rangers once again, implying that the Lux and Lone Star "impostors" were in fact agents of the Cloak Society sent to try and destroy the New Rangers from within.

"The Rangers of Justice, in conjunction with the mayor's office and the city council, have declared martial law in Sterling City," a newscaster reported. "In addition to the curfew already in effect, a full-scale manhunt is currently underway for any and all persons who can be linked to the Cloak Society. Roadblocks have been set up on all roads leading out of the city, and helicopters are patrolling our borders. Citizens are urged to stay in their homes and follow any directions given to them by the Rangers or Ranger-appointed Deputies. Remember, no matter how well you *think* you know someone, they may in fact be a highly trained Cloak operative. It's important that you report any suspicious behavior to the Ranger hotline listed at the bottom of the screen."

"Great," Amp said. "Just what those untrained idiots need: absolute authority on the streets."

"That hotline probably goes directly to Cloak," Mallory said. "They're completely bypassing the police."

"And spreading fear," Gage added. "That line about not trusting your friends and neighbors—they're cultivating paranoia."

"It's going to be madness," Lux whispered. "Imagine being able to send Deputies to the doorstep of any person you'd ever been angry at."

"We could get out if we really wanted to," Bug said. "Misty could help us, or we could just fight through the roadblocks."

"They're not worried about us escaping," Alex said. "They know we won't leave the city. This is just an act. They're showing off how much control they have."

Onscreen, the newscaster continued.

"The following footage is a taped message from Lux,

whose return was announced before the Cloak interference at today's groundbreaking ceremony."

In Carla's living room, the real Lux jumped to her feet as Novo the shape-shifter stepped in front of a microphone. Alex could only imagine what it must have felt like to see not just a copy of yourself, but one that seemed to exude the sort of strength and vitality that had been sucked out of you.

"I am here tonight to inform the villains of this city that no longer will the Rangers sit idly by waiting for your next move. We are coming for you. We will find you. We have help."

Beside her, Titan appeared, holding a large silver metal case. On the top was a small symbol in black: two daggers laid across one another to form an X.

"The Guild of Daggers," Alex said. "This must be what my mother was talking about. They're working together on something. They—"

Alex stopped as Novo pulled a weapon out of the case. It was a sleek, matte-gray rifle with a boxy containment unit on the back. It pulsed with a deep-purple light.

"Impossible," Gage whispered.

"This is a fully functional prototype for what we're calling 'the Umbra.' It's an ingenious crime-fighting tool developed by our resident weapons expert, Shade. This device does not shoot bullets or lasers, but a *synthesized,*

nonlethal energy bolt that immediately transports anything—or anyone—it touches to a state-of-the-art prison
facility designed to house superpowered criminals. For
security reasons, we are not currently at liberty to say *where*
this facility is located. While the use of this weapon is a last
resort, if the villains of the Cloak Society do not turn themselves in, we have no choice but to use drastic measures. At
an accelerated manufacturing speed, we will be able to arm
our ever-growing squad of Deputies with these weapons in
the near future."

She paused for a moment, as if waiting for an unseen
audience to take in this information. In the living room,
there was barely the sound of breath.

"No, no, no . . . ," Lone Star repeated. His hands were
shaking.

The camera zoomed out as Novo aimed the gun at a
mannequin onscreen. She fired. There was a low, resound-
ing electronic sound. An inky black splotch grew over the
mannequin's chest, until it covered the figure completely.
Then, suddenly, it was gone—melted away.

Alex just stared at the television. Again, it was a per-
formance meant only for them. To show them they'd been
outsmarted. If Cloak and the Guild of Daggers had managed
to synthesize Phantom's energy—and from the demonstra-
tion it seemed that was *exactly* what they'd done—what
would keep them from creating *countless* weapons? They

wouldn't even have to stop at Umbra Guns. They could have bombs, missiles—weapons that could send entire cities into the Gloom.

Novo stared straight into the camera.

"Turn yourselves in, and we will show you the mercy of justice. But if you force us to hunt you down—if you endanger the lives of countless civilians in your selfish attempts to defeat us, we promise you that you will know true fear." She paused, and Alex was sure he could detect a twitch of a smile as she added, "And gloom."

OVERHEARD

"Carla, Lux," Lone Star said, "we need to speak in private. The rest of the team stays up here for now."

"There's the office over here," Carla said. Then, after thinking about it for a beat: "Or we can go down to the basement. It might be a bit more private."

"No offense, *sir*," Alex said, "but you can't call us your teammates if you're going to shut us out of whatever you're planning to do next."

"I understand your concerns."

"If you really understood, we wouldn't have shown up to the groundbreaking like we did today," Mallory said.

"They did try to warn us, Star," Lux said.

"We did what we thought was best. You know that, Lux."

Carla raised an eyebrow and turned to her brother. Lux frowned, but nodded. She turned to Alex and Kirbie and the others. "Just give us ten minutes to talk and we'll be back. We won't do anything without consulting with you all first."

And with that, the three adults were gone.

"This is ridiculous," Mallory said. "They've only been out of the Gloom for a day. There are months—*years* of background they need to know."

"Lone Star said to trust him and—," Kyle said.

"No," Amp said, getting to his feet. "Mallory's right. They may look at us as their junior team still, but we know way more about what's happening right now than they do." He made a beeline for the basement door in the hallway.

"They're not going to be happy if they find out we've been spying on them."

"We shouldn't *have* to be spying," Alex countered as the others followed Amp down the hall.

"Shhhh," Amp said. "Everyone just shut up and let me do my thing. I need to concentrate."

He placed his left hand on the door to the basement and held his right palm out toward the others. Voices from downstairs started to pour out of him, amplified.

"How bad is this, really?" Lone Star asked. "How are things looking from inside the government? Isn't there anyone opposing the Rangers' growing control?"

"In your entire tenure as a Ranger, did anyone *ever*

come out and say they didn't want you protecting the city?" Carla asked. "There are people against giving the Rangers so much power, sure, but they're in the minority. And it's not exactly an open topic of conversation. You get around enough people who are die-hard in favor of every suggestion and decree the Rangers are making and you start to feel like maybe they're right."

"It's herd mentality," Lux said. "They've got enough implants in the system to sway anyone who might be on the fence."

"Wait . . . who *heard* what?" Misty asked on the first floor.

"No, *herd*," Alex said. "Like you'd herd sheep or cows or something."

"Cloak's like a virus," Kyle whispered. "It just keeps spreading."

Carla started talking again.

"What's their end goal? To take over the city? The country? World domination?"

"All of the above," Lone Star said. "Maybe even more."

"Don't you have other superhero friends or something you can call in as backup?" Carla asked.

"No one who could take on Cloak. And I wouldn't be surprised if half the 'heroes' we know about are now running around the city as Deputies. We don't want to risk giving ourselves away."

"Ah. Now there's something that's *not* going in their

favor. All these 'Deputies of Justice' suddenly have rank over the *actual* police. I've been in contact with the commissioner. We haven't spoken directly about the situation, but I can tell he's not pleased with the way things are going. Neither are his men. If we had to, we could probably get some sort of police presence to back you."

"That's something that could totally help us," Kyle said.

"It would certainly look good if we had the police on our side," Gage agreed, adjusting his sling with a scowl. "We could use some kind of government agency backing us."

Alex nodded. He didn't want to put the police in harm's way actually fighting Cloak, but there was surely some way that they could help him and the others out. *If* they could get the police on their side.

"What about the National Guard or FBI?" Lux asked. "Where are they?"

"They were here after Justice Tower fell," Carla said. "*Everyone* was here. But when Dr. Photon showed up with his new teammates, suddenly all the agencies backed off. I think they thought it was a lucky break. No one was sure whose jurisdiction the Rangers and Cloak fell under to begin with. It's not like any of them were trained to deal with supervillains. That's always been *your* job."

Alex could imagine the High Council congratulating one another upon hearing this statement. Their theories had been right. The Rangers *had* made the city weak in some ways. With them out of the equation, it had been so easy for Cloak to swoop in and take over.

Carla continued.

"Give it to me straight: if it came down to a fight, would you two be able to defeat Cloak and the New Rangers together?"

"Just the two of us against all of Cloak?" Lone Star asked. "There's no way we could take them on. Not like we are now."

"But we've got the Junior Rangers and the Cloak defects on our side, too," Lux offered.

"They're *children*," Carla said. "I have two of my own their age. I don't care what kind of powers they have or what they've been through to get here. They shouldn't be put in danger. I've *never* approved of your use of children as soldiers."

"They're our *teammates*," Lone Star said.

"I'm surprised they made it this far alive. In fact, I can't believe someone didn't step in and stop you the first time you unveiled Amp as your sidekick, much less formed an entire *team* of underage superheroes."

"Their actions have saved countless lives."

"And the others? The ones who were trained to murder and become, what, twelve-year-old dictators? You do realize that one of them killed their former teammate today. I imagine you won't be so quick to defend them when it's *you* they've turned on."

Misty and Mallory shifted on their feet uncomfortably. Alex didn't breathe. He felt like he'd been punched in the stomach. Kirbie looked at him and shook her head to try to dispel the words from sinking in, but it was too late.

"We kind of saved her brother's life," Misty whispered. "*Starla* should be thanking us."

"I *trust* them," Lone Star said. "Every one of them. If you had any idea what they've been through the last month, you would too."

"STOP IT!" Lux shouted. "Both of you. There's a group of psychopaths posing as both the good guys and the bad guys right now. They've got the city in a vise. They have *at least* one Umbra Gun and claim to be able to make more. Now what are we going to do about it?"

There was silence for a few moments. In the first-floor hallway, everyone was growing restless.

Lone Star's voice started to drift out of Amp's hand again.

"The city has turned on us. We don't have any powers. Maybe . . . maybe it's time we start thinking about turning ourselves in."

"What?" Lux asked.

"Victor . . . ," Carla said.

"Maybe they'll even just take me," he continued. "Then they'll have a full set of Rangers. I'm powerless. It's not like I'll do them much good other than speaking engagements and propaganda. It could buy you all some time."

"He's lost it," Kirbie whispered.

But Alex didn't think that was the case. It wasn't so much giving up as it was desperation. He'd wondered plenty of times if handing himself over to his parents might help to save his friends and teammates. There was something very familiar to him about Lone Star's hopelessness.

"There has to be another way," Lux said.

"We can't fight them," Lone Star said. "I won't watch any of those kids get banished to the Gloom. Or killed. I don't even know which is worse. You heard what Novo said. You know what's coming next, right? They'll wage a fake war between Cloak and the Rangers. They'll tear down this city to find us. This might be the only way we can protect people from being harmed."

Huddled in the hallway, Alex and his teammates listened grimly. None of them spoke, but Kirbie walked away, back into the living room, where she paced back and forth. She disappeared for a few moments before returning, holding Alex's trench coat.

"The Gloom Key was at the lake house, right?" she asked.

"It was," Gage said. "I can't say if it still is."

"We need that device. If they have a real Umbra Gun, we need a way into the Gloom."

"But Phantom's energy left our bodies," Mallory said. "Does the key even work anymore?"

"Gage, is there a *chance* the Gloom Key still works?" Kirbie asked.

"Of course," Gage said. "There's always a chance."

Kirbie turned to Alex. "Do you trust me?"

"Of course I do," Alex said, without having to think about the question at all.

"Good. Then let's go."

"My mother knows we're a threat now. She'll probably torture Photon until she's pulled every secret from his head. Cloak might already know about the lake house."

"Are you trying to talk me out of this?" Kirbie asked.

"No," Alex said. "I just want you to know what we're getting into."

"Kirbie, no," Kyle said.

"Lone Star might have given up, but I haven't." Kirbie headed toward the back door. "It's night, the city's under lockdown, and Misty can't travel to and from the lake house in one trip. I can carry Alex. We'll grab the Gloom Key and get out of there."

Before anyone could talk her out of it, Kirbie was in the backyard, with her eyes to the sky.

"There's even plenty of cloud cover."

"This could be a trap," Kyle said as he and the others followed her outside. "They could be waiting for you there."

"I doubt it," Alex said. "Cloak's furious. They'll want action. Even if they've already found the place, they wouldn't sit around waiting for us. They wouldn't even know how recently we used it as a base. We could have moved on weeks ago."

"Wait," Amp said, stepping forward. His voice was stern, authoritative. He tossed something to Alex. A communicator.

"Notify us the second anything goes weird," he said as Alex slipped the device over his ear. "And get back as soon as you can."

"Don't worry," Kirbie said. "I've been taken prisoner by Cloak twice. It's not going to happen again."

"Here." Gage fished around in his coat pockets before pulling out the device he'd used to track Lone Star in the Gloom. He tapped on it a little clumsily, bracing it against the side of his sling. "I've set it to detect heat signatures, so you're not going in there blind. You should be able to use it once you get within two hundred yards or so of the base."

"Thanks, Gage."

"Maps, notes, blueprints," Amp said. "Whatever you can grab that might help us. And then you're out of there."

"Laser pistols. Gassers. Really anything from the garage would be great," Gage added.

"It's dangerous," Kyle said.

"This is something we can actually do," Kirbie said. "If we're turning ourselves in, what's the difference anyway? Do you want to become one of Shade's brainwashed puppets? I won't. I've had her in my head once, and I won't let it happen again. I'm going to fight this until my last breath."

"Just be careful, Kirbs." Kyle offered a small smile. "I can't believe you're going to leave us to deal with telling Lone Star and Lux. You'd better go now, before they realize what's happening."

And with that, she was a golden bird, huge and majestic, her talons around Alex's shoulders as they flew into the night.

BLACKOUT

They stayed above the seemingly endless quilt of dense gray clouds as they soared across the city. At first Alex had trouble breathing normally, but he soon got the hang of it. He couldn't help but let all his anxieties and fears float away, into the night air that chapped his lips and kept his eyes half-squinted. Every so often the cover would break, and suddenly he had stunning views of places in Sterling City he'd never seen before. He wondered how Kirbie ever managed to stay on the ground when she could have views like this all the time.

It took them almost half an hour to get to Silver Lake, the northernmost neighborhood in the city. When they got close, Kirbie let out a shrill call and they began to descend.

Alex whipped out the device Gage had given him, scanning the area around them.

"I'm not getting anything on thermal yet," he shouted so Kirbie could hear. Then, taking a closer look at the screen, he squinted in confusion. "Wait, that can't be right. . . ."

Before he could investigate further, they were flying through the clouds, the thick, damp air filling his lungs. And when they finally emerged into the open, he saw that the device hadn't been malfunctioning. Far ahead of them were the house and garage on Silver Lake. Or at least, it was the place where these buildings *had* been. Now there was nothing but embers and thick black smoke.

Kirbie let out another call, breaking Alex's stunned silence. He looked back and forth between the ground and the device in his hands.

"I'm not seeing anyone," he said. "Just the burning buildings."

Still, Kirbie circled the site a few times before landing near the edge of the water, where the dock had jutted out into the private cove. Now the dock was gone, leaving a few splintered boards behind. Half the water was still frozen over from the day before, the other half a slushy, melted mess.

"I didn't see anyone either," Kirbie said after she morphed back into her human form and started making her way up the sloping bank. Thick curls of black smoke swirled upward all around them as Alex followed. They passed the propeller from the boat that had been sitting in the garage the last time Alex had seen it. Now it was wedged into a tree a dozen yards away. He recognized the destruction that Barrage's powers could cause. A mixture of fire and pressure and explosive force that broke apart everything it touched.

The garage had been leveled. It was nothing but a pile of debris smoking on top of a black foundation. Alex's thoughts tore over the scorched pieces of wood and metal and concrete, picking through the destroyed building and sending embers and ash flying. His face and hands stung as tiny bits of orange rested on them, fading to dark gray smudges. In a few moments he'd dismantled the shell of the garage that remained and began sifting through the ruined tools and equipment, the items darting in front of his face as fast as his brain could latch on to them. Kirbie stayed back, watching as the items flew like mangled metal birds through the air before her.

Minutes ticked by as Alex continued, growing more frustrated, focusing more intensely, until in one wave of thought he sent all the refuse in the air flying backward and deep into the wooded area behind the garage. He started in on what remained on the ground, sifting and searching and plowing through the brittle, seared matter until finally he found it. The Gloom Key, with the huge Excelsior diamond mounted on top. Half a plastic cooler was melted around it. He smiled.

And then he turned the device over with his thoughts. The containment unit that had held Phantom's dark energy was punctured. Empty.

The Gloom Key was useless.

"Of course . . . ," Kirbie said, stepping up beside Alex.

"We didn't even get a chance to see if it would still work now that Phantom's gone," he whispered.

Alex furrowed his eyebrows together and concentrated. The Excelsior diamond flew out of its mounting and hovered in front of them. He let the rest of the device fall to the ground. It was useless now. The diamond lit up as it reflected the small fires and embers surrounding them. Not long ago, he would have given anything to have the Excelsior. It had been his primary target on his first mission, back when everything seemed so easy, so black and white. *Get into the vault. Steal the diamond. Prove your worth. Make your parents proud.*

"If I'd known how much trouble this thing was going to cause . . . ," Alex trailed off, staring at the jewel.

"What?" Kirbie asked. "You would have done things differently?"

"Not everything."

Kirbie turned to the place where the house had stood. There was less remaining of it than the garage. Alex took the communicator and radioed back to Amp, telling him that the Gloom Key was a dead end and that they'd be back soon.

"They know about the underground tunnel now," Kirbie said. "If they know about this place, they know about it, too. They know about everything."

"Not Carla's. We're still safe there."

"For now."

"We could just fly away," Alex said. Kirbie turned and stared at him. He wasn't even sure where those words had come from, just that at that moment all he wanted to do was leave, to put everything behind them.

"I know," he continued. "We can't."

"Why not?" she asked.

Alex shrugged. He didn't think she was actually looking for an answer. She'd never run away. She'd brought them all the way out here in the name of fighting until the end, after all.

"I don't know," Alex said. "Because it's not the right thing to do."

"Congratulations, Alex Knight," she said. "You're a superhero. I was right about you all along."

"Yeah. And look what you got for trying to talk sense into your enemy."

"Where would we go?" she asked. "What would we do if we weren't trying to save the world?"

"I don't know," Alex said. "What do normal kids do? Go to school? Take math tests?"

"Play sports. Perform in musicals. Get detention."

"Oh, I've had detention. I had to be a moving target for the others while they were shooting paintballs at me."

"Oh yeah?" She gave a small smile. "Once I snuck out of Justice Tower for a flight. I had to clean the entire inside of the dome as punishment."

"I guess that just means we definitely aren't normal kids."

He started to sift through the ashes of the house, but it was quickly apparent that it was of no use. They weren't going to find anything they could use there. Their lists and blueprints, Gage's notes—everything was gone. He sighed, staring at the clouds.

"You doing okay?" she asked.

"Yeah," Alex said, but even he could hear that it wasn't a very convincing answer.

"Look, I'm not going to push you or anything, but I want you to know that what happened at the groundbreaking wasn't your fault, okay? It was an accident. We're practically in a war right now, Alex. I'm surprised none of us have been hurt more than we already have. And we . . . we never should have done things so quickly, without proof or knowing what Cloak was up to. You tried to stop us, but we were so sure that just having Lone Star and Lux back would fix everything that we ignored all the warning signs."

"What if . . . ," Alex started. "What if it wasn't an accident, though? What if it was my Cloak training, or something like that? I don't want it to happen again."

"There," Kirbie said, squinting her hazel eyes a little. "What you just said. Doesn't that prove you didn't mean for Phantom to really get hurt?"

"But—"

"I know you pretty well, Alex. I could tell you were one of the good guys when you didn't even know it yourself. If you wanted me to, I could talk for the next hour about how much I believe that what happened today wasn't on purpose, or how even if it was, it probably saved a ton of people in the long run and definitely helped us out, or how I'm pretty sure that Cloak wouldn't flinch if one of the Junior Rangers bit it in the middle of a fight—but I'm guessing this is all stuff you already know and don't want to hear me talk about. So instead, just know that all of us still trust you and everything. Nothing's changed."

Alex stared at her, his mouth parted slightly. The blue tint of his vision had rolled away as she spoke, leaving her in full color.

"Please say something, or else I'm going to keep talking and end up feeling really dumb."

"Thanks," he said. "Really. I needed that."

"Good."

"Now we just have to figure out how to save the city. And how to get Lone Star back to being more of a super-hero."

"And if we can't do that, we'll defeat Cloak without him."

"That's treasonous talk," Alex said, though he wasn't sure if he was using the word "treasonous" correctly.

Kirbie shrugged. "I guess I've picked a few things up from you in the last few months, too."

Alex started to respond defensively, but her smile stopped him.

"We should get back," she said. "Is there anything else we need to do while we're here?"

"No," Alex said. "I think we've gotten all we can from this place."

They were halfway back home when Kirbie, in her bird form, jerked to the side suddenly, looping around and diving through a break in the clouds. Alex's feet flew back, his coat whipping around his legs. He was disoriented, hardly able to tell up from down as they plummeted toward the earth, landing on the top of some tall structure.

"What's going on?" Alex asked, getting to his feet, braced for an attack. He looked over the side of the roof. They appeared to be on top of a school auditorium.

"Don't you notice anything weird?" Kirbie asked. When

it took Alex a moment to respond, she continued, "There aren't any lights on anywhere, Alex. It's a blackout."

Of course. A darkness had settled on the city. For as far as Alex could see, there were no streetlamps on, no lights in the windows.

"This is crazy," he said. "I guess my father might have been able to do something to the power grid. Or Photon could have—"

"Shhh," she cut him off. Her features were shifting, changing, her ears pointing outward and hinting at transformation. "There's something happening over there."

A block away, four Deputies were dragging a family out of their home. Dogs were barking. Alex could hear the family—a man and woman, a teenager, and two kids who looked much younger than Alex—all screaming and shouting. There were no police, no flashing lights. Only the Rangers' Deputies and a black paddy wagon.

"Crap," Alex said. "What do you think it is?"

"I don't know. But if the Deputies are doing it, it can't be good, right?"

"How far are we from Carla's?"

"Far enough that they'd never be able to track us there," Kirbie said. "What do you say? I could blow off some steam with a good fight right now."

Alex didn't respond, but gave her a sly grin.

"Let's do some hero work."

She transformed as she leaped into the air, swooped around, and then grabbed Alex, flying down the block. She released him with a pendulum swing of her talons, sending him rocketing toward one of the Deputies, a middle-aged man who never saw Alex coming. The boy's feet struck against the man's chest, sending him sailing backward through the air.

"Sorry to drop in on you." Alex grinned.

"Seriously?" Kirbie asked, as she landed beside him. "*That's* your line?"

The remaining three Deputies—and the family— looked stunned for a moment, and Alex and Kirbie didn't give anyone time to make a move against them. A telekinetic blast knocked the wind out of a woman in blue and silver, while Kirbie took out a teenage girl who appeared to have the ability to produce strobe-light effects from her eyes. All of them were carrying Cloak-issue laser pistols.

That left only one Deputy. Alex sent a telekinetic bolt into the man's stomach, but he didn't budge. Kirbie rammed a shoulder into the man's back, to no effect. They continued trying to knock him down for a few more seconds, using a variety of powered and non-powered attacks. Finally Kirbie stopped.

"What are you?" she asked. "Some kind of human boulder?"

The man, who had appeared to be stunned into still

silence throughout the attacks, spoke up.

"I have a very strong center of gravity."

"That is *not* a superpower," Alex said, and with a few stray thoughts, he had four laser pistols pointing at the man's head.

Kirbie turned to the family. They'd sent the two younger kids inside. A middle-aged man and woman stood on the lawn, in front of the teenage boy, whom they appeared to be hiding.

"What do you want?" the man asked.

"Want?" Kirbie was confused. "Just to stop whatever *they* were doing."

"I know who you are," the woman said. "You're criminals."

"You have no idea," Alex murmured.

"Why were they here?" Kirbie asked, ignoring her teammate.

"You can't have him!" the man said, taking a step forward.

Alex zeroed in on the still-standing Deputy. He tapped one of the guns against the man's forehead.

"What were you doing here?"

The Deputy stammered a bit before words finally came out.

"The kid's been drafted," he said, his voice several pitches higher than it was before the four weapons were floating around him. "We had orders to collect him. The whole family if they gave us trouble. It's an honor to be wanted by the Rangers."

Alex turned to the three civilians on the lawn, his face twisted in confusion.

"It was just a rumor," the woman said. "Some kids at school made it up to give him trouble."

"Did you call the police?" Kirbie asked.

"I *am* a police officer," the woman said. "Trust me when I say there's nothing that calling the police would have done but get good officers in trouble."

"Oh, come on," the teenage boy said, pushing through his parents. He clapped his palms together in front of his chest. Both hands erupted into flames. "I can take them. They're just kids."

Alex pointed a finger and lifted him into the air. The boy's smug self-assurance faded into fear. The fire disappeared. Still, Alex was impressed with his guts.

"We're *not* here to hurt you," Kirbie said, casting a chiding look at Alex. The teenager sank back to the ground.

"Do you have a car?" Alex asked.

"Out back," the boy's father said. His voice wobbled just a hint.

"I'd suggest getting out of the city. I know the people after your son. They don't give up easily."

The family stood there in silence before nodding and hurrying inside. The woman stopped just before entering.

"Thank you," she said.

Kirbie and Alex turned to the remaining Deputy.

"Who ordered this?" Kirbie asked.

"One of the higher Deputies. An Alpha."

"You're kidding me," Alex said.

"Cloak never was one for original ranking systems, I guess," Kirbie said.

"And this blackout. I'm guessing that was you guys, too?"

"U-uh . . . ," the Deputy stammered. "All I know is that right before they sent the squads out, everything went dark."

"Squads?" Kirbie asked. "Plural?"

"I don't know how many. A few dozen, maybe?"

"And they're all collecting people?"

"Yeah," the Deputy said. He averted his eyes from theirs. "Anyone with powers. Or people rumored to be speaking out against the Rangers."

Alex swallowed hard. Even if his teammates were there with him, there was no way they could stop every Deputy sent out. He felt useless as he glanced around the yard. His thoughts focused on a garden hose and wrapped it around the standing Deputy, tying it tight. The other three remained down.

"Please, please. I won't tell anyone about you if you let me go safely," the Deputy pleaded. "Honest."

"You *will* report this. Not to an Alpha. To the New Rangers," Alex said, mustering up his most authoritative voice. "As soon as you manage to get yourself free, you go straight to them. That's the price of us letting you go."

The man looked confused, but nodded hurriedly.

"Good," Alex said. "When you talk to Shade, tell her that her son is coming for her."

"We should get out of here," Kirbie said.

"Yeah, let's—"

A pounding from inside the paddy wagon interrupted him. He and Kirbie looked at each other, then hurried to the big black vehicle, flanking either side of the back. Kirbie nodded to Alex, who wrenched open the doors with his thoughts.

There was a series of gasps. Alex looked inside to find a dozen sets of eyes looking at him, maybe more—it was difficult to tell in the darkness. The captives stared back at them, unsure of what to do.

"This is crazy," Kirbie whispered.

"They're not just building a new police force," Alex said. "They're drafting an army."

14

FLIGHT
PRACTICE

It was late by the time they finally got back to Carla's house and landed in the backyard. They briefed everyone who was still awake. Lux and a few others were waiting for them downstairs, candles providing flickering light in the living room. Lone Star and Carla had apparently already gone to bed, which was just as well for Alex—he didn't want to have to endure a lecture. Alex doubted any of them would sleep well knowing that there was an Umbra Gun out there but once again no way into the Gloom. On the plus side, their encounter with the Deputies *had* gained them four laser pistols.

Lux frowned at Kirbie and pulled her to the stairs.

"I know we shouldn't have—," Kirbie started.

"I trained you better than this," Lux said. "I know you were listening in on us talking. I don't blame you for trying to figure out a way to help the situation. For wanting to fight. But what would we have done if you hadn't come back? What if . . ."

Her voice trailed off.

"I'm sorry," Kirbie said.

"Don't pull anything like that again," Lux said. Her words were harsh, but her tone was softer than before. "Ever."

Kirbie nodded, and they climbed the stairs.

Alex stayed in the living room, tossing himself onto one of the couches. Amp was on the one beside him. As they lay awake, Amp spoke.

"It kills me that I'm not out there right now, knowing what the Deputies are doing."

"That's probably what Cloak was hoping for," Alex said. "Draw us out, then attack us. We lucked out with the ones we ran across. They didn't get a chance to call for backup."

"You're probably right. Half of us would end up in the Gloom by dawn."

"If the Guild of Daggers created a new Umbra Gun, Gage can probably turn it into a new Gloom Key," Alex said. He was thinking of Amp's parents, and what the loss of the device meant for their future. "I mean, that's what he did with the last one. It doesn't mean we're locked out of the Gloom forever."

"Yeah," Amp said quietly. "But I'm not getting my hopes up."

Neither of them spoke for a minute.

"Thanks, though," Amp said. "For thinking about it."

"Yeah, man. Of course." He was glad to envision a family reunion that turned out happy for a change.

A chiming clock woke Alex in the middle of the night, and he lay awake, trying unsuccessfully to go back to sleep. Every time he closed his eyes, all he could see was the surprise on Phantom's face before she melted into the shadows, and the hatred in his mother's eyes once she'd disappeared. He tossed and turned, and then just lay there, staring at the ceiling, trying not to have a single thought and hoping that sleep would sneak up on him.

There was a thump somewhere outside. Alex was off the couch in a flash, at the window, ready to raise an alarm and wake everyone else if necessary. He was just about to yell at Amp when he realized that the man in front of the backyard garage was Lone Star, dressed in dark clothes. Alex watched as he climbed up the side of the garage with impressive agility, then stood on the edge, eyes closed. He took a deep breath and leaped, falling to the ground below and landing like a gymnast completing a dismount. He stayed like that a few moments before jumping to his feet and making his way back to the top of the garage. Again, he stepped off the edge, only this time he held his arms out at his sides. He fell as if he were going to belly flop into a pool, his body scrunching together and bracing itself for impact against the ground at the last possible second.

Lone Star stayed crouched low to the earth. He pounded a fist on the grass.

Alex was furious. First Lone Star had cut them out of his planning, and now the man was outside doing some weird training regimen and risking being seen by someone overhead or passing by. And what if the Ranger sprained an ankle, or broke a rib? Alex quietly slipped out the back door.

Lone Star noticed him approaching just as he started to climb up the side of the garage again.

"I didn't set off an alarm or something, did I?" he asked.

"No," Alex said. "I heard you . . . hitting the ground."

Lone Star shook his head as he flung himself over onto the roof of the garage. That was when Alex realized what the man was doing.

"You're trying to fly, aren't you?"

Lone Star didn't respond but looked up at the sky, staring at something in the distance.

"There's Pegasus," he said, pointing to a clump of stars. "The flying horse."

"Next to Andromeda," Alex said. "But she's behind the clouds."

"You know the constellations?"

"I spent a lot of time up on the roof when I could get out of the underground base. Staring at the sky. It was a lot easier to find things at the drive-in, though. No houses or trees."

"Amp told me," Lone Star said. His lips curved up just a bit in a small, sad smile. "Of all the places I imagined the Cloak Society hiding, I have to say I never expected it to be beneath an old drive-in theater."

"That was kind of the point," Alex said.

Lone Star nodded. "I used to sit in the dome at the top of Justice Tower and look at the sky. That's how I know the stars so well."

"You shouldn't be out here." Alex suddenly felt strange telling Lone Star what he should and shouldn't have been doing. Even if he had taken over and ignored Alex and the others, he *was* still a legend. "I mean, you know . . . Someone could see you."

"I'm keeping my eyes open. No paddy wagons have been by. No sign of Cloak."

"You heard what Kirbie and I saw, I guess."

"The house has thin walls," the Ranger said.

"Aren't you going to yell at us for leaving?" Alex asked.

"And risk waking half the block? You're not stupid, Alex. You know how risky that was. And you're probably smart enough to know that running off like that put not only yourself but all of us in danger. Your friends could have gotten seriously hurt if you were tracked back here."

Alex shrugged. He hadn't really thought about those things. When Kirbie asked him to go, he'd just known that he wanted to do something, anything to help out.

Lone Star's posture straightened, as if he were about to perform a perfect dive into an unseen pool.

"Don't worry about the ground," Alex said. "I'll catch you."

"Are you sure?"

"If you don't trust me, you'd better regain your powers quick or you'll end up with a face full of dirt."

Lone Star smiled wider this time. He leaped from the rooftop with his eyes closed. His trajectory was high and far, his body curving gracefully. Alex could tell he'd trained in acrobatics, like the other Rangers—his form was flawless. For a moment, he seemed to hover in the air, and Alex believed that maybe he *had* suddenly regained his powers. But then he began to fall, plummeting toward the grass and dirt below. He flashed in Alex's mind. Blue energy sparked and caught the man a foot from the earth.

Lone Star opened his eyes. They lit up, until he realized that it wasn't his own power that was keeping him afloat.

"You're good."

"Thanks," Alex said, waving his hand and twisting Lone Star's body until the man was standing in front of him. "I've had to get much better in the last month, but I've still got a ways to go in terms of control and strength. I've learned a lot from the Junior Rangers, though."

"I imagine they've learned just as much from you. I can tell by the way they move and strategize now. Amp came out to talk to me earlier, and I didn't know he was there until he was beside me—didn't make a single sound when he approached. That must be something they picked up from you and your team."

"We helped each other out," Alex said. "We did the best we could."

Alex had all but forgotten how angry he'd been when he started outside. He realized this was his first time alone talking to the leader of the Rangers of Justice. It was different from when there was a group. Lone Star didn't have to keep control of the room or show his authority. And it was far different from the brash, egotistical man that the High Council had spoken of—the one who'd destroyed half of Cloak, including Alex's grandfather, in a ball of light and fire a decade ago. He was just a guy, talking.

"I've had my powers since I was about your age," Lone Star said. "I haven't felt so chained to the ground in almost two decades."

"I bet it's hard."

"What about you?" Lone Star asked, leaning against the side of the garage. "The Junior Rangers trust you. You've helped save them more than once. But at great cost. I know a little bit about what it's like to have to turn your back on your family, but nothing like what you must have gone through. How are you faring now that you're fighting on the other side of things?"

Alex was quiet, thinking this over and wondering how best to answer the question.

"My mother used to always talk about how the Rangers had it so easy. The people followed you blindly, showering you with praise. She said you made them weak with your help. They depended on you too much. And the reasons we would be called supervillains and bad guys was because we'd make them see that. But eventually they'd serve us out of respect for our power, or out of fear. I guess I always thought it would just be a lot simpler to be a Ranger than a member of Cloak. But I don't think that's really the case. I mean, I know these are really extreme circumstances, but still."

"What I do—what *we* do—sounds easy," Lone Star said. "Stop the bad guys. Keep the people safe. Make sure life can progress without someone threatening to turn half the city into a frozen wasteland. But it's more complicated than that. When people imagine what the Rangers of Justice are like, they believe us to be these saint-like figures incapable of doing evil. They think our superpowers also grant us the ability to know the difference between right and wrong so well that there's never a question in our minds as to what choice or decision we should make. But that's not how it works. We're only human. We're as confused as the rest of the world."

Alex couldn't believe what he was hearing. Here was Lone Star, model of all that was good, admitting that he made mistakes. That sometimes he didn't know what the right thing to do was, or if there even was a right thing to begin with. Alex felt somehow relieved.

"How do you do it, then?" Alex asked. "How do you figure out the best thing to do when someone's going to get hurt no matter what you choose? Even if they are the bad guys."

Lone Star smiled a bit.

"You don't ever figure it out. Not really. You'll always wonder if you should have done things differently. But you know this already. You made a choice to turn your back on Cloak."

"I don't regret that," Alex said.

"Then you're thinking about today. About what happened to Phantom."

Alex nodded. Phantom, and the future.

"Alex, if anyone is to blame for that incident, it's me. That was an accident."

"I guess a part of me is afraid it wasn't."

Lone Star's face hardened. When he spoke again, his

words were chosen very carefully, his voice a level deeper than it had been before.

"I want you to listen to me carefully, Alex. To do something like that—to take the life of another person—is a conscious thing. I know. Ten years ago in Victory Park I made that decision. Even if it was fueled by rage and grief and fear, it was the choice *I* made. They called me the *hero* of that battle, but I felt like I had become what I hated. I'd turned my back on everything I held close. It's something I've had to live with every day since then."

"But what you did at Victory Park . . . you *saved* the city. Not to mention Lux and Photon. If Cloak had managed to defeat all of you, who knows if anyone could have stopped them? You *were* the hero that day."

"So does that make it right?"

Alex didn't have an answer. On one hand he knew the fate that Sterling City had been saved from, but he also knew the anguish of living through it in the underground base. The orphaned Omegas. The death of Julie and Titan's mother. His own parents' desire to have him as prepared as possible for any situation.

"Exactly," Lone Star said in response to Alex's silence.

"We'll face Cloak again," Alex said. "Soon. What am I supposed to do if I can save a bunch of people but have to hurt some of my former teammates to do so? Or my parents? How would I live with myself afterward?"

Lone Star placed a hand on Alex's shoulder and stared down at him intently.

"It's my goal that you'll never have to make that choice. Any of you."

In that moment, Alex could see why the Junior Rangers spoke of Lone Star with such high regard, as if he had every answer to every problem in the world. And Alex, for the first time all day, felt hopeful.

SCYLLA AND
CHARYBDIS

By early afternoon the next day, lights were coming on across the city. Cell towers and phone lines were strangely affected by the loss of power, however. The city's communication was temporarily cut off.

The Cloak Society was tightening its reins.

"There's a storm coming," Alex said. He stood at the windows, looking out onto Carla's backyard.

"Normally I'd say you were being a little dramatic, but under the present circumstances I would have to agree," Gage said.

"No, I mean literally. It looks like it's about to pour."

The sun was hiding behind dark, heavy clouds. Most of the team was sitting around downstairs. Lone Star was napping in one of the bedrooms. He'd been up most of the night keeping watch over the house and trying to jump-start his powers in some way, to no avail.

"How can they get away with this?" Kyle asked. "I mean, if they were dragging people out of their homes all night . . ."

"They run the media, and they've cut off the only forms of communication most people know about," Amp said. "People probably think they're isolated incidents."

"Or they don't care," Alex said. "I'm guessing the New Rangers can get away with most things if people think it's for the greater good."

"Besides, it's martial law now. Everything they do is technically legal."

"We're boxed in. Misty's now our only reliably stealth transportation."

"I am *not* just some kind of human escape vehicle," Misty said. "Even if I *am* good at it. Besides, I've been stretching my powers with the eight of us. I don't know if I could handle Lone Star and Lux as well. I know he's not as powerful as he was before he went into the Gloom, but the dude is still, like, five times my size."

"Lone Star acts like he's completely lost hope," Kyle said quietly, running a hand through his blond hair.

"He'll be okay," Alex said. And he believed it.

"So our choices now are basically face the Cloak Society

head on or let the city—and then the *country*—fall, right?" Amp asked. "That's a real question, because the way I see it, things are looking pretty crappy for us."

"We can't even worry about the rest of the country right now, I don't think," Mallory said. "We just have to focus on stopping Cloak here."

"We're sailing between Scylla and Charybdis," Gage said.

"Who and what?" Kyle asked.

"They're from Greek mythology," Gage answered. "Two sea monsters on either side of a narrow channel of water. In *The Odyssey*, Odysseus has to steer his ship between them, knowing that no matter which side he gets closer to, death awaits. They're really more metaphors than anything else. Odysseus is one of the first epic heroes of literature. I figured that would have been Ranger 101."

"So what happens?" Kyle asked. He seemed genuinely interested, as if Odysseus's decision might offer a solution for all of them. "Which way does he choose to go?"

"He sails closer to Scylla, since the other path was so dangerous that his entire ship would definitely have been destroyed."

"He makes it out?"

"Yes. But he still loses half a dozen of his men to the monster."

"The lesser of two evils," Bug chimed in as he rubbed

the back of a finger over Zip, who perched on his knee.

"That probably would have been a simpler idiom to use, yes," Gage said. "Sorry to spoil it for you, but the entire crew except for Odysseus ends up dying pretty soon after that anyway, so I wouldn't put *too* much stock in that as an example."

"It's an apt comparison," Lux said, coming in from the hallway.

"We were just discussing our options," Kirbie said. Misty sat beside her on the couch, braiding her blond locks.

"Or lack thereof," Gage murmured.

"Keep going." Lux leaned on the back of the couch.

"What do you mean?" Kyle asked.

"The eight of you got more done in the last month working together than seems possible," Lux said. "Seeing all of you fight together yesterday—if I didn't know better, I'd swear you'd been training as a team your whole lives." She turned her eyes to Alex. "You said they'd be expecting us. We didn't listen. And I don't know what we should do now. So I want to know what *you all* think we should do. Because you made it this far together. Actually, hold on."

She disappeared into the hallway and returned with Carla and Lone Star, the latter of whom leaned against the wall, bleary-eyed.

"What is it?" he asked through a yawn.

Alex looked around, locking eyes with his teammates.

They nodded, or just stared back, or smiled a little, despite what was ahead of them. Alex jumped to his feet.

"What do we know?" he asked.

"They've got a new Umbra Gun," Gage said.

"The way Lux—sorry—*Novo* spoke on the news, it sounded like they were planning on making a bunch of weapons."

"It could be a bluff," Gage said.

"We can't take that chance," Amp said. "Can you imagine trying to go up against Deputies armed with those things? Even if they didn't end up shooting each other, there's no way we could risk that."

"Then we need to act. Soon." Alex closed his eyes, racking his brain. "The Guild of Daggers is helping them with the weapon creation, but they're based out of New York."

"Wait," Kyle said. "Could we, I don't know, recruit them and make some sort of deal to get them on *our* side instead?"

"We don't exactly have their phone numbers," Gage said. "Besides, there's nothing we could offer that the High Council couldn't trump. They're probably as afraid of Cloak as we are. It's too far away for us to stop production, but maybe we can cut Cloak down before they ever get a shipment."

"*Then* we go after the Guild." Misty smacked her fist into one of her palms.

"They've lost their way into the Gloom, right?" Kirbie asked. "I mean if we could get the Umbra Gun from them somehow, we could use it *against* them."

"We'd have to have Photon back on our side first," Alex said. "That gun's metal. If he's under Shade's control, it's not going anywhere she doesn't want it to be."

"Can we assume that they can turn it into a bomb like the last one?" Mallory asked.

"Undoubtedly." Gage nodded. "That's far simpler than the construction of the gun itself."

"That makes my mother our main target," Alex said. "She'll have the gun, and she'll be controlling Photon. We'll need to incapacitate her and get him back on our side. That's the goal. We need him."

"We can't afford to lose people to the Gloom," Amp said.

"I can keep us shielded." Alex started pacing back and forth. His mind was racing. "I've deflected Umbra Gun bullets before. She might not even fire. I sent my father into the Gloom when she shot at me in Justice Tower, and they won't want to have anyone melting into the shadows either. We'll just need to break her connection with Photon in some way."

"A Gasser?" Kyle suggested. "Or we could use one of the Tasers on her."

Alex shook his head.

"I tried that at the museum. She'll see them coming and dodge, or use Photon to deflect them."

"Actually, we should rule out all weapons with electronic components," Gage said. "One electromagnetic pulse and they'll be worthless. Same with communicators. I'm guessing it was Photon who took out the power grid last night, not Volt."

"I'll do it," Amp said. And as he spoke, Alex could see him putting things together in his brain, forming a plan. "Like when I faced off with the horde of Legions at the Cloak mansion. A high-frequency tone focused directly on her. She'll hardly be able to think, let alone control someone else."

"Yes!" Alex cried. "That's perfect."

"If we can keep her preoccupied," Gage said, "I'd suggest getting Photon as far away from her as possible. Maybe we can break her hold on him with some distance and a few familiar faces. He seemed to be somewhat conflicted when the Rangers first showed up yesterday."

"No problem," Misty said. She flicked her curly red hair back. "As long as he doesn't have, like, metal bones or something, I can get him somewhere else once Shade's distracted."

"How do we *find* them?" Kirbie asked. "How do we take them by surprise?"

"They'll show up wherever we tell them to," Alex said.

"There's no way Cloak's going to turn down a fight—not when they think they've got us so outpowered. Plus, the city thinks they're unstoppable right now. We just have to challenge them."

"Television," Kyle said. "They've been using it against us this whole time. What if we issue them a challenge on TV? For the soul of Sterling City. Everyone will know. It'll spread. Cloak will *have* to show up. We'd just have to get on the air."

Gage shrugged. "That should be relatively simple."

"We give them a half-hour notice. Don't let them have time to plan anything."

"Just like their surprise press conferences," Kirbie added with a grin. "We use their tactics against them."

"We need some way to take the Deputies out of the equation," Amp said, his fingers twitching. "The last thing I want is to be gassed by one of them while I'm focusing on Shade."

"We need a force of our own," Alex said.

"Look hard enough and you'll find rebels in even the most utopian setting," Gage said. "Think about it: Who has a grudge against the New Rangers' private security force?"

"The Sterling City police!" Kyle exclaimed. "Carla already said they weren't happy, right? Can't we get *them* to handle the Deputies?"

"The police commissioner and I go way back," Lux said.

"He's a good man. We can trust him."

"Do we have any info on him?" Kirbie asked. "Any Cloak relations?"

"He's as clean as they come, as far as I know. We've done thorough background checks on him. If he's under their thumb, I don't know that I would trust *anybody* in the city."

"We need a way to talk to him alone," Alex said.

"That's not a problem," Carla said. "He's working sixteen-hour days right now. Just visit him sometime after dark, once the curfew's in effect. Most of the force will have been sent home by then, I imagine. The Deputies are the ones enforcing this whole no-one-out-after-dark policy."

"Headquarters is on the other side of the city, right?" Misty asked. "It's a long way to mist." She eyed Lone Star. "And you're very heavy. But I can get us in once we're there if it's a small team and someone can tell me where his office is."

Lone Star stepped forward, raising his hands up. He looked like he was still trying to process the rapid flow of information.

"Whoa, whoa. You all are talking about a head-to-head battle with the Cloak Society—do you have any idea how dangerous that is? We almost didn't defeat them a decade ago and we certainly couldn't yesterday."

"We also knew how dangerous it was to go into the Gloom and rescue you," Amp said. "We didn't do that just to call it quits after one setback. I didn't leave my *parents* in that place just to give up when things got rough."

"Amp, think about this," Lone Star said.

"We can face them," Alex said. "We can defeat them. One on one. Power for power."

"Lux and I don't have powers, though."

"But you still have arms and legs, right?" Alex asked. His voice rose in volume. Frustration was bubbling up inside him. He had to convince Lone Star that he could still fight, even without his powers. "I've seen the Junior Rangers at work. The fact that they can fight hand-to-hand and bounce around like acrobats means that you must be able to, too."

The others stared at Alex and Amp. Bug looked shocked that either of them would talk to the leader of the Rangers in such a way. Even in his current state, Lone Star was a man who commanded a certain level of respect and awe.

"It's not your power that defines you," Alex said, more softly, calming down. "It's your actions. That's something I've had to learn recently."

"He's right," Lux said. "We've gotten so used to our powers that we've forgotten they're not what make us Rangers."

Lone Star turned his head slowly, locking eyes with everyone in the room before nodding.

"I can see now how you managed to do everything you've accomplished so far. But this needs to be planned out. We can't just rush into battle without all our bases covered."

"Where do we make our stand?" Amp asked.

"To carry on with Lone Star's baseball metaphor, my first reaction is a stadium, but that seems a little *too* formal," Gage said.

"You guys, isn't it obvious?" Misty asked. She waited for someone to respond, and when they didn't, she rolled her eyes. "Victory Park! It's the perfect place. Kyle will have his pick of plants and trees, and, you know, there's *history* and stuff there."

"I want to make sure we all know what we're talking about here," Lone Star said. "This is so dangerous . . . it's something I never wanted you to face as Junior Rangers. Or that *anyone* would have to face, for that matter. I want you to know that there's nothing wrong with backing out of this. If *any* of you don't want to risk this fight, you can stay behind."

Everyone stared at him. They all knew what he meant. They could be hurt. They might not even make it out of a fight like this. A quiet fell over the room, until the youngest among them finally spoke.

"With all due respect, Lone Star." Misty grinned. "You don't know us very well."

"If we fail," Gage said, "this will go down as a heroic win for the New Rangers. They'll twist the story to make us the villains. It'll give them that much more power and sway."

"Then we don't fail," Kirbie said. "We can't."

"We choose Scylla. We don't let the whole ship go down."

"Except we don't lose six teammates, Gage," Mallory said. "You've got to start choosing your metaphors more carefully."

Gage gave her a grin.

"We save the city," Kirbie said.

"We save the *world*," Alex suggested.

"It would help if we had any sort of evidence that connected Cloak to the New Rangers," Amp said. "Just for a worst-case scenario. Something we could leave behind."

"Everything was incinerated at the lake house," Kirbie said, falling back against the couch. "And all of *that* was just our notes and stuff."

"Shade seems a little crazier than normal," Mallory said. "What else was she saying onstage? Anything we can use?"

Alex's thoughts raced. He started babbling everything he could think of.

"The Umbra Gun, the Guild of Daggers, how they want to make us suffer by watching the city fall, how the people were so quick to believe them . . ."

"Too bad the microphone wasn't on for all that," Lux muttered.

Alex nodded. Shade had ripped out the microphone.

Even if someone *had* managed to capture video of the whole thing, there'd be no sound. And what would it show? Just the heroic Shade taking down another bad guy. If only they had video of the New Rangers *before* they were the new Rangers.

"Wait," Alex said. He stopped. Something his mother mentioned popped into his mind. They hadn't always planned on becoming Rangers. That had been a new development, something they'd come up with after Alex had defected.

"What are you thinking?" Amp asked.

"The Cloak Society doesn't wear masks." Alex started across the room.

"Well, we know *that*," Kyle said, seemingly deflated.

"No, you don't understand. I've got it." Alex found his Cloak trench draped across a chair. He slid two photos out of the inside pocket. "We've already beaten them."

PROOF

It took a few days for them to put together the information Alex had in mind. In that time, things seemed to stay the same in Sterling City—meaning, things were still bad but the city hadn't been sucked into the Gloom or anything.

They hated to wait. But it was worth it.

What Alex realized as he and his teammates discussed how and where they would make their final stand was that he'd been carrying proof of Cloak's connection to the New Rangers ever since he'd left the underground base. He had photos. In one picture, his parents stared into the camera, grinning. They held him between them, nothing but a brown-haired infant. On the back was Shade's handwriting: *Alex—6 months.*

That was a start—their "son" Titan was blond, after all—but it really wasn't much. The other photo was far more condemning. It was the Polaroid that had hung on the Rec Room wall in the lake house, a picture Alex had pocketed before the groundbreaking ceremony. It had been taken less than a year before: Alex, Mallory, Julie, and Titan, all four of them wearing their black Beta uniforms with grinning silver Cloak skulls on the chest.

The people of Sterling City knew that skull all too well now. They just never imagined their hero, Titan, wearing it.

From there, Alex's brain bloomed with possibilities. In taking the identity of the Rangers, Cloak had overlooked all the years of evidence that had piled up. Every time Cloak had gone anywhere in public together, they were exposed to surveillance cameras and recordings. It had never occurred to them to hide their identities because they saw no reason to: soon the world would know them as their Cloak rulers, anyway. That was something Alex and his team could take advantage of.

Between Alex, Mallory, Misty, and Gage, they created a list of all the places they'd recently been to on Thursday outings—those brief hours every week when they'd been allowed to leave the underground base and see movies or go get ice cream. They figured out places the High Council had been together, too. And then, they went hunting.

Carla and the former Betas carried out the assignments,

since theirs were the faces least likely to be recognized. From across the city, security tapes went missing. In a bookstore on the south side of town several rows of shelves toppled over mysteriously. By the time they were put back in order, the computer hard drive that held all the store's backlog footage was missing. In the arts district, someone managed to melt through a museum's thick basement window and make off with several components of its security systems. And on the western edge of Sterling City, a checkout clerk swore she saw a box of tapes float through the air as she locked up.

Back at Carla's, the Junior Rangers watched hours and hours of footage, putting together a sort of highlights reel. Phantom and Shade were clearly visible shopping together at a high-end boutique. Barrage and Volt picked up rare, special-order books for the Tutor. The Beta Team threw popcorn at one another as they exited a movie theater.

Evidence, all of it. Proof that the New Rangers weren't who they said they were.

One of the tapes came from an outdoor shopping center. Alex was with Kirbie in the upstairs den as she discovered it.

"Look!" Kirbie shouted, jumping to her feet and pointing at the parking lot on the screen. "It's you. I mean, it's *all* of you."

Sure enough, the Betas stood at the back of a black SUV

as Barrage and Shade talked to them. Alex shook his head. It seemed so long ago.

"This is good stuff," Kirbie said. "Not only does it have all of you guys, but it's got Shade and Barrage, too. Look, you can see them both clearly getting back into the car together."

"Do you know what day that was?" Alex asked.

"No, should I?" She trailed off as she fast-forwarded through the footage. "Wait, is this when . . ." The camera angles changed a few times as she sped through, until suddenly she saw herself, chasing after a skeezy-looking man carrying a purse.

"Yup," Alex said.

"This is the day I ran into you at the mall," she said quietly.

The camera angle shifted again, and they saw the whole encounter play out. Alex was nervous for some reason as they watched. There was no sound, but he remembered the scene like it had happened yesterday. He'd lied to Kirbie, telling her that he was thinking of leaving Cloak, even though he'd had no intention of doing so at the time. It was almost funny now given the mess they were in. Eventually, she'd flown away to her team, and Alex had gone back to his.

Kirbie paused the video and smiled a strange, small smile.

"What?" Alex asked.

"Nothing."

"Oh come on. We're almost, like, at the end of the world."

"No, it's nothing," she said. "I was just remembering how I thought I could turn you into a Ranger, and we'd all just ride in and take Cloak by surprise and save the day. I was so . . . I don't know, what's the right word? Just dumb, I guess?"

Alex wrinkled his brow as he stared at her.

"Are you kidding?" he asked. "If I'd never met you—if I'd never *fought* you—I don't know if I'd ever have realized what the Cloak Society was really all about. I would have raided Justice Tower along with them. I wouldn't have been able to see just how *insane* my family is."

"You did this on your own, Alex."

"No," he said. "I did it with you by my side. And with Kyle and Amp. With everyone."

Kirbie smiled and let her eyes drop to the floor. Her golden hair was usually in a ponytail, but it was down now, falling over her shoulders.

"If—no, *when* we make it out of all this, what are we all going to do? You'll stick with us, right? As a Ranger?"

"I don't know," Alex said. "I don't think any of us have really thought about it much since we've been so caught up in what to do about Cloak. I mean, of course we'll figure something out. But me and Mal and the others, we weren't really brought up for that kind of spotlight. Besides, there's so much we were trained to do that's not even *legal*. We'd have to completely relearn everything we know if we were going to be some kind of superheroes."

"I don't think that's true," Kirbie said. "Look at all the good you've done in the last month."

"Are you talking about things like destroying museum exhibits and crashing press conferences or just generally causing a public panic anywhere I go?"

"You *know* what I mean."

"Let's just make it through the next few days," Alex said. "Then we'll have all the time in the world to figure out where we all belong in this city."

When they weren't collecting data and research and evidence, they were training. Nothing that would give them away—there would be no giant, flailing trees or window-breaking bursts of sound—but they could shoot targets in the backyard and spar.

A few hours after watching the video with Kirbie, Alex sat against a wall in the basement with Amp. They watched Lux and Lone Star train. The two Rangers had very different ways of fighting. Lux was an acrobat, lithe and agile, twisting her body at lightning speeds as she jabbed forward with a bladelike palm. Lone Star was a brawler. He was all fists and grunts, throwing his body at the swinging sandbag in the room with seemingly no regard for himself.

Alex had never been especially good at fighting hand to hand—that was always something Titan and Julie had excelled at. He was impressed by how naturally it seemed to come to both of the Rangers. Alex kept a few things he'd brought down from around the house darting about through the air, giving them plenty of moving targets. They seemed in high spirits.

"Remember that time the robber dressed in a weird animal costume got you in a headlock at that jewelry store?" Lux asked. "You know, the one in the modified mascot costume."

"That wasn't my fault," Lone Star said. "I was flying. How was I supposed to know he could jump that high?"

"He *did* call himself the Jackrabbit." Lux tossed her pale hair back as she slammed her leg against a floating couch cushion in a swinging kick.

"I thought he could punch really fast." He smiled and loosed a mighty right hook on a decorative pillow zigzagging in front of him. "I didn't expect him to have gas-powered springs in his boots."

"You're just lucky Photon was there to rip him off you."

Alex smirked at the exchange and willed the soft targets to dive and move at a faster pace.

"Hey," Amp said to him. "Can you hear anything weird?"

Alex turned to the Junior Ranger, who was pointing a finger out in his direction. He shook his head.

"How about now?" Amp moved his finger so that it was in line with Alex's chest.

Alex shivered. Suddenly it was like he had a silent drum pounding in his ribs.

"Whoa, weird," Alex said. "I can't hear it, but I can *feel* it. Is . . . this safe?"

"Totally," Amp said, looking pleased with himself. "Just trying to work on making the most focused audio stream I can."

He got a mischievous look in his eye, and before Alex could say anything, the Junior Ranger flicked his wrist, drawing his finger in a quick line across Alex's face.

Alex felt like he had his head shoved into the world's most powerful speaker for a split second.

"Gah!" he shouted, clutching his ears. Near the center of the room, one of the pillows exploded as he lost control of his telekinetic powers.

"Hey, hey," Lone Star said, his voice low and chastising as feathers floated in the air all around him. "What are you two up to?"

"Dude, Alex, I'm so sorry," Amp said. "I didn't think it was that bad. It was half the power I've been practicing with." He lowered his voice. "That should be enough to throw Shade off, at least."

Alex took his hands off his ears and narrowed his eyes. Amp started to speak.

"Whatever it is you're think—"

He was cut off by a series of five cushions and pillows smacking against his body.

"Alex, that's hardly fair," Lux said, trying not to smile.

Amp was just starting to climb out from under the pile of cushions when Gage swung open the door at the top of the basement stairs.

"We're done with the footage," he said, rubbing the dark bag under one of his eyes. "We've got everything we can. The plan can move forward as soon as you're ready."

REBELS

After the sun had been down for several hours, Lone Star and Lux squeezed into the backseat of Carla's SUV while Misty and Alex sat in the far back trunk. Fortunately, the windows were already darkly tinted, meaning that if they kept their heads down, they might be able to make it to the other side of town without rousing any suspicion. Maybe.

"Please don't let this end up being some sort of high-speed car chase," Carla said as the garage door opened. She tightened her hands around the steering wheel. "I really like this car."

"If we just stick to the plan and all stay calm, I'm sure we'll be fine," Lux said, though Alex couldn't help but wish she'd sounded more sure herself when she spoke.

"Besides," Lone Star added, "you did a great job jetting us away in that van the other day. I'd say you've got a knack as a getaway driver."

Carla stared at her brother, not amused, before starting the car.

The city was eerily quiet and seemed darker than normal, even with the streetlamps back on. Rain had fallen earlier, and heavy clouds still floated thick in the sky, obscuring the moon and stars. Alex watched the wet street pass by through the back window of the SUV, illuminated every few blocks by the vehicle's brake lights. The streets around them were ominously serene.

"I've got Deputies up ahead," Carla said as they drew nearer to town, driving through the financial district. "But they've got a couple of kids or something with them. I think they're making an arrest."

As they got closer, the scene began to make sense. Two Deputies had three college-aged citizens lined up against a wall, laser pistols drawn. One of the civilians wore a shirt that said WE DIDN'T VOTE ON PHOTON. Above them was one of the giant posters of the New Rangers. Horns and mustaches had been drawn on all the figures. In neon-green letters, someone had spray-painted over parts of the text so that it read NO RANGERS. JUST US. And in the white space on the side of the poster was a giant skull painted in dripping silver.

Everyone but Carla kept their heads down as they drove past, slowly.

"Should we help them?" Misty asked.

"That's a bad idea," Lone Star said. "The best thing we can do for them is continue on our mission."

Alex pressed a finger over his lips to Misty and concentrated on the two laser pistols pointed at the civilians. He waited until their SUV was a few blocks away, then pulled the weapons out of the Deputies' hands with one thought and pushed the two lackeys to the ground with another. The three kids made a break for it. Carla turned a corner, and Alex couldn't see them any longer.

"That was a Cloak skull, right?" Alex asked. "That can't be coincidence."

"They've adopted it as a symbol of rebellion against the Rangers," Lux said. "It's not exactly uncommon in a situation like this. 'The enemy of my enemy is my friend,' and all."

"Great. Cloak groupies."

"Will you all please stay down back there?" Carla commanded more than asked as she noticed Alex's head in the rearview mirror. "I thought you were supposed to be masters of stealth."

They continued in silence for a few more blocks as they drew closer to the heart of the city, where the streetlights and building marquees kept the roads better lit. An electronic billboard on the side of a building flashed a single message: CURFEW IN EFFECT. AS YOUR EVER-VIGILANT PROTECTORS, WE ARE WATCHING.—THE RANGERS OF JUSTICE.

"Well, *that's* comforting," Alex muttered.

"Misty," Carla said, her voice steady, but with a slight edge. "You're on deck. I've got a roadblock up here."

"Got it!" Misty said. She reached over the backseat and grabbed Lone Star's and Lux's shoulders, while Alex held on to the sleeve of her coat. "Ready."

The car stopped in front of a female Deputy standing in the middle of the street and waving a glow stick. Her partner approached the driver's side of the car, one hand on his belt holster.

"Now," Carla said, as she began to roll down her window.

The four people in the back atomized, until they were nothing but a thin haze that settled on the seats and floors in the dark of the car.

"You'd better have clearance to be out here, ma'am," the man said in a thick Texas drawl, "or else you're going to be meetin' a bunch of new friends soon. Or I guess I should say 'cell mates' instead."

He smiled a wide, self-satisfied grin, looking positively giddy to have stopped someone. Carla pulled a leather rectangle from her jacket pocket and shoved it in the man's face.

"I'm chief assistant district attorney of this city, young

man," she said, her voice firm and annoyed. "I have full clearance to be out."

"Well, well, well, now," the man said. "I don't know about that. You did say *assistant*, right? Not *the* district attorney. Maybe I need to call this in to the Rangers and make sure that an *assistant* is high enough on the food chain to be out at night."

Carla pulled her ID back inside the car and narrowed her eyes.

"I'm sure Photon and Lux have nothing better to do than field the questions of a Deputy who didn't bother to learn who does and does not have the right to be on the streets tonight. Especially when the person you're asking about is a city official who specializes in the prosecution of criminals, making every second you keep me here an obstruction of *justice*. So by all means, call this in and find out if you're doing your job or not. I can wait. I'll just make sure that when a Cloak henchman goes free because my time was wasted at this checkpoint, you're the person who gets to explain why to the Rangers."

The Deputy stuttered for a bit before taking a few steps away from the SUV and waving them on. As they drove away, the others began to materialize in the back-seats.

"You were *amazing*," Misty said as she put everyone back together again. "Even I was kind of scared of you."

"Now you see why I wanted Starla as a Ranger," Lone Star said with a grin.

Carla glared at him in the rearview mirror, and then let out a long breath.

"If that's who we've entrusted the city's future to, we're doomed," she said.

"They'll learn," Alex said. "My mother will whip them into shape. Trust me. I've seen her do it with the unpowered Unibands back at the Cloak base. We're just lucky she hasn't had time to devote to these guys."

They drove on, until finally they came to police headquarters. Carla parked in the alley out back, far from the lenses of any security cameras, her SUV blending in with the shadows.

"All right," Alex said. "Misty, you know the way around inside?"

"Please," Misty said. "Thanks to Carla's help, I know this place inside and out."

Everyone in the back grabbed on to one another. Lone Star held a hand out to Carla. She looked skeptical for the first time that night.

"Don't worry," Misty said. "I do this all the time."

"I just don't want to come out of this on the other side with my head on someone else's body," Carla said, taking Lone Star's hand.

"Huh," Misty said as she began to break apart. "I wonder if I could do that."

Before Carla could protest, they were shooting out of a cracked car window, flying over the parking lot and through a vent in the top of the roof. It was dark and hot as they sped through the ventilation system and into a hallway, where they paused just briefly before traveling to a room at the end of the corridor.

They rematerialized in the commissioner's office. Alex closed the blinds on the windows looking out into the hallway with a flick of his thoughts. Carla doubled over, staggering, reaching out to the wall for support.

"I think I'm going to be sick," she muttered.

"What in the—," the commissioner started, jumping up from his desk. Alex recognized him from photos and news broadcasts, an older man with dark, wrinkled skin and salt-and-pepper hair slicked back neatly. He reached for his desk drawer, but when his eyes fell on Lone Star, he paused, staring at the Ranger.

"Commissioner, please don't be alarmed," Lone Star said, raising his hands up in front of his chest to try and calm the other man down. "It's Lone Star. You know me. I've just come to talk."

"Don't be alarmed? You tell me that after you just *appear* in my office? I saw the look-alikes on the news. How am I supposed to know you're real?"

The man eyed Lux, who was dragging a chair over for Carla. Alex could see him doing calculations in his head and wondered if he might call for help or try to pull a weapon on them. Not that it would matter—he could have the man immobile in an instant, but he didn't want to have to resort to that.

"I can vouch for him, sir," Carla said, but the man's face didn't look very relieved by that. Instead his eyes drifted over to Alex and Misty. He gave them curious looks.

"Not only have you shown up after having *no word* from you for a month, but you've brought a missing little girl and a boy wanted on suspicion of being a Cloak agent with you. And I'm supposed to remain calm."

"I believe Alex is wanted in connection to my disappearance, too," Lone Star said. "Which is obviously not the case."

The commissioner turned his gaze back to Lone Star and regarded him with suspicion.

"All right," he said. "If you're really Lone Star, prove it. Tell me something only you would know."

"You once gave me a bronzed version of the official Lone Star action figure as a birthday gift, only on the base's engraving you misspelled my name. L-O-A-N. Loan Star. You realized the mistake right after you'd given it to me and took it back to be corrected."

Everyone was silent for a moment. Finally the commissioner spoke.

"That was the *engraver's* fault, not mine." He sat slowly

back down in his chair. "It's good to see you. I hadn't let myself get up too much hope that it was actually you after seeing how things went down at the press conference. Lux, I assume this is the real you, too."

"You never misspelled my name, but you did once ask me on a date to the Mayor's Ball. I said no."

The commissioner winced a bit.

"Well, now that we've gotten all that out in the open, someone tell me what's going on in this city. It's been a rough few weeks, and I'm guessing that two missing super-heroes showing up in my office looking like they've been put through the wringer doesn't mean things are going to start looking up anytime soon."

Lone Star and Lux briefed him as quickly as possible, leaving out the Gloom entirely and simply explaining that Cloak had them trapped and a group of Junior Rangers and former Cloak kids had managed to rescue them. Alex finished up the rundown, explaining who Novo was and exactly how they'd managed to have *two* Luxes at the groundbreaking ceremony.

When Alex was done, the commissioner sat back in his chair, sighed, and rubbed his temples with thick fingers.

"I appreciate you coming here to tell me this," he said slowly. "And I really am glad you're alive. But I just don't see what I can do. My hands are tied as far as the New Rangers go. The mayor and city council have handed them the city on a silver platter. I'll happily tell everyone I know that you're the real Rangers, but it sounds like I wouldn't get very far before being silenced."

"We're going to make a move against Cloak," Lux said. "To right all of this."

"Good. Do it. Then I can start trying to get this city back to normal."

"We need officers," Lone Star said. "Men and women with an allegiance to you, not to the New Rangers. We've heard that there are some among the police force who aren't exactly happy with the way the Rangers have taken over security in Sterling City."

"That's an understatement," the commissioner said, getting up from his desk and walking toward the front windows of his office. He peeked through the blinds as he spoke. "I've got officers who've had badges for decades suddenly outranked by people barely old enough to drive. A lot of these men and women weren't even happy about the Rangers when *you* were in charge, much less now."

"Could you find out who they are and mobilize them if you had to?" Lone Star asked. "Soon."

The commissioner let the two blinds he held open snap shut, turning to Lone Star.

"What *exactly* are you planning?"

"A battle for the fate of Sterling City," Alex said. "More or less."

"We need to take these Deputies out of the equation," Lux said, stepping toward the man. "But it would have to be a fast operation. We don't want to give Cloak time to retaliate. We need your men and women to take them into custody."

"On what grounds?" The commissioner spread his arms wide. "I don't like this any more than you do, but I'm not putting my officers at risk just to have *them* all dragged out of their homes in the middle of the night and thrown into some secret prison." He crossed to a window near his desk, glancing down at the parking lot below with a wary eye. A long sigh escaped his lips. "Do you have any idea how many of my people I've lost just because they questioned a Deputy's actions?"

"If our plan fails, this city is doomed anyway," Alex said.

"We don't need them to actually be *arrested*," Lone Star added. "They just need to be detained for a few hours."

"You know they're getting their orders from criminals," Lux said. "What more do you need?"

"*Proof* that they're criminals," the commissioner said, his voice growing louder. "I can't just call in a couple dozen officers and tell them Lone Star visited me in the middle of the night and told me the New Rangers are actually supervillains."

"Here." Alex tossed a small USB drive onto the commissioner's desk. The commissioner raised an eyebrow. "That's proof that there's a link between the Cloak Society and the New Rangers."

"All right, kid, you've got my attention. What's on it?"

"Surveillance footage. On that drive you'll find all sorts of video showing known members of the Cloak Society and the New Rangers hanging out together. Buying *groceries* together. Pictures, too. It should be enough to convince your officers."

"Maybe," the man said, raising an eyebrow.

Alex wrapped his thoughts around one of the photos in his pocket and pushed it up in front of the man's face. The commissioner looked surprised, then quickly scowled.

"The Beta Team," Alex said. "Cloak's junior squad. You'll recognize me *and* Titan, but you know the girl with black hair, too. Julie. Titan's sister. She stayed underground to serve as one of the city's villains. You've got a video of her appearance when Cloak crashed the Rangers memorial a few weeks ago, right? You'll see that she is who I say she is. And I'm sure you've already noticed that we're all wearing Cloak Society uniforms. Even Titan."

"I've read the police reports for the incident at Silver Bank in September," Carla said. "Officers cleared the area, but more than one of them reported seeing a blond boy from a distance who had the ability to rip a fire hydrant out of the ground. Sound like anyone you know?"

"There was some cell phone footage taken of that bank incident that was never released to the public," the commissioner said. His voice was soft but his eyes were growing wide. "Didn't want to cause a panic or anything like that. I'm betting if I watch it now *looking* for Titan, I can find him."

"He'd probably be hard to miss," Alex said. "He likes to be the center of attention."

"Could we get a copy of that cell phone video?" Carla asked.

"I'll have someone deliver it to your office first thing in the morning." The commissioner's face went hard. "Can you do it? Beat them, that is? I've been in the same room as Shade and Volt. You can sense they're powerful. Predatory even."

"I believe we can," Lone Star said.

"We have to," Alex said. "Or the city will be theirs. And that's just the beginning."

The commissioner shook his head and rubbed his temples again, closing his eyes.

"I can have officers for you. When is this going down?"

"Tomorrow," Lone Star said.

"Well," the commissioner said with a slight smirk, "I guess I'd better start making the arrangements."

18

ACTION
FIGURES

"You know what's kind of strange?" Alex asked. "I think this is the first normal house I've ever been in."

He flicked a piece of popcorn up into the air. From across a coffee table, Bug's eyes flashed and Zip raced through the room, snatching it in her legs.

"That's super weird," Bug said. Zip tossed the morsel into a nearby trash can and landed on his head, watching for the next piece of food.

They sat on the floor in the upstairs den at Carla's house. None of them had been able to sleep after returning from the police station, and so they passed the time together, trying to think about anything except the battle ahead of them. They'd gone through tomorrow's plans over and over again, until they were etched into their thoughts. Now Alex just wanted to not think, to not worry about consequences or outcomes. From the way his teammates acted, he was sure they felt the same way. Gage and Kyle played chess as Kirbie flipped mindlessly through a stack of comic books. Misty and Mallory were downstairs somewhere. Amp paced around, sat for a few seconds, and then resumed pacing.

"What was your room at the underground base like?" Bug asked.

"Small." Alex flicked another piece of popcorn, this time directing it around the room with his thoughts. Zip followed after it. "Well, at least it felt small."

"My workshop was practically the size of this house, though," Gage chimed in. He moved a piece across the board. "Checkmate."

"Ugh," Kyle said. "That's three wins for you. I think I'm done."

"Don't give up now. You're actually much better than most players I've gone up against. You even managed to capture one of my bishops."

"What about you?" Alex asked Bug.

The boy hadn't volunteered much information about his life before he'd shown up at the lake house other than that he doubted anyone really missed him. Bug was quiet for a few seconds, and then shrugged. "I spent most of my time outside, so my room was really big." He smiled, eyes flashing. "Think fast. Zip's on to you."

Alex flicked his finger, and the popcorn Zip was trailing broke into two pieces, jetting off in opposite directions.

"Hey," Bug said. "No fair."

There was a creak from the staircase, and Alex turned to see Mallory. She held her hands out in front of her. The tip of each finger was decorated with gobs of blue and white and gold.

"What happened to you?" Alex asked.

"Misty," Mallory said. "And Rangers of Justice nail art. Or at least it was supposed to be."

"Oh, no, no, no." Kirbie shook her head. She jumped up and ushered the other girl away. "Let's find you some nail polish remover."

"I think it was her first time. I should've realized I was in trouble when she wanted to test it out on me."

The two of them disappeared into the bathroom just as Misty put herself together in the middle of the room.

"All right, Kirbie," she said. "It's your lucky day. I— Hey, where'd she go?"

"I think you may have claimed your only victim for tonight," Amp said, taking a seat where Kirbie had been and leafing through a few comics.

"I need a new opponent if you'd like me to teach you how to play chess," Gage suggested.

"I'm *not* spending the night before tomorrow learning to play *chess*, thanks," Misty said, throwing herself onto the couch.

"I'm telling you," Carla's voice came from the stairs, "he's a superfan. He's got stuff I didn't even know *existed* until the internet. I'm guessing half of it wasn't even licensed."

Carla, Lux, and Lone Star came up. They nodded hello to the others as they crossed the den to an adjoining bedroom, the one that Alex had found himself in following the groundbreaking ceremony.

"I thought we had a legal team that kept stuff like that from happening," Lux said.

"If so, you need a *better* one."

Alex leaned back to get a better view, watching as Lone Star stepped into the bedroom, staring at the poster of himself framed on the wall. On the bookshelf, there were all kinds of Rangers of Justice trinkets. Action figures, mugs, postcards, a model of Justice Tower—it was practically a shrine to the Rangers.

Lone Star stood very still just a few steps inside. Finally he spoke.

"I thought you never told him that I'm . . . that his *uncle* is Lone Star."

"I didn't," Carla said. "In fact, I made it a point to hardly ever mention the Rangers at all. He came to this on his own. And he's not the only one. Most of his friends are the same way. He's ten years old and the Rangers are practically his world. He was inconsolable the day Justice Tower fell."

Alex and the others began to move closer to the doorway, trying to listen in on the conversation. Misty was the only one of them who gave up on stealth altogether, sticking her head halfway into the bedroom.

Lux walked over to the bookshelf. As her fingers slid over the edge of a Rangers lunch box, a smile appeared on her face, at first small and sad and then growing into a full-on grin. It faded quickly as she picked up a stuffed doll in her likeness.

"This thing is hideous," she said. "I definitely never signed off on this. Look, this doll is wearing high-heeled boots. How would you fight crime in high-heeled boots?"

"You know, the people haven't abandoned you. You just have to remind them of who you are, and what you stand for," Carla said. "I don't want to see toys of Shade and Titan in my son's hands."

"You won't," Lone Star said. "We'll make sure of it. We have to."

Alex looked over at Amp, who grinned.

"Now come back downstairs," Carla said. As she turned to the door, Misty sublimated, disappearing. "If you're addressing the world tomorrow, we need to clean you up a bit first. You look like you've been trapped in another plane of existence for a month."

Lone Star smirked and made for the stairs. Carla and Lux followed.

"When we're done with Cloak, we can go after those toy makers," he said.

"The true villains," Lux agreed.

When the adults were halfway down to the first floor, Misty put herself back together in the bedroom, looking for the doll Lux had been talking about. Alex could hear her shuffling things around on the shelves as Mallory and Kirbie joined him back at the table, smelling of rubbing alcohol and laughing about something Alex hadn't heard.

"After tomorrow, do you think we'll get our own action figures?" Misty called into the den where the others were gathered.

"I don't know how they'd show off your powers," Mallory said. "Or mine. Or Alex's for that matter."

"Kirbie could have interchanging parts," Bug said. "A wolf head and claws. I don't know how they'd do the bird, though."

"The ingenious Gage," Kyle said, "featuring a lab coat full of Gassers. Superbrain not included."

"Yours could come with a seed packet," Gage suggested.

"Amp's could have a speaker in its chest!" Misty said.

"Oh yeah? What would it say?" Amp asked.

"Stop! In the name of justice!" Alex proclaimed, with exaggerated authority.

"No, no," Mallory jumped in. "What'd you say when you used your powers against us for the first time? At the bank . . ."

Amp's eyes fell to the carpet. He tried to hide a smile.

"Boom."

"Yes! That's it!"

"Boom!" Kirbie cried out with a grin. "I forgot you were trying to make that a thing. Your signature line."

"It wasn't a line," Amp said in feigned defense. "It was my special move."

"What's this?" Misty asked. She stood in the doorway of the bedroom, holding a plastic case in her hands.

"Oh, whoa," Kyle said, coming to her side. "That's the old Rangers of Justice video game!"

"Wait, what?" Mallory asked.

"Yeah. It's supposed to be really bad. I've never even seen a copy before. It came out a few years after Victory Park. I think it's a collectible item now. It's super rare."

"The Rangers were totally embarrassed by it," Amp added. "Lone Star hated it. Apparently some company took a bunch of sound bites from interviews and used them in the game without their knowing it. They had to stop selling it in stores."

"How did I miss this when I was going through all their stuff earlier?" Misty asked, her face practically glowing with excitement. "Can we play this thing?"

"We should be able to," Kyle said. "The console up here is backward compatible so it'll play older games."

Misty was on the ground in front of the TV in an instant. As she tossed the case aside, Alex pulled it to his hands with his thoughts. The front and back were covered in cartoon images of Lone Star, Lux, and Photon battling a horde of dragons and robots.

"You've got to be kidding me," Alex murmured.

Onscreen, an image of the three Rangers appeared, squared off and pixilated. The game had obviously been made for an older system. The graphics were so bad that if it hadn't been for the flashing "Rangers of Justice" title, Alex might not have been able to make out who the people on the television were supposed to be at all.

"Welcome, Rangers of Justice!" Lone Star's voice boomed from the speakers.

"Ahhh, turn it down!" Kyle whispered as the others searched for the remote. "I do *not* want Lone Star taking this before I get a chance to play."

Misty pressed a few buttons, and then the game started up. It was a side-scroller, her player not one of the actual Rangers, but instead a generic male character dressed in blue and white.

"You don't even get to play as Lone Star or someone?" Alex asked. "Lame."

"I didn't even get to pick between being a boy or girl," Misty said. Her tongue stuck out the side of her mouth a bit as she mashed on the controller, taking out waves of opponents.

"Was that a lizard man who just attacked you?" Bug asked. Zip landed on his shoulder and stared ahead, as if she was watching the gameplay, too. "What's with these bad guys?"

"It wasn't originally supposed to be a Rangers game," Kyle said. "That's how it came out so fast. The people who made it just changed the main characters' clothes and added in the opening credits and stuff. I've read a lot about this game. If we get to the castle, you fight Dracula and Frankenstein. I think it's level three."

"Frankenstein's *monster*, actually," Gage corrected.

"What*ever*." Kyle shoved Gage's arm a little.

"Oh, I'm definitely making it to level three," Misty said. "Hey, I think this is two-player. Who wants to beat up lizard men with me?"

Kyle joined in, and over the course of the next hour they all took turns swapping in and out, plowing through the enemies. Alex found that his real-life combat skills didn't exactly translate to the video-game world—his character kept falling into holes or vats of lava instead of taking out the enemies.

He'd passed on the controller by the time they got to the final level, some space station full of high-tech robots with jets in their feet and spinning blades for hands. The walls and floor were all a dull gray. The doors opened and closed with slight *fwoosh* noises. He couldn't help but be reminded of the underground base. As if on cue, new enemies showed up onscreen. They were all identical figures dressed from head to toe in black, with masks obscuring their faces. Alex half expected that the next person to appear on screen would be a digital version of his mother or father, a pixelated trench coat flowing out behind them. For a moment his heart jumped, and a tingling anxiety coursed through his veins.

That'll be us tomorrow, he thought. *One last level.*

The entire room cheered when Misty took out the final dark figure, paving the way for the big boss battle. Alex watched the enemy's body on the screen, lying on the blank gray floor. It blinked twice, and then disappeared. He shuddered.

19

LIVE

BROADCAST

The next morning, breakfast was quiet. Everyone sat around the dining-room table, staring at their plates and bowls. Alex went over the day's plans again in his head, imagining that the others were probably doing the same. Each of them had an important role to play in the coming hours, and everything needed to go off perfectly. There could be no setbacks, no misfires.

Lux and Kirbie led them through a morning meditation session, everyone focusing intently. Alex snuck a peek during all the deep breathing. Even Misty was serious, her lips pressed tightly together. A little later, just before they were supposed to regroup, she cornered Alex in the upstairs hallway.

"Aren't you going to warn me about how dangerous this is and how I need to be extra careful and stuff?" she asked. "Or try and tell me there's another way we can do this without me?"

"I think I stopped doing that, like, the third time you saved our lives," Alex said. "I don't know if you noticed or not, but no one thinks of you as the youngest person on the team anymore. You're just one of us."

Misty looked like she'd been ready to argue with him, but instead just threw her arms around his chest and hugged him.

"I'm scared," she said softly.

"I know," Alex said. "Everyone is."

"Nu-uh," she countered. "You're not. Lone Star's not."

Alex pushed her away from him and crouched, getting down to her level.

"Don't tell any of the others, but I'm scared, too," he said. "So is Lone Star. Everyone is. But we just have to keep going and remind ourselves that what we're doing is right."

"I guess so."

"If you're having second thoughts . . . ," Alex started, but Misty's posture changed. She stood tall and stared at him as if he was about to suggest something utterly ridiculous. He smiled. "Yeah, I didn't think that would be the case."

Lone Star poked his head around the corner.

"We're all ready in here. What about you two? Alex? Misty?"

"My *name* is the—," she started, but didn't finish. "Of course I'm ready. Let's go."

Alex followed her into the living room, where everyone had gathered. They certainly looked like a ragtag group, with Kirbie in her Ranger uniform under a hoodie, Mallory wearing her Beta fatigues under her Cloak trench, and the rest of them in strange combinations of clothing they'd been wearing when Justice Tower fell, or had taken from the lake house, or rummaged out of closets in Carla's home. Alex was looking at the gathered force that would decide the fate of the city. There was a chance that they'd never be in the same room together after today if things went terribly wrong.

"Does anybody have any questions?" Lone Star asked. He waited for someone to speak up, but they just stood there, quietly looking at one another.

"We won't go down without a fight," Amp said. "If we go out, it'll be in a blaze of glory. We fight for the city, and its people."

"For truth," Alex said, recalling old posters of the Rangers.

"For peace." Kirbie nodded.

"For justice," Lone Star said. His voice was resolute.

"There he is." Carla smiled.

"All right," Amp said. "Let's move."

Carla tossed Lone Star a set of keys.

"My SUV's in the garage," she said. "Lux, here are the keys to the van. It's parked around back. The rental company is dropping off a car for me but . . . You're sure there's nothing else I can help with?"

"You've got your own work to do," Lone Star said. "We'll be in contact."

"Everyone who's coming with me, let's get moving." Lux turned and headed toward the garage. Everyone but Gage, Misty, Lone Star, and Alex followed.

"Your team's leaving," Gage said.

"I know," Alex responded. "I just . . . I guess I just wanted to say good luck." Then he grinned. "Don't screw up. We're all counting on you."

"You too," Gage said, smiling. "We'll see you in a bit."

"Right," Alex said. He turned to join the others.

Lux dropped them off in pairs at various locations around downtown Sterling City. Kirbie and Alex walked the streets with sharp eyes, careful to avoid any Deputies for the time being. Kirbie kept her hood up. Alex kept his face sunk down into the turned-up lapels of his trench coat. He glanced at his watch every few seconds.

"There's an electronics store a few blocks away," Kirbie said. "We can watch the broadcast from there."

"Perfect."

They walked in silence for a while, and then they were inside the shop, pretending to browse around. Finally, there was static in Alex's communicator.

"We're a go," Gage's voice crackled.

Alex looked at Kirbie, took a deep breath, and made his way to a huge wall of televisions at the back of the store.

Lone Star's face suddenly appeared on all the TV screens, replacing normal daytime programming. It would be everywhere in the city—electronic billboards, the screens in the backseats of taxis, along with every other television with a cable or satellite connection. He'd be impossible to miss. In the electronics store, Kirbie and Alex joined a huddle of customers all staring at the wall of TVs in confusion. Alex used his powers to gently press the volume buttons on several of the monitors, dialing them up so no one would miss a word of what was about to be said.

Lone Star smiled. It wasn't like the sparse moments of happiness Alex had seen from him in the last few days. This was the full, ear-to-ear grin he used to flash at public events and in glossy magazine photos—the smile the people *expected* to see. When he spoke, his voice was a rich baritone, commanding but gentle.

"People of Sterling City—good afternoon. My name is Lone Star of the Rangers of Justice. Despite what the so-called 'New Rangers' would have you believe, I am alive and well and look forward to serving you in the future. But I'm not here today to address you. I am speaking directly to the Cloak Society—including those who have tricked you into believing they are heroes. Shade. Volt. Titan." From around the store, Alex heard people gasping. "You've deceived the good people of this city into trusting you. They believe you fight for them, when in truth you care only about your own petty plans for domination over humanity. But I am here to stop you. I am here to challenge you."

His face grew serious, his eyes narrowed and chin jutted forward.

"Victory Park in half an hour. A battle to decide the fate of Sterling City. It's time we finish what we started a decade ago." More gasps from around the store. "If you *don't* show, the people of this city will surely know you all to be cowards. If you truly want them to believe that you're the saviors of this city, you'll be there."

The screens all went to white noise, then switched back to their regular programming. There was a moment of silence in the store before chaos broke out as everyone inside made a break for the front entrance.

"That's our cue," Kirbie said with a grin.

They made their way outside, where Kirbie leaped into the air, taking her huge bird form. Alex stretched his arms out at either side as she looped around and grabbed him amid a crowd of gasping onlookers. The time for anonymity and subtlety had passed. This was the endgame.

Kirbie flew them high over the rooftops and toward the park, where they could see their plan in effect. Victory Circle, the street that looped around the park, had been cleared, and all streets leading to and from it were now cut off with police cars and barricades. There were a dozen roads blocked by huge trees that had apparently grown out of the asphalt itself—Kyle had worked quickly.

Alex and Kirbie kept their eyes to the ground. All around, people were heading away from the park. There were only a handful of people running *toward* it, and almost all of them were dressed in the uniform of the New Rangers' Deputies. This was what Alex and Kirbie were looking for—their job in the moments after the broadcast was to assist the police the commissioner had recruited in any way they could. Luckily, it looked as though law enforcement had everything under control. The Deputies seemed to be panicking, and were not used to having their authority challenged by other people. Especially not other people with badges and weapons and riot gear.

Kirbie let out a shriek, and they dove toward the top of a short building near the east end of the park. On the west end, Bug and Mallory would be doing exactly what they were, communicating with the officers and helping wherever they could. Kirbie dropped Alex on the building's roof and landed beside him in her human form as a familiar voice boomed through the air.

"Citizens of Sterling City, this is Lux of the Rangers of Justice." Her voice echoed off the buildings around the park, her words flowing out of Amp's body at an impossible volume. They were in the park somewhere. Kyle would be beside them, keeping them protected. "Please exit Victory Park and its surrounding blocks in a calm and orderly fashion. Those remaining will be taken into custody by the Sterling City police. We thank you for your cooperation."

"I hate that we have to be so menacing," Kirbie said. "It sounds so much like the stuff your mother has been spewing."

"Whatever gets them out of the line of fire," Alex said, his eyes sweeping the crowds below. "They'll either thank us after all this is over or we won't be around to hear them complain about it."

"Wait, look," Kirbie said, pointing to what appeared to be some sort of scuffle on the street a few blocks away. A team of four police officers was arguing with two Deputies. One of them Alex had never seen before, but the other was impossible to miss: Novo in the form of Del, her waist-length auburn hair twisting in the air all around her as she shouted something at the people trying to arrest her.

"We've got to—," Alex said, but before he could elaborate, Kirbie had him in her talons again, flying them over and around a handful of buildings until they were on the rooftop above the group.

When they landed, the Deputy they didn't recognize was climbing into the back of a police paddy wagon with little resistance. Novo followed. But just as she was about to step up into the back of the trailer-like vehicle, her hair shot out and twisted around two of the officers' waists, flipping them over her head and into the back of the transport. She shoved another of her captors inside and closed the doors behind them with a flick of her head. In an instant, Novo's hair was around the remaining officer's neck. She slammed him against the outside wall of the building nearby.

"Who ordered this?" Novo asked, her voice deep and monstrous.

The officer shook his head as best he could, but said nothing. Novo's hair formed a spike in the air that smashed into the wall beside the officer's head, embedding itself there. Chunks of mortar and brick dust fell to the ground.

"Start talking, or this is going to get *really* uncomfortable for you." The hair spike pulled out of the wall and hovered in front of the man's left eye.

"Use your telekinesis on her," Kirbie said.

"I *can't*, remember?" Alex said. "There's something about her powers that—"

"Then use it on the officer!" Kirbie said in a barely contained shout. Across the street, the policeman's face was starting to turn strange colors.

Alex focused on the man and pulled with one hard thought. Novo wasn't expecting such resistance, and the officer slipped through her tendrils and floated up, onto the rooftop across from Alex and Kirbie, looking terrified as he gasped for air.

Novo licked her lips as her sneer turned into a smile.

"Is that little Alex Knight playing around with the police?" she asked, her eyes darting around. "Come out, come out. Or do I have to come and find you?"

She started forward, only to stop after a few steps, looking annoyed. She raised a hand to her ear, where there must have been some sort of communicator Alex hadn't noticed.

"This is . . ." Novo's face went blank for a second. She'd been so many people lately that Alex wasn't surprised she'd forgotten who she was *supposed* to be at that time. "This is *Del*. I think—"

She stopped, listening to whoever was speaking on the other end of the communicator.

"Yes, but A—" she started once again, more emphatically this time, but was apparently cut off. "Of course, Shade. I'll be right there."

She lowered her hand from her ear and looked around at the windows and rooftops up above, scowling. Alex and Kirbie slipped back away from the edge, out of sight.

"Don't go anywhere, Knight," Novo yelled. She sighed loudly, then turned her back on them and sprinted toward the corner. Alex peeked over the roof. As she rounded the building, Novo changed. Gone was her Deputy uniform and Del's appearance, replaced by athletic clothing and her true form—a narrow face, blond hair, and piercing eyes. She sprinted past another unit of officers, who regarded her as a simple civilian out for a run, turned another corner, and disappeared.

"She's headed away from Victory Park," Kirbie said. "Cloak must be regrouping before they head to fight us."

"Maybe we should go after her," Alex suggested. "Take her out now."

"That's not the plan. Besides, it could be a trap."

Alex nodded. They didn't have room for improvisation. The others would be counting on them.

Kirbie morphed, and they were in the air again, on the lookout for any more disturbances as the seconds to battle ticked by. But the Deputies were under control. After a few flyovers, they felt sure that all civilians had made their way out of the park. They found Kyle, Lux, and Amp in an expansive lawn that would give them plenty of open terrain to fight on. They wouldn't have to worry about ambushes and could be more mindful of one another and come to aid when necessary. Mallory came out of the trees, and Bug followed her, his eyes bright and metallic as countless insect sentries scoured the area around them, searching for any signs of approaching danger.

Kyle got on his knees, sitting on his feet with his hands on the ground. He murmured words that Alex couldn't make out, his fingers dug into the earth, mingling with the roots and soil.

"What's he doing?" Alex asked.

"Preparing for war," Kirbie said.

There was a swirl of wind, and Gage, Lone Star, and

Misty assembled in front of them. Misty exhaled a long sigh when they were all solid.

"I'm not saying I'm tired," she said, "but that was a *lot* of misting around."

"Good job," Alex said. "All of you. That was perfect."

"And now we wait," Lone Star said.

"Bug's got eyes all around," Mallory said. "We should see them coming."

Lone Star nodded and turned away, walking the perimeter of the tree line and stretching his arms and back. Alex took a few steps from the Rangers. Mallory and Gage joined him at his sides, watching the sky.

"Thanks," Alex said. "Both of you. For sticking by me. I know it hasn't been easy."

"Don't be dumb," Mallory said. "We should be thanking you."

"I guess I'm just trying to say that it means a lot to me that you're here right now."

"She's right, Alex," Gage said. "I'm not one to be overly emotional, but I can't imagine being anywhere but here."

Alex smiled, despite knowing what was to come.

Gage continued. "That's not *exactly* true. I could imagine being in plenty of other places right now. Many of which don't include battles that will potentially decide the fate of humanity. Places where they've never heard of the Gloom."

"Places where people have never seen your face on the news or a wanted poster before," Alex added.

"Cities in mountains," Mallory said. "Or on beaches, even."

"When this is all over, I think we all need a vacation. Except since I've never actually been on vacation, I don't know what we would do."

"I want a clean workshop," Gage said.

"I just want my own room," Mallory said. "Do you have any idea how much Misty kicks in her sleep?"

They all laughed a little, quietly, nervously. Then they just stood there together for a few moments.

"You've got weapons, right, Gage?" Alex asked.

"You don't have to worry about me," Gage said, lowering his goggles over his eyes. "I can take care of myself. Even with only one functioning arm. You worry about keeping your mother occupied and us out of the Gloom."

Alex nodded.

"I'm going to put up a telekinetic shield around us. Just in case there's some sort of surprise attack. I have to do something, or I'll go crazy waiting."

He raised his hands and started gathering energy together. *We can do this,* he told himself. *We have to.*

Then Alex blinked, and the world changed.

ALEXANDER THE
KING

Alex stood on the open lawn in Victory Park, but he was alone. Where Mallory had been a half second before, there was nothing but grass. He did a double take. *Green* grass. He could see the world in *color*. The greens and yellows and reds of the plants and trees were so vivid that they seemed unreal to him. That's when he realized that his powers felt strange. The telekinetic energy was everywhere—the earth beneath his feet felt as though it were *made* of the stuff—and yet, he couldn't see it. Not like he had every day since his powers had developed.

He spun around in circles, confused, looking for the others, panic gripping his chest.

"They're not here."

It was his mother's voice, at once all around him, as if spoken from every direction.

"Don't worry. We haven't harmed them yet."

And then she was there in front of him, where before there had been nothing. She materialized out of the air, sitting in a floating chair that looked as if it were made completely of glass. She wore a T-shirt and jeans, clothing he'd only ever seen her wear on the most relaxed days growing up. The light from the sun created a sort of halo around his mother's dark bob of hair. Alex was suddenly aware of the fact that it was warm outside, as if it were spring.

"This can't be real." Alex blinked.

"No, my darling boy," Shade said. "It's not. We're in your head. I thought we could have a moment to ourselves before this fight you've forced upon us gets underway. Just you and me. Mother and son."

"How is this possible?" Alex glanced around nervously. Where were his teammates? If this was in his head, what was happening in the *real* world? Was he just standing there, staring into space?

"It's not a very *practical* use of my abilities. It takes an awful lot of concentration that's usually unnecessary when I can just let my voice ring out in your head, but then this is a special occasion. Just think of it as a lucid dream, or a trip through your own imagination. I doubt the others even realize anything's odd about you. I'm influencing the way you comprehend time. Seconds feel like minutes. It's a very useful trick. It works wonders when it comes to interrogations."

Alex stared blankly at his mother for a few moments before his lips spread in a smirk. The sky above them crackled with blue lightning. From nowhere, a cage appeared, imprisoning Shade. The space around them seemed to shrink as his thoughts squeezed in, encasing the borders of the open lawn with popping blue energy.

"If we're in my head, I'm in control," Alex said.

"For the most part, that's true," Shade said from behind him. He turned and there she was, standing just a few feet away. He looked back at the cage, only to find it empty. "But I'm very good at navigating other people's minds. I wouldn't bother with any more traps. It was a good idea, but it was *only* an idea, if that makes sense. As you said yourself, none of this is real."

"Give me one reason I shouldn't force you out of here right now." The sky lit up with energy and grew closer to the earth. Alex imagined that thunder would follow and suddenly there it was, so loud that it shook them both.

"Because then you'd never hear what I had to say. We're about to meet on the battlefield. If something were to *happen* to either of us, would you really want to have missed this opportunity to speak to your mother? I know I'm not your favorite person in the world right now, but I think you owe me one last little chat."

Alex opened his mouth to immediately dismiss this idea but was struck by what his mother was implying. They were about to fight each other. It was very possible that one of them, even both of them, might not survive. Or worse, he thought, one of them might die at the hands of the other, by accident or by design. It had happened with Phantom so quickly, in an instant. And when faced with the idea that this might in fact be the last time he ever spoke to his mother, part of him said, *Yes, stay in this moment while you can.* Even though he knew deep down inside that the woman in front of him was the enemy and someone who couldn't be trusted, she was also his mother.

"Make it fast," he said through gritted teeth.

Shade smiled.

"Let's go somewhere a little cozier, shall we?"

A bright light suddenly radiated from his mother's eyes, causing him to raise his arm against the glare. When he uncovered his eyes, he stood in his old bedroom in the underground base, beneath the Big Sky Drive-In. Every detail was exactly as he remembered it, from the humming of the overhead light to the pictures pinned up on the wall—there were even piles of his dirty clothes lying around on the floor. The room smelled so *familiar*. A flood of memories rushed through his mind. He could see faint outlines of himself working at the computer and curled up in bed reading. And of his friends on the Beta team—Misty and Mallory milling around, laughing, helping him cut out newspaper clippings to hang over his desk. Even Titan and Julie, from better, friendlier days. They were like ghosts, barely visible shadows of a less complicated time.

Alex began to panic. For every thought that said, *No, this is wrong,* there was an equal force inside him saying, *Don't you want to just climb into your old bed and forget all this ever happened?* He couldn't tell if it was his mother's doing or his own subconscious.

"Stop trying to soften me up with old memories." He rubbed the side of his head and steeled himself. "It won't work."

"That wasn't my intention. I just miss this place. This time. With my son." His mother leaned against his desk, dressed now in her Cloak mission attire, and looked with admiration at an origami swan cradled in her hand.

"I guess it must be a strange sensation to suddenly be *home* after being gone for so long," she continued. The swan began to flap its white, blue-lined wings and glide through the air. "This was one of the first pieces I taught you to make after your powers developed. You went through half a notebook before you got it right using your telekinesis, but we were both so thrilled when you'd done it. Your father, too. Do you remember that?"

"This isn't my home anymore," Alex said, ignoring her question. "Why are we here?" His voice was loud and caused the air around them to pop with blue sparks. He tried to calm himself down and think rationally, but he didn't even know how to begin to do that. They were inside his head. None of this was real. And yet, it *felt* real. And all the anger he'd built up against his mother and Cloak and his past was now all mixed up with the smell of recycled air and the sight of the room he'd spent most of his life in.

"For you to remember," Shade said. "What it was like before everything went wrong. All the dreams and hopes we had. How proud and useful and *safe* you felt down here. It's been difficult for you since you've been gone. I don't have to be a telepath to know that—it's written on your face."

Alex remained silent. He *was* tired. Even if he put on a brave appearance for all the others. A feeling of longing welled up inside him, and he had the sudden urge to hug his mother. He bit his tongue, dispelling the emotion and reminding himself that this was all just some weird delusion. He couldn't trust anything here. Not any strange feelings, and certainly not his mother.

"You've been trying to outrun your past, Alex, but the past will always be there. It's one of the few things in life that's permanent. You can try to cover it up all you want. You can put on a new uniform and do everything the opposite of how we raised you, but your history is still there." She waved her hand around his room. "It's here. Unchanged in your memories. A part of who you are."

She motioned to the mirror above the sink in the corner. In his reflection, he was wearing a Cloak uniform, the silver skull grinning at him. But it wasn't just in the mirror—his clothes had changed. He reached up to his chest and let his fingers trace the hard outline of Cloak's mark, as he'd done hundreds of times before.

Shade bent down and picked something up off the floor, then walked over to her son.

"If you'll allow me," she said, reaching out to his shoulder. Alex flinched. "Don't worry. I'm not going to hurt you. I just want to make sure you're complete."

She placed two silver bars on each of his shoulders, the markings of rank within the Cloak Society he'd ripped off and left behind the night he'd decided to flee the underground base and warn Kirbie of the impending attack on Justice Tower. The bars fastened themselves to the coat as if by magic, glinting under the fluorescent light.

"There now," Shade said. "All better."

"You're wrong," he said. "It's what I do *now* that matters. Not my past."

Shade reached out a hand, slowly, and tousled Alex's hair.

"My brilliant son. You're right, of course." She smiled at him before stepping away to the door that led out of the room. "Come with me, Alex. I want you to see something." The door slid open. The paper swan flew after her.

The exit opened not into the concrete-and-steel hallway of the underground base, but a huge open space of dark marble and pillars. The walls were made of glass, looking out at the sunny skyline of Sterling City. There was something familiar about the place that Alex at first couldn't pin down, until he realized that it was strikingly similar to the twelfth floor of Justice Tower, where Cloak had left him to die as the building had begun to fall apart.

It took his breath away.

"It's only an imagining of what it will look like eventually, but it'll have to do. We've only just had the groundbreaking, after all."

Shade was now dressed in her Ranger uniform. She stood beneath a gold starburst that floated high above her in the center of the room. It spun slowly, casting a warm spotlight around her.

"Of course it won't just be Sterling City," she said, gesturing to the outside world. "Pick a place. Anywhere you like. You've spent your whole life in this city. Don't you think it's time to travel a bit? We have people everywhere, Alex. Our core has always been here, underground, but our reach is farther than you could imagine. We have plants all over the country, all over the *world*. Sterling City was always just the first rung of the ladder."

Outside, the buildings flickered and morphed. He and his mother were in Los Angeles, and then Chicago, then looking out at Big Ben and the Eiffel Tower, the streets of Moscow and glittering lights of Tokyo. Alex's head spun, not just because of the rotating skylines, but the implication behind each change: Cloak's headquarters could be in any of these places. Their rule could span continents.

"Let's get down to business, Alexander. What I'm offering you is a free pass. A clean slate. I'm giving you the chance to rejoin our ranks with no questions asked. We can put the events of the last few weeks behind us."

"I don't want—," he started.

"Just hear me out."

"I thought you'd have come up with something new by now. I'm not coming back to Cloak to be your mindless slave."

"You misunderstand," Shade said. "I'm not offering you a place back on the Beta Team with the promise that one day you'll be in charge. I'm offering you a place on the High Council. Not as my subordinate, but as my peer. Not as someone who takes orders but as someone whose thoughts will shape the future of this world. Look at everything you've done in the past month. Even though it was all against us, I'm *impressed* by what you've accomplished. You were obviously born to lead, Alex. And as you know, the High Council is a little low on membership these days."

The origami swan flew in front of Alex's face and landed

on an outstretched palm. Phantom's. She'd appeared out of nowhere. The woman smiled at the bird. She looked up to Alex, and then both she and the paper turned an inky black and flaked apart, drifting through the air and into the shadows of the room.

"That was an accident," he said firmly, but his hands were trembling at his sides.

"Was it?" she asked. "If you say so. Do you know what she said to me, when I was in her head just before she melted away? She pledged her allegiance to Cloak for the last time. 'For the Glory,' and then she was gone." Shade's voice was firm but her eyes looked sad. "Even in her final breaths she could think only of us. Her family. The common good. If you really regret what happened to her, what better way is there of showing that than by honoring her dying words?"

Alex said nothing. His knees shook.

"Just think of it, Alex," his mother continued. "You'd be ordering Titan and Julie around. I know you'd like that. You could do anything you wanted. Could *be* anyone you wanted." She pointed to his chest. His Cloak attire had been replaced with a Ranger uniform. "Even a Ranger. You could create your own team."

In the place where Phantom had stood, a long table materialized. Gathered around it were Kirbie and Gage and all the others he'd spent the last month training with and fighting alongside. All of them were dressed as Rangers and staring at the head of the table, where Alex now stood. His mouth fell open. Their eyes widened, waiting to hang on his every word.

"It's a tempting offer, isn't it?" Shade whispered, suddenly beside him. "We don't have to go through the bother of fighting today. You can prevent any more casualties in this rebellion against us. Come and rule by my side, Alex."

"And what about them?" He pointed to the others sitting at the table. "Are they to be reprogrammed to be my servants?"

"Half of them would follow you on their own. You must know that by now. They'd need only the slightest nudging. The others could be taught to appreciate what we're doing."

"You're asking me to betray my friends and what I think is right."

"I'm asking you to come home," Shade said. "You've seen how easy it was for this city to turn over everything to us. And it's been, what, only a month? The city has embraced us. The *world* will welcome us." She stepped closer to him. "Your father and I miss you. I want my son to stand beside me in the spotlight. To love me." Her voice started to wobble. Alex thought she might cry. "To love me as I love him."

Alex didn't say anything, just stared at the ground.

He was afraid to open his mouth. If he did, he wasn't sure what would come out. For a moment, nothing else mattered—not the future, or the past, or even his teammates. The only thing in the world was Alex and his mother and the glimmer of a future where they lived happily alongside each other. As a family.

And then the reality of the situation crushed him. She was talking about brainwashing his friends. About taking over the world. This whole thing in his head was a setup. She was probably just acting.

And even if she wasn't, he'd seen what she'd done to Sterling City. She—the Cloak Society—had to be stopped.

"For a long time, I wanted nothing more than to please you and the rest of the High Council," Alex said. "Sometimes I just wanted to be a normal boy, with a normal family. To not have to worry about entire cities. And these past few weeks—I've missed you and Dad. You're my family. You'll *always* be my family." He raised his eyes to hers. "But that doesn't mean I have to agree with you. Now . . . now I just want to be me."

"You can be, my son." Shade's eyes were wide, bordering on manic. "You can be the *best* you. Alexander the king. The warrior. The savior! The tyrant! Don't you see the endless opportunities before you? You can have anything you want. Just say the words."

"I'll try my best to make sure you don't get hurt." Energy started pouring from his eyes.

"What?" Shade asked, breathless with anticipation.

"Mother," Alex said as his fingers curled into fists. "Get out of my head."

The air exploded with blue energy, sending Shade smashing through one of the windows and out into nothingness. She disappeared as the room began to fall apart around Alex, the floor and ceiling crumbling until there was nothing there but a haze of blue energy all around him. Just energy and a single word, his mother's voice, in his head and all around him.

Disappointment.

His eyes shot open as he gasped for air.

"Whoa," Mallory said. "Are you okay?"

Alex took a few deep breaths, looking around. No one seemed to have moved much since he'd last seen them. It was as if no time had passed at all.

"How long have I been standing here?" he asked.

"I don't know. Maybe a few minutes? I thought you were just focusing on getting the shield up. Is everything okay?"

"Yeah," Alex said. "Everything's fine."

He blinked a few times, trying to calm himself down, but every time he closed his eyes, he saw the skylines of different cities. Cloak operatives across the world, his mother had said. When he'd met her on the stage at the ground-breaking, he'd been afraid to really use his powers against her. But now he knew he couldn't be afraid. He had to do everything he could to stop Cloak. The world depended on him, and on his team.

"You guys," Bug said, his eyes shining. "They're coming."

VICTORY
PARK

The New Rangers emerged from the trees, all four of them walking with chins held high, the golden starbursts on their chests gleaming in the sunlight. Shade's eyes rested on her son for only a beat before scanning over the others. She gave no indication that they'd just had a lengthy conversation inside his head. For a second he wondered if he'd dreamed the whole thing.

They stopped just past the trees. Volt's fingers twitched at his sides, sparks of purple falling from them. Titan carried a metal case, his expression smug. Photon's face was blank, ready for his master's commands.

"We've got Omegas flanking us," Bug said. "Legion to the east and Novo to the west."

"We know our targets," Amp said quietly. "Stick to them, but keep an eye on your teammates."

"You know," Shade said, "we were going to let you enjoy your freedom a little while longer."

"We won't sit idly by while you plot to take over the world," Lone Star said, stepping forward and pointing a finger at them.

"Spoken like a true Ranger. I must say, Star, that I've missed your unique sense of bravado. Pity you don't look so well." She turned to Photon. "EMP."

The brainwashed Ranger closed his eyes and shot his arms out. Alex's earpiece powered down. Just as Gage had predicted, their electronics were wiped out by a single electromagnetic pulse.

"Well *that* didn't take long," Alex murmured.

"Electronics are out across the park," Photon said.

"Excellent," Shade said. "Titan, if you please."

Alex tensed up. Titan flipped up two levers on the case in his hand, and lifted the top open.

"Insulated against electromagnetic waves," Gage said. "That must be the Umbra Gun."

"I know what you're all thinking," Shade said, wagging a finger. "You'll just pry this gun out of my fingers and take it, right? First of all, Photon can keep it in my hands. But just in case . . ." She pointed to a silver cuff on one of her wrists. "There's a small microchip buried inside all this metal. The gun is rigged to become an Umbra Bomb should the need arise." She pulled out the weapon, holding it up for everyone to see. "But it'll also go off if the gun isn't within five feet of me at all times. You take it, and everything goes boom. All of us and half of Sterling City are in another plane of existence. Now, if anyone wants to go ahead and give up, it'll save everyone a lot of trouble. Honestly, I don't know why you've bothered with all this. Even if you succeeded in defeating us, the entire city would be against you."

"You don't get it," Lone Star said with a smile. "We're not here to beat you. We've already done that."

Shade said nothing, but one of her eyes twitched.

"You gave us a way to win," Alex said. "You told me yourself. Cloak had never intended to become Rangers."

"What—," Shade started.

"We have video and photo evidence connecting the Cloak Society and the New Rangers," Lone Star said. "You and Barrage out in public together. Volt and Phantom running errands."

"Titan in his Cloak uniform throwing a fire hydrant at me," Kirbie added.

"It's already mailed out to every government agency and media outlet in the state. And beyond."

"As we speak, *our* operatives are hand-delivering it to the CIA, FBI—even letters you've never heard of." Lux couldn't help but smirk.

That was mostly true. Their "operatives" were really just Carla in a rental car driving to the closest big city with copies of the footage they'd put together *and* what the commissioner had sent to her office.

"You're done," Lone Star said. "This whole sham is over. We didn't broadcast it because we figured it'd cause you to run. We're only here to make sure you don't slither away and come back in another ten years."

Confusion fell across all of the New Rangers' faces. Shade took a step forward, sneering.

"You're lying."

"Read our minds," Alex said. "It's over."

His mother was enraged. Then she laughed. "You may have changed our plans, but we are far from beaten," Shade spat. "We've made our way this far and by God, I won't stop fighting until this entire world is bowing before me. I am a third-generation member of the Cloak Society, and I will destroy this city before I give it back to the Rangers."

For a brief pause, her speech reminded Alex of one he'd given on the steps of Silver Bank. Then the sound of his mother's voice overwhelmed him. At first he thought she was screaming in his mind, but then realized that it was his ears that were being assaulted.

"I am a third-generation member of the Cloak Society, and I will destroy this city before I give it back to the Rangers."

He turned to see Amp standing behind him with his palms held up to the sky. Shade's voice boomed out of his body, echoing her speech through the park and out into the streets. Alex stared dumbly at the Junior Ranger, who smiled before letting loose the entire monologue again.

"I will destroy this city."

Anyone within a half mile would hear it.

Shade's body began to tremble with rage. She spoke only a few words.

"No quick exits."

Alex's father grinned. He raised one arm. A bolt of crackling purple electricity flew through the air so quickly that it was nothing but a flash to Alex as it passed by him. Misty had just enough time to gasp before the electric blast hit her, snaking over her body. She let out a strange, startled noise before falling backward, her curly red hair frizzed out around her.

"Misty!" Alex yelled out.

The Cloak Society charged.

In all his training, Alex had never been on the field with so many different people at once. It could easily devolve into chaos, but they had a plan. Kyle disappeared into the trees. Kirbie made a beeline toward Titan, in her wolf form, her teeth chomping at the air in anticipation of attack. Alex and Amp sprinted toward Shade. Lone Star carried Misty off the field while the others stayed back, ready to take on the Omegas.

Something huge and hulking came through the trees:

on top of a giant, spidery creation of twisted roots and branches and tree trunks almost two stories tall stood Kyle, who held thick clumps of vines in one hand like reins. His other hand was out, fingers spread wide as he muttered to himself, directing the giant plant creature. The behemoth moved with shocking speed, and that, coupled with the unexpected sight of a monster made up of parts of Victory Park itself, caught Volt and Titan by surprise. One thick arm reached out and wrapped Titan in its clutches, lifting him high into the air, while another slammed down onto Volt, roots growing over the man's body, pinning him to the ground.

Shade bared her teeth and her eyes flashed. Above her, Photon raised one arm and pointed straight ahead.

"I hope you don't mind," she said. "I've invited some old friends to help."

Out of the trees walked a dozen figures that Alex recognized immediately. Their silver bodies reflected the light of the sun and trees and grass around them. Their eyes stared forward, vacant. Alex could even name some of them. Storm Lad. Ms. Light. And Amp's parents—the Guardian and the Sentry.

Walking toward them were the *statues* of the old Rangers that lived permanently in Victory Park. Photon had breathed life into their metal forms. Through the trees behind Shade, Alex could see a few more of the figures stepping down from pedestals and platforms in the memorial sculpture garden and walking across the park to serve as Cloak's disposable soldiers.

"What?" Alex whispered.

"Don't look so surprised," Shade said. "You *did* arrest our Deputies. I look forward to interrogating each police officer personally once this is over to figure out who is and isn't on our side. The disloyal will be made an example of. You have yourselves to thank for that."

The statues charged forward, some carrying tree branches, others carrying weapons that had been sculpted into their hands. Alex concentrated on one of the forms, straining his thoughts as he lifted it off the ground. He swung the twisting figure back and forth, knocking others off the battlefield. There was a low electronic pulse as Shade fired the Umbra Gun, aimed at Kirbie. Alex caught the dark energy bolt just in time, deflecting it into one of the moving statues instead.

"Maybe I trained you a little *too* well with all those rubber bullets back home," Shade lamented as the statue melted into the Gloom.

Amp's metal parents charged straight toward him. A sonic blast bounced off his father. They were just like Titan, immune to his powers.

"Kyle, cover me!" the boy shouted.

The plant monster lurched forward, but Photon twisted

his hand and brought the statue of the Guardian flying up through the air. It tackled Kyle, sending both of them falling to the ground with a thud. Kirbie started after him in her wolf form, but Titan stopped her, batting at her with a thick piece of wood he'd pulled off Kyle's plant creation as he escaped its grasp.

"Bug Bomb!" Alex shouted over his shoulder.

Bug nodded, and out of the trees behind Shade came a swarm of insects, buzzing around her eyes, mouth, and ears. She yelled, but opening her mouth only gave the insects a new place to explore. She swatted at them desperately. Across the lawn, the statues started to move more slowly. It was an unexpected attack, but more importantly to Alex, it would keep his mother occupied without actually hurting her. At least not much.

Behind Alex, Lux and Lux's mirror image, Novo, were facing off against each other like two sparring twins.

The real Lux kicked high, slamming the sole of her boot into the Omega's nose—into a reflection of herself. The attack left an imprint on Novo's face, which quickly scrambled and re-formed.

"You must *really* hate looking at yourself," Novo said, jeering. "That almost hurt."

Novo's arm shot forward, wrapping around Lux's neck like a tentacle. The genuine Ranger choked.

"You know, I think I'm going to *enjoy* being you."

"Stop, Novo," Gage shouted as he caught up to the two of them. He stood in front of the Omega, a tree branch in his one good hand, lab coat billowing in the slight breeze. "Let her go."

"HA!" Novo laughed. "Oh, this is wonderful. The broken little inventor whose toys are all useless thanks to big, bad Photon. You're going to come at me with a stick, now, is that it?"

Gage rushed forward, branch reared back, letting out a battle cry. Novo tossed Lux aside and grabbed his unbroken arm, holding him up to her eye level.

"It'll take more than that to get rid of me," Novo seethed, her words a mixture of high and low voices all speaking at the same time. "I'm going to take my time with you. Shade may want your mind, but the rest of you can be as mangled as I want it to be."

"Do you really think I can't design something without EMP protection?" Gage asked. He smiled. *Fiat Lux.*

There was a whirring inside his goggles.

"What, is that some sort of Latin curse or—"

Twin lasers shot from the sides of Gage's goggles, searing holes into Novo's face. Novo let out a shriek, her image turning in on itself and regenerating, this time as her own face and not a copy of Lux's.

When she re-formed, she found Mallory, whose jaw was clenched and hands shaking, as if she was holding in an immense amount of energy. Then, as Novo's entire body shot toward her, she unleashed a supercharged subzero blast that flash-froze the Omega. Novo's body smoked like dry ice, her face distorted—an abstract sculpture with vaguely human elements.

"Beat the boss once," Mallory said, "and it's a lot easier the second time."

One frozen appendage still held Gage in the air.

"Cold," Gage said, his teeth chattering, "Very c-c-cold."

He shook his body, until the thin fingers around his bicep shattered and he fell. He let out a cry as his broken arm hit the ground.

"You okay?" Mallory asked.

"Fine," he said, though his voice was full of pain. "Go help the others."

She hesitated briefly before running farther up the battlefield to Alex. He had his arms outstretched, trying to direct one of the metal statues, but was sweating against Photon's powers.

"Protect Amp," he called to her as she approached. "I've got this."

He turned his attention to Volt—now free from the plant monster's clutches—and swung the metal statue at him, slowly enough that if it actually hit his father, it would just knock him down for a bit. Volt dodged and sent an arc of electricity flying through the air at his son, who raised a telekinetic shield just in time.

"Incoming!" Lone Star shouted from somewhere behind them.

Alex looked over his shoulder to find Legion tumbling in front of Bug, clones rolling out of him. Lone Star followed behind, swinging and kicking and brawling with copy after copy as they vanished one by one. But the Ranger looked as if he'd been beaten to a veritable pulp. Already one of his eyes was swelling shut and his bottom lip was busted and bleeding. Bug started forward to help him, but one of the Legions held out a strong arm, clotheslining the boy. The Omega was on top of him in an instant.

"Sorry, Bug boy, but this is it for you," Legion said. "We can't just let you keep spying on us with all your little flying friends."

Before Bug could respond, another Legion separated from the one holding him down. The copy moved so quickly that he was little more than a blur as he solidified, snatching Zip out of the air.

"NO!" Bug shouted.

Legion bared his teeth as the clone closed his fist around the dragonfly. When he opened his hand again, Zip fell to the ground, motionless.

Bug didn't say anything at first. He just shook, and his eyes began to glow an intense golden green. When he did finally speak, he had only a question.

"If a copy came out of you, you must be the *actual* Legion, right?"

There was a near-deafening buzz in the air, and suddenly Legion was covered in hornets. He tried to bat them off, but they were a seemingly endless cloud of eyes, wings, and stingers. Clones fell out of him but vanished as they hit the ground, all writhing in agony. He ran blindly into the brush, away from Bug and the battle.

Bug picked Zip up and stood silent for a moment. The insect's body curled in on itself. Her beautiful, fragile wings were crushed. Bug swallowed hard as he moved her to the foot of a tree, where he brushed some soil over his fallen companion, whispering a few words. Then, with a crown of hornets circling his head, he continued to fight.

A few yards away, the statue of the Sentry that was attacking Amp began to slow, and then smoke. It took a step forward, but in doing so its leg cracked and broke off.

"Go!" Mallory said from behind Amp. A few beads of sweat had crystallized around her hairline. "Stop Shade!"

"This is for my parents," he said.

A wave of ear-piercing sound shot out of his hands, all focused on Alex's mother, the woman who was now on her knees with the Umbra Gun in one hand as she swatted insects away with another. When the sound reached her, she shrieked, shaking her head.

All around the battlefield, the statues stopped moving.

Alex wrapped all the energy he could muster around Photon, who floated above Shade, looking as if he'd been stunned himself. With a wave of his hands, Alex ripped the Ranger from the sky, sending him flying across the lawn. He landed near Lone Star, bouncing twice before stopping. Lone Star and Gage were at his side almost immediately.

"He's unconscious," Gage shouted back to the others.

There was an explosion at the other end of the clearing, erupting from the entrance to the once-secret underground tunnel.

Barrage, Alex thought.

The metal drain fell on the ground not far from Alex, who picked it up with his thoughts instinctively and sent it flying toward Volt. It was within a few feet of hitting his father's head when Alex realized the repercussions of such an attack and changed its course. The drain dipped and turned, bouncing off his father's shoulder. As Volt staggered backward, falling to the ground, Alex watched smoke and dirt billow up out of the tunnel hole, followed by Barrage and Julie and a dozen armed Unibands.

Alex made it to the middle of the battlefield, where Lone Star, Lux, and Gage hovered over Photon. Barrage sent waves of explosive energy balls that smashed against Alex's telekinetic forces, creating a cloud of fire and debris. Alex planted his feet and peered through the dust. Kirbie was in her bird form, swooping down and picking up

Unibands, throwing them this way and that and into one another. Finally she picked Julie up by her hair and flung the girl into the trees, which closed in around her—Kyle was controlling them from somewhere.

"What's the story, Gage?" Alex asked.

"He's out of it," Gage said, nodding at Photon's still form. "I don't know. I've never exactly dealt with someone who's had their brain tampered with."

Alex glanced back at his mother, still pinned down by Amp and Bug. If she got to her feet again, he couldn't protect Photon *and* handle the Umbra Gun.

Lone Star slapped the side of Photon's face.

"Come on, old friend," he said. "You've gotta wake up."

"These Unibands," Lux said, "they don't have powers, right? Just weapons?"

"Laser pistols and Tasers and things, yes," Gage said.

Lux nodded. "Good. I've got some pent-up aggression I'd like to take out on them."

She left their side, sprinting toward the few Unibands Kirbie had left standing. She moved faster than Alex had expected, her palms smashing against noses and feet sending her opponents flying, even as she dodged all kinds of attacks.

Barrage let out a shout, clutching a shoulder where his coat was now scorched, smoking slightly. Mallory was hurling superheated energy at him, drawing his fire away.

"All right," Alex said. "I'll keep a shield up around you and—"

Something slammed into him, sending him tumbling to the ground. It was Bug, unconscious. Alex checked to make sure the boy was still breathing, and then looked up to see Titan grinning at him. Farther up the battlefield, the insect army around Shade's head dissipated.

"Crap," Alex muttered. Amp was now the only thing keeping Shade down. Alex had to keep Titan occupied.

He sprinted directly at the metal boy. To collide with him would no doubt break half the bones in Alex's body, but seconds before the two of them hit each other, he used his powers to give himself a boost. He jumped over the boy. Titan's feet dug deep grooves into the ground as he skidded to a stop.

"Gagh," Titan groaned. "Just stand still so I can snap you like a . . . stupid twig."

"That wouldn't be very smart of me, now would it?" Alex asked.

"You think you're so *clever*, don't you?"

"Well, you've always been the brawn, so that *does* make me the brains."

"Ha," Titan scoffed. "If you were half as smart as you think you are, you'd have checked your three o'clock."

Alex spun to his right just in time to see Julie flying toward him from the trees. He ducked and pushed her away with his thoughts, but she managed to drag her claws across his left shoulder. Before he could counterattack, Titan was on him, holding him up with one hand around his neck.

"Well?" Titan asked. "Where's all your smarts now?"

"Not just smarts," Alex half gagged through Titan's grip. "I've got *friends*, too."

Kirbie swooped low and pecked her oversized beak at the back of Titan's head. Alex used the moment of confusion to let loose a mighty telekinetic blast that sent Titan into the trees, splintering several trunks. But he was hardly fazed by this and started back after Alex almost immediately.

"Don't you ever get knocked out?" Alex asked. He raised Titan into the air, anger and fear pouring out of him as his thoughts tightened around his opponent. Beside him, Kirbie was in her wolf form, trading swipes with Julie.

"I will skin you and make you into a rug, little doggie," Julie spat.

Kirbie tackled her with a bone-rattling roar. The two toppled over each other. Farther back, Shade was crawling on the ground, hands clasped over her ears from Amp's continued assault. The Umbra Gun sat on the ground in front of her. Alex wondered briefly if he could somehow pry the bracelet off his mother's wrist, but Titan was struggling in the air, and he had to keep his energies concentrated on the metal boy.

"Barrage," Shade shouted, pain tingeing her voice. "Take out Amp."

Several crackling orbs of red energy shot forward from Barrage's palm, sailing straight for the Junior Ranger. There was only one way to stop Amp from taking a direct hit—one that he probably wouldn't survive. Alex hurled Titan forward to intercept the attack. Titan and the very air around him erupted into flames as Barrage's fireballs slammed into his son's body one after the other, each exploding with the force of a small bomb, pushing him out of Alex's grasp. Titan fell to the earth, thick black smoke trailing behind him.

Alex stopped and stared at the wall of dirt and debris where Amp had just been standing. The tree branches were now crackling with fire. He searched for movement. The whole battlefield seemed to pause. And then, something emerged.

At first Alex thought that it was one of Photon's statues, but there was no denying that it was Titan once he got a look at the rage on the boy's face. The entire upper half of his body had been burned away, leaving nothing but shiny metal. The flames reflected off his arms and torso as if they were dancing on his body. He dragged an unconscious Amp on the ground behind him. Alex wasn't sure if it had been the force of the explosions or Titan who'd knocked out the Junior Ranger.

"You . . . ," Titan growled at Alex with narrowed eyes.

Alex could just make out the hint of white teeth through Titan's sneering lips. It was impossible for him not to think of the grinning silver skull of Cloak, as if it had come to life and manifested on the battlefield before him. Titan tossed Amp to the side. Julie ran to her brother, her arms turning human and fleshy again.

"Titan," she said tentatively, reaching her hand out. When her fingers met the searing-hot metal of his arm, she yelped, pulling them back and to her mouth.

"Don't touch me," Titan muttered. His every movement seemed to be made through intense pain as he lumbered toward Alex.

Off to the side, Shade was regaining her composure. Her hands were shaky as she tapped at something on top of the Umbra Gun.

"Do you have *any* idea how much that hurt?" she asked, shaking her head. She turned her gaze to Alex. Her eyes went silver. Inside Alex's head, it felt like his brain was being torn apart. There was a high, piercing ringing that was penetrating his thoughts. He fell to his knees. "I'm betting you regret your decision to turn down my offer earlier."

He forced his mother out, pushing her thoughts away with a wave of telekinetic energy. Still, the attack had done its damage. He felt stunned, discombobulated, and looked around the battlefield for help. Kirbie was taking on Julie and Titan by herself. Mallory held off Barrage and a handful of Unibands beside Lux. Lone Star and Gage were dragging Photon toward the edge of the battlefield, out of harm's way. Everyone else was either knocked out or missing.

"A Taser," Gage was shouting. "Get me a Taser."

"I'm on it," Lux said. She charged one of the Unibands, weaving between laser blasts before finally catapulting herself feetfirst into the henchman's chest. Lux disarmed him of several weapons and gave him a swift kick in the side before returning to Lone Star and Gage.

"I didn't know which one for sure," she said, dropping the haul beside them.

Gage picked up one of the gun-like items and looked at Photon.

"Will this work?" Lone Star asked.

"What have we got to lose?"

An electric bolt shot into Photon's body, causing him to convulse on the ground for a moment. And then, nothing. The Ranger remained unconscious. Lux and Lone Star stared at him, waiting, but there was only his quiet breathing.

"Okay," Gage said. "We need to get him as far away from here as we can. If you two—"

Photon sat up, gasping for breath, causing the others to jump back in surprise. He patted at his body, as if he hadn't felt it in a very long time and needed to be sure that it was actually there.

"Photon!" Lone Star shouted. There was a hesitation in his voice. They couldn't be sure it was actually their teammate and not some Cloak puppet.

"Lone Star?" The man looked up at him, recognition dawning.

"Is it really you?" Lux whispered.

Photon looked around the battlefield, blinking. Finally his gaze landed on Shade, who was staggering toward Alex. Photon's eyes widened and his fists clenched together.

"We should get you out of here," Gage said. "We don't know how long—"

"No," Photon said. "I've seen everything that woman has done and I haven't been able to stop it. Until now."

With that, he shot up into the sky, hovering in the middle of the battlefield. He raised one hand, and all around him Uniband weapons floated into the air. With a flick of his wrist, they became nothing more than a mangled ball of scraps. Around the lawn, the Ranger statues began to move again, this time attacking the Unibands, holding them off the ground as they kicked and struggled.

"You!" Shade shouted, her eyes wide and bloodshot, her hair a tangled mess standing out in every direction thanks to Bug's previous attacks. "You're mine." Her eyes went silver, her limbs shaking.

"Not anymore," Photon said.

He twitched his fingers. The metal bracelet around

Shade's wrist shattered, and the Umbra Gun flew out of her hands and up to him. He gave it a quick once-over before a piece of the weapon detached itself and disintegrated. The bomb was disarmed.

From the ground, Barrage shouted in rage, sending a series of blasts at the Ranger. Photon dodged. As he did, the Umbra Gun turned in midair, and he used his powers to fire off a single round. The dark energy hit Barrage in the stomach, the icy black seeping over him.

"No," he grunted. "No, no, no!"

"Dad!" Julie shouted, running toward him, but Titan reached out and grabbed her arm, holding her up in the air. She tried to wriggle out of her brother's grasp as she shouted at him. "What are you—"

"It's not me, you idiot," Titan said, glaring at Photon, who had taken control of his metal body. Several of the nearby Ranger statues ran to the brother and sister. They wrapped their arms around the pair before becoming lifeless once again, forming a cage around the siblings.

"Wrangle up what's left of Cloak," Lone Star shouted. "We're taking them in."

Across the battlefield, Barrage melted into shadow and disappeared. Julie screamed.

From the trees, a stream of purple electricity shot up and zapped Photon. He cried out, plummeting toward the earth, then landed in a heap in front of Lone Star, the

Umbra Gun falling beside him. Mallory and Lux sprinted toward the direction of Volt's charge.

Alex turned to face his mother, but she was nowhere to be seen. Gone.

"Where's Shade?" Kirbie asked, running to his side. "Where'd she go?"

"This way," Alex shouted, already headed toward the trees. "We can't let her get away."

He got several yards before Kirbie's talons were on his shoulders, lifting him off the ground. They climbed into the sky. Together they would find his mother. Together they would keep her from escaping.

THE FATE OF STERLING
CITY

They soared over the trees and paths and lawns of Victory Park. The air dried out Alex's eyes as he tried to catch sight of his mother. She had to be somewhere near them. The tunnel underground was all but caved in after Barrage's explosion, and Photon certainly wasn't going to be flying her anywhere. They had to find her before she made it to a vehicle and had a chance to escape. This would be their only chance. If they didn't catch her now, Alex had no doubt that the next time he saw her she'd be putting some other plot into motion. It would be too late.

Kirbie began to dive, causing Alex's body to jerk back. Her avian eyes had spotted Shade, who ran toward the edge of the park, almost to the street. Alex focused on his mother as they drew closer, preparing to stop her dead in her tracks.

Shade must have sensed they were there. She turned and fired several shots from a laser pistol over her shoulder at them. Caught off guard, Kirbie swooped and twisted, making sure the shots missed Alex, but a stray bolt hit one of her wings and sent the two of them tumbling down side by side. Alex lost his telekinetic focus on Shade as his body was torn from Kirbie's grip, and he found himself falling very quickly to the ground below. He covered his head and pushed at the earth with his thoughts, landing with a relatively soft thud on the grass.

Kirbie alighted beside him, changing back to her human form.

"You all right?"

Alex nodded, already on his feet, moving in the direction they'd been flying. "We have to get her. If she disappears into the city, we'll never be able to find her."

They sprinted wordlessly through the park and out onto the street, where Shade began to fire at them once more.

"Now who's running, huh?" Kirbie shouted as they chased after her, weaving to avoid shots from her laser pistol. "There's nowhere for you to go."

Alex tried to wrap his thoughts around his mother's feet, but with the fall and her lasers and the slight ringing in his head from her previous psychic attack, he was having trouble focusing on the fast-moving woman. Instead he brought everything he could down around her. She leaped over streetlamps that he sent sweeping toward her, and dodged trash cans.

"Why, dear, it's like you're not even really *trying* to hit me," she shouted over her shoulder as she jumped on and then over a flying park bench.

They reached a grassy section of land, where Shade turned and stopped. Her eyes flashed, and Alex heard Kirbie make a strange noise behind him. He turned to see her frozen, though her eyes were wide.

"I can't move my—," she started, but something small and black exploded in the grass in front of her, causing her to fly through the air. She landed in the bushes clear on the other side of the street at an entrance to Victory Park.

"Kirbie!" Alex shouted.

"I'm okay," she yelled back, but as she tried to stand, she stumbled forward, one of her legs giving out.

"I swear that girl has nine lives," Shade said with contempt. "I wonder what number we're on now."

"You . . . ," Alex muttered, clenching his fists.

"Oh, come now, son. It was only a concussion grenade. The only weapon I had left. Perhaps I should just shut down her brain and—"

Alex shot his hands forward, hitting his mother with a bolt of telekinetic energy that sent her flying onto the steps of the building behind her. She let out a groan as she landed on the cement, and Alex pulled the laser pistol from her hand, tossing it far from her reach.

Shade let out a small, angry laugh.

"Of course we'd end up here."

For the first time, Alex realized where they were. Shade was getting to her feet on the steps of Silver Bank, where he'd failed to open a vault door weeks before and had then saved the life of a Junior Ranger. Where the unraveling of all the things he knew to be true and right began.

Alex felt a small tug at his thoughts. It was something that would have gone unnoticed to anyone who hadn't grown up with a telepath for a parent. He immediately let his powers flare up around his mind, imagining it in a powerful blue box of energy, one that his mother could never break through.

"Don't worry," Shade said. Her voice was tinged with defeat, but Alex wasn't about to let his guard down. "I honestly just wanted to know what you were thinking. Do you realize what's so amazing about that imaginary blue box you keep your secrets hidden away in?"

Alex stayed silent. He'd never really thought much about it. It was a simple use of his powers, something he'd done many times before. But he didn't know how it worked, really. Just that it *did*.

"That box doesn't exist," his mother said. "It's fueled by your powers, sure. But it's imaginary. You can't keep your brain locked up. There's no way to wrap your entire mind in telekinetic power without killing yourself. What keeps me out is your *belief* that I can't get in. That's all."

Alex glanced to the side. Kirbie was still struggling to stand.

"You know, your father was still fighting back there when I left. He could be *dead* now. Don't you care about that?"

"Of course I do," Alex said. "And if you were worried about him, why did you leave?"

"To survive," Shade answered immediately, her voice growing harsher. "To carry on our mission."

"Just turn yourself in, Mother. Please. I'm asking you as your son, not your enemy."

"So we're back to this stalemate?" she asked. "They can't keep me locked up. There's no place that can hold me. They'd never even *get* me to a facility if they had one. Their minds would be mine. I'm more powerful than any other person on this planet, Alex." She shook her head. "Except for you, right? So it's *your* choice. Are you going to end me here and now, or let me walk free across this earth? Because I guarantee if you do that, you have not seen the last of me. The Cloak Society lives on. It's in my blood. It's in *your* blood. We will lurk in the shadows until you have all but forgotten about us, and *that* is when we will strike. We have rebuilt ourselves before, and in Phantom's name I swear we will do it again."

Alex's mother glowed a brilliant blue in his vision. He held her there, a fragile body, as pure energy streamed out of his eyes. He lifted her, almost subconsciously, off the ground, until she floated a few feet in the air. She was right.

His thoughts tightened around her.

Shade winced, staring back at him. She smiled, then closed her eyes and tilted her head back, raising her face to the sun.

Alex let her go. She dropped to the stairs with a thud.

"You'd like that, wouldn't you?" Alex asked softly. "For me to kill you. To prove that I was the weapon you'd raised me to be. It'd be like some sort of final proof you were right. But I won't give you that satisfaction."

Shade let out a grunt, staring up at him with narrowed eyes. Her words dripped with pure spite. "So, what *are* you going to do, son?"

"Nothing," a baritone voice said.

Alex turned to find Lone Star behind him, the Umbra Gun in his hands. There was a deep electronic sound as he fired the weapon.

Shade's eyes went silver as she scrambled to her feet, but it was too late. The bolt of dark energy hit her in the chest and began to spread over her body. She reached out to Alex and managed to take a few steps toward him before the oily black seized her legs. As she stared at her son, her eyes faded back to normal. Human.

"For the glory," she said, her voice betraying the smallest

hint of a tremble as the darkness rose over the sides of her head, framing her face.

"Hail Cloak," Alex whispered instinctively, his eyes wide.

And then his mother was nothing but a silhouette that melted onto the ground and scattered into the dark corners of Silver Bank and the shrubs and his own shadow.

Alex didn't move. He felt as though he couldn't, as if some force was keeping him frozen in place. He stared at the spot where his mother had just been standing. There were only steps there now. They were the same steps he'd stood on during his first mission when he'd proudly proclaimed himself to be Alexander Knight, fourth-generation member of the Cloak Society—a moment that now seemed like it had happened long ago, or in some sort of waking dream.

His body shivered. It was an unexpected sensation, since he wasn't particularly cold. It was simply that he didn't know what else to do, couldn't even figure out how he was supposed to think. More than anything, he suddenly felt lost.

Lone Star stepped next to him. He stood beside Alex for what seemed like a long time before finally speaking.

"I'm sorry, Alex. If you have to hate someone for what just happened, you can hate *me*. But know that your mother's fate rests on my conscience, not yours."

Alex couldn't speak. He turned to look for Kirbie. She was standing with one foot twisted awkwardly to the side as she leaned on Misty, whose hair was wild and sticking out in every direction.

"Is everyone okay?" Alex asked. His voice was wobbly and parched. "My father?"

"For the most part, everyone's fine," Lone Star said. "A little battered and bruised. We have Volt. Barrage is in the Gloom. I think the Legion boy got away. Everyone else is captured. We lost Zip. Bug's pretty inconsolable right now, but Mallory and Kyle are with him."

Alex nodded. "What about Amp?"

"He's got a few bad burns, but he'll be fine." Lone Star reached a hand out to put on Alex's shoulder. "Lux and a few police officers are taking him to the hospital just in case. Gage went with them. I think his arm needs to be looked at again. What can I do for you?"

"I'm ready to go home," Alex said. It was the first thing that came to his mind.

"Of course," Lone Star said. "Where do you mean?"

Alex looked up at the man and exhaled a short laugh through his nose.

"I have no idea."

EPILOGUE
ONE MONTH LATER

Alex Knight stared at his father. Volt sat across from him, behind a thick layer of bulletproof glass. In the background was a small wooden bed and table piled high with books and journals. The room itself was covered in black rubber tiles. The man who could conduct and control electricity had been rendered powerless by a few materials from a hardware store.

Neither of the two spoke for what felt to Alex like a very long time. He couldn't get over how different his father looked with several weeks' worth of beard on his face. The whiskers made him look warmer somehow.

Finally Volt broke the silence.

"Has there been any word about your mother?" His voice was piped in through speakers hidden somewhere in the walls.

Alex hesitated at first, unsure whether this was something he was allowed to tell his father. But there was nothing, really, that Volt could do with the information, and deep down, Alex didn't want him having to wonder about his wife's fate.

"No," he said. "But we can get into the Gloom now that Gage and Photon have reverse engineered the Umbra Gun. We've been in contact with Amp's parents, so we've got eyes on the inside."

"You mean they're still alive in the Gloom after all these years?"

"Not *very* alive, from what I hear," Alex said. "They're scouring the Gloom looking for Mom. So far they haven't found any trace of her. Or Barrage. They've got Ghost locked away inside there somewhere, though. There's been talk of sending a team inside, but . . ."

His voice trailed off. Volt nodded.

"It would be dangerous. Not worth the risk."

"I'm sure she's all right," Alex said. He hoped this was true, despite everything that had happened. "She's not exactly someone who gives up."

"I have no doubt that she's plotting her way back into this world right now." Volt smiled to himself, looking at the floor. It was a sad look, one that Alex couldn't easily interpret. "The Gloom must be a nightmare for her. Old enemies as wardens. An entire world to rule, but no one to rule over. It's quite the prison."

Alex stared hard at his father. There was a question that had been lingering in the back of his mind for some time now, but it wasn't one that he knew how to ask. He wasn't even sure he really wanted to know the answer. His eyebrows drew together, crinkling his forehead. Volt took notice.

"What is it, son?"

"I just . . . Obviously Mother used her powers to control people and get her way. She told me that she did it to other Cloak members sometimes. Pushed them one way or the other. Is it possible her powers were influencing people around her even when she didn't know she was doing it?"

"Are you asking because you want a free pass for the first twelve years of your life?"

"No," Alex said, meeting his father's eyes. "I'm asking because I want to know if she was controlling you all this time."

Confusion flashed on Volt's face before being replaced by a small grin. His eyes looked almost proud.

"Son," Volt said slowly, "does it matter, really? What's done is done. The Cloak Society as it existed for generations is no more. Even if I *wanted* to blame my actions on your mother's powers, how could I do that knowing that you were able to break away from her influence? Not only hers—the influence of all of us. How weak would that make me look?"

Alex wasn't sure what to make of that answer.

"I'll let you know if we find her," he said. With that he rose from the uncomfortable metal chair he'd been sitting in and made his way to the door. Just before he reached it, Volt spoke again.

"When did she tell you that? About using her powers against the High Council sometimes."

"Not too long ago," Alex said. "I was sitting in the same room you're in now. Only I was cuffed to a metal chair."

Volt started to say something several times, then stopped. Finally he sighed.

"I hope that in the end, you find some of what we taught you to be worthwhile."

Alex was still, searching his father's face, trying to crack it. He knocked on the metal door twice. It slid open with a slight *whoosh*, and he left.

"Did you get the answers you were looking for?" Photon asked. His fingers flew over an electronic screen in his hands, though he was looking at Alex.

"I don't know," Alex said. "I think so."

They stood in the lowest level of what had once been the Cloak Society's secret underground base, home to the High Council's apartments, the formal dining room where Alex had taken countless meals, and a handful of maximum-security cells. Now the entire level was a prison, the base's brig. His father still lived there, but in a cell. Novo was held in a huge pressurized glass chamber in Phantom's former quarters.

The world was still trying to figure out how to react to the crimes of the Cloak Society. The footage Alex and his team put together and sent out had played over and over again on the news, which had helped people understand why the New Rangers suddenly disappeared, but had opened up an unending slew of questions. Until someone figured out what to do with the supervillains, they'd remain there, on the bottom floor of the place they had once called home. Photon served as their jailor and temporary overseer of the underground base. He'd taken Shade and Volt's old apartment as his own and cut off all unauthorized access to the bottom level.

"Gage's design for Volt's cell was genius in its simplicity. I believe he said he was inspired by a room the Omegas had designed for Amp."

"Yeah, except with acoustic tiles instead of rubber."

"He hasn't been any trouble." Photon nodded his head toward another door. "Not like those two."

Barrage's old apartment had been reinforced with titanium plating. Now it was home to his children, Julie and Titan, until other arrangements could be made.

"How are his injuries?" Alex asked, gesturing toward the door. "Last time I looked in, he was still a little . . . gross."

"Much better," Photon said. "Have a look for yourself if you like."

Alex lifted a hatch on the door and peered in through a rectangle of thick glass.

Titan sat on a couch, staring at a television. His skin was pale pink and smooth, and he had no eyebrows that Alex could see. The hair on his head grew unevenly in blond patches. When he noticed Alex, his face contorted. He was off the couch in an instant, hurtling toward him. When he got within a few yards of the door, he was jerked backward, tumbling over the couch and into the back wall.

"The magnetic field's holding," Alex said, looking at Photon.

"He won't be getting anywhere close to the door unless I allow him to."

When Alex turned back, Julie was standing in front of the small window. Her black hair was twisted out in several directions, her eyes and smile wild. She said nothing but dragged one clawed finger back and forth across the metal door. A screeching sound filled the air.

"That *noise*," Titan yelled from somewhere at the back of the room. "I'm so sick of that stupid noise."

"All right," Alex said, letting the hatch slam shut. "I'm ready to go back up."

"Back to your room, or to the first floor?" Photon asked as they stepped into the elevator.

"First floor. We're all meeting in Gage's workshop before we head out."

After the battle with the New Rangers, Alex and his fellow Cloak defects were left in a strange position. As members of Cloak, they'd always had the High Council to direct them. In the days after Justice Tower, their goals had been clear, even when they didn't know what action to take. Rescue the Rangers. Defeat Cloak. But no more. So while Lone Star, Lux, Bug, and the Junior Rangers moved into hotel rooms and regrouped, drawing up plans for a new headquarters, Alex, Mallory, Gage, and Misty went back to the underground base to help oversee everything that was happening in their former home.

City officials took in the Gammas. The remaining Unibands were arrested. Many of them claimed to have never been willing servants of Cloak—that Shade had turned them into mindless drones—but there was really no way to know for sure. Carla and her team in the city would be spending months just trying to figure out if it was even possible to put them all on trial—though they'd already begun proceedings against Misty's mother, who police had captured as she attempted to flee town. Between that and trying to help out all the people Cloak had detained or flat-out kidnapped during their short reign, her office was overwhelmed. The Tutor was the only person whose processing had been easy. As someone with the power to never forget a single thing he'd read, he made a deal to go on record with an oral history of the Cloak Society. In return, he was promised that the rest of his life, though lived under constant scrutiny, would be spent somewhere comfortable and full of books.

Alex found Gage and Mallory in the first-floor workshop. The inventor's arm was still in a cast, signed by all of his teammates from the battle in Victory Park. Misty had decorated the signatures. Alex's sparkled with blue marker. Small yellow flowers surrounded Kyle's. Lone Star's shimmered with gold glitter.

"Your painting's gone," Alex said, nodding to the blank wall above Gage's workstation.

"The Rembrandt?" Gage asked. "Technically it was my father's, but yes. They took it out this morning. Apparently it actually belonged to a museum in Boston. I think half the Tutor's library has already been claimed by various institutions and private collectors across the globe. We've accidentally created quite a stir in the art world."

"Apparently being stolen by Cloak made them even bigger collector's pieces," Mallory said. "People are so weird."

Alex looked around. "Do I need to go pull Misty away from the TV again?"

"That reminds me," Gage said. "We're not actually *paying* for that satellite feed right now. I should talk to Photon about getting us an account or something. I'm guessing it would be frowned upon if he found out we were stealing television."

"She's down there changing," Mallory said. "We went shopping with the Junior Rangers this afternoon while you were going through stuff in the War Room." She took a white box off one of Gage's workbenches and held it out to him. "Here. This is for you."

Alex looked a little confused but took the box and lifted the lid off with his thoughts. He dug through a few layers of tissue paper before pulling out a navy peacoat. On the right chest pocket was a small golden pin in the shape of a starburst.

"The Rangers had them made for us," Mallory explained. "We all got one." She pointed to a stool by Gage's workstation, where two more coats had been tossed.

Alex smiled and slipped it on. It fit perfectly.

"I don't suppose it's bulletproof or has protective plating in it like the trench coats do," he said.

"You can just *enjoy* the present, Alex." Mallory shook her head. "You don't have to go into battle wearing it."

"I can always see about reinforcing them later, if you like," Gage added.

Misty appeared beside Alex. She wore a dark sweater and jeans under her Ranger-supplied peacoat, with a giant purple-and-gray-plaid scarf tied around her neck. A shiny silver headband held her hair back. She looked up at Alex expectantly.

"You look really nice, Misty," he said.

She seemed to be satisfied by this answer, and only then

noticed that he had on his peacoat as well.

"Look!" she said, pointing at his gold starburst. "We're twinsies!"

"Oh, good. Everyone's here," Photon said as the doors to Gage's workshop slid open. "We should get going if we don't want to be late."

"It's a pity there are so many of us," Gage said, grabbing his new coat and tossing Mallory hers. "I'd like to ride in one of the Italian sports cars before they're taken away."

Photon raised an eyebrow.

"If you want, I can take you out in one tomorrow," he offered. "We can have a little joyride to take a break from cataloging the armory. I admit that I've been wanting to get behind the wheel of a few of these machines while they're still here."

"YES!" Gage blurted out immediately. He composed himself a bit before adding, "I mean, if we have the time."

"If all the cars are going, pretty soon Misty will be our only way of getting around again," Alex said as he followed the others into the garage, which connected to the surface through a long underground tunnel.

"I am *not* your taxi," Misty said. She let out an exaggerated sigh. "We're going to have to have a serious talk about misting privileges sometime soon."

Tremendous crowds milled about the arts district north of Victory Park. They stopped at pop-up shops and sipped hot cider. Music played from speakers dotting every block. Chatter filled the air. After pulling into a reserved parking spot, Photon left to find Lone Star, and Alex's group met up with Kirbie, Kyle, Amp, and Bug near the front of a stage. Everyone was wearing their new coats.

"They all fit!" Kirbie said.

"These are *amazing*," Misty said.

"They're great, right?" Kyle asked, looking down at the golden starburst over his heart.

"Definitely," Alex agreed. He pointed to the canvas tote bag Kirbie had over her shoulder. "What's in the bag?"

"It's in case I want to get some souvenirs or something," she said. "It's a *celebration*, Alex."

She nodded up to a banner at the top of the stage that read WINTER FEST.

"Didn't the city just have a street fair last month?" Mallory asked. "A *Fall* Festival?"

"Yeah," Kyle said, "But it turns out we kind of ruined it by showing up at the museum and picking a fight with Cloak."

"Oh yeah. I guess we did."

"Besides," Amp said, "everyone wants to celebrate the return of the *real* Rangers of Justice."

They chatted for a while. Gage bought the Junior Rangers popcorn as thanks for the coats, and Alex bought Misty popcorn because Gage hadn't. Finally the music stopped, and the crowd burst into applause as the police commissioner took the stage.

"Good evening," he said. "And welcome to Sterling City's first Winter Fest."

Everyone cheered.

"Now, I know I'm not the person all of you are here to see, but I want to take a moment to acknowledge something. You'll notice that many of the people you'd usually see standing up here with me are absent. It is the utmost priority of the city government to flush out all remaining officials with ties to the Cloak Society. Many of them simply disappeared following Cloak's defeat in Victory Park, but I assure you that those who remain will be discovered."

There was a smattering of applause across the crowd.

"But you can read about that later. Without further ado, I'd like to hand things over to our special guests."

The Rangers of Justice were an awe-inspiring sight as they climbed the side stairs onto the stage. A golden cape hung from Lone Star's shoulders. Light glinted in his eyes and glowed around his palms as he waved to the crowd. Behind him, Photon grinned. Lux's hair shone with an unnatural brightness, as if there was a strand of light for every hair on her head. Their powers were returning. Slowly, but returning nonetheless.

It took several minutes for the crowd's excitement to die down enough for Lone Star to speak.

"Thank you, Commissioner, and good evening, citizens of Sterling City and beyond." His voice was rich and low. "There are many changes in our future. Historians will look back at this period of time and judge us based on what we do or do not learn from the Cloak Society's rise and fall. The very question of *how* the Rangers of Justice fit into this city—even this world—needs to be examined, and subjected to some sort of regulation."

"You're our protectors! Our superheroes!" someone shouted from the crowd. Others joined in, until Lone Star was thumping on the end of the microphone, trying to calm everyone down.

"We have been called those things many times," Lone Star continued. "But it wasn't me, or Lux, or even Photon who you have to thank for Cloak's defeat." He raised his palm, and a light spread out from it, falling on Alex and the others. The people around them stepped away, forming a circle around them. "These eight heroes are the reason any of us are here today. Even when I thought all hope was lost, they persevered. Where there was nothing but darkness, they believed in the light."

Their golden pins shone. Alex was caught off guard by the sudden attention and tensed up. He'd never actually been in the spotlight before—had hardly ever been out in *public* without some ulterior motive. His eyes widened and mouth fell open a bit.

"Smile, Alex," Kirbie said, pushing his shoulder. "You look terrified."

The Junior Rangers all stood with perfect posture, their smiles wide and their chins up. Bug was beaming, but he looked down sheepishly. Gage was unfazed, and Misty grinned from ear to ear. She performed a small curtsy. Alex's eyes met Mallory's. The girl seemed hesitant, but after looking at each other for a moment, her lips curled up in a big smile.

"These are your true heroes," Lone Star said from the stage. "These are the people who rescued us. And every day that we live from now on, we owe in part to them. Ladies and gentlemen, I give you the future of Sterling City."

In the crowd, someone started clapping, and then suddenly there was a roar of applause, followed by shouts and cheers. Alex looked up at Lone Star, who grinned back at him, applauding along with everyone else. He felt his cheeks burn as he smiled, and the sound of the crowd washed over him.

After the speech, Alex and the others were swarmed with well-wishers and reporters. Everyone wanted to know their names, their powers, where they'd come from, and what they were going to do next. All of them were quite overwhelmed, and with Lone Star's blessing and a little help from Misty, they snuck away from the street festival and ended up on the steps of the Sterling City Library, catching their breath.

"I think I talked to more people tonight than in the rest of my life combined," Alex said.

"You really didn't do much talking." Amp had a joking grin. "It was more 'staring straight ahead and nodding.' We're really going to have to work on your public speaking skills."

"Some of us weren't trained to be TV-ready," Mallory said. "But you've probably got a point."

"We should get hair and makeup people!" Misty said.

"How's life underground going?" Kirbie asked. "It's weird not seeing you guys every waking moment."

"It's great to have my own room again." Mallory turned to Misty. "No offense."

"None taken," Misty said. "You snore."

"That's totally a lie."

"It's nice to be back in my workshop," Gage said.

"I have to admit, though, it's a little . . ." Mallory struggled for the right word.

"Boring?" Amp suggested.

"Yeah. I guess."

"All I wanted when we were trying to defeat Cloak was to be worry free," Alex said. "But now that I'm not fighting for my life half the time, I feel kind of lazy. Or at least like my powers are getting rusty."

"We should start training together again," Amp said. "We've barely scratched the surface of how we can work together."

"Too bad we've scared every wannabe villain out of town for now," Kirbie said. "I could use a good fight."

There was a moment of silence before Alex spoke again.

"Hey, Kyle. Have they made any progress trying to find Legion?"

Kyle shrugged.

"Not really. I mean, I hear the police have gotten a few tips and stuff, but they haven't really turned up anything." He paused for a beat, and his eyes grew a little wider. "But *I* could definitely look into it and see if anything stuck out to me."

"We should probably follow up on any leads the police checked out," Bug added. "In case we see something they missed."

"It's entirely possible they stumbled on some sort of Cloak safe house and didn't even realize it," Mallory said.

"But we know how Cloak operates," Alex said, standing up. "We can track Legion down. We've done it before and we can definitely do it again."

"And who knows what's coming next?" Amp jumped to his feet. "Cloak probably accidentally inspired a whole new generation of supervillains. I mean, you said Shade mentioned that Cloak had people across the country, right?

What if they band together? Even if they don't have super-powers, they'd still be a huge threat."

"Plus, there's still the Guild of Daggers in New York," Kirbie added with a grin.

"Tomorrow," Kyle said. "No, tonight. I'll start looking into it tonight."

"If you come to the underground base, I can help you hack into any of the files the police won't hand over to you," Gage suggested.

"Gage," Kyle said with a sigh, "that's definitely not at all legal."

"Yeah, but it'll get Legion," Misty said. "I mean, it's not going to hurt anyone if we look at a couple of things online, right?"

"We're going to have to have a really serious talk about superhero ethics," Amp said, shaking his head.

"We'll come over tomorrow," Kyle said, ignoring Amp. "I wish we had some sort of shuttle set up between the hotel and the underground base."

"I could look into the possibility of rerouting the trans-portation system that currently leads to the safe house through the Gloom—," Gage started.

"NO!" half of them shouted in unison.

"It was just a thought," Gage murmured with a smirk.

"We can just build a *new* base," Misty said. "With giant rooms and closets, and a swimming pool, and Kyle could have a big garden, and—"

"Whoa, whoa." Amp cut her off, glancing at his watch. "Let's talk closets and pools tomorrow. Lone Star and the others are probably wondering where we are. We should get back."

"Let's walk," Kyle said as he and the others got up.

"But it's *so far*," Misty said.

"It's like, five blocks at most," Mallory corrected her.

"Come on, Misty," Bug said. "I'll buy you a hot chocolate."

The girl let out an exaggerated sigh.

"Okay, fine."

They all started down the steps except for Kirbie, who grabbed Alex's coat sleeve and held him back.

"Do you have a second?" she asked.

"Of course," he said. "I've got nothing but time."

She reached into her tote bag and pulled out a small package wrapped in brown paper.

"Here." She handed the bundle over to him.

"What is it?"

"You could probably just *open* it and find out."

Alex stared at it, turning the package over in his hands. He took a few deep breaths, leaning on the meditation techniques Kirbie had taught him and the others on the lawn of the lake house. The blue tint faded from his vision. Whatever it was, he wanted to see it as clearly as possible.

Carefully he tore open the wrapping. Inside was a uniform top. It was dark gray, with the familiar texture of a fabric woven with protective ballistic fibers. He unfurled it, holding it out in front of him with his powers. There was a hood connected to the back collar. On the chest was a small white starburst with a gleaming golden sword on top of it, right over where his heart would be.

"I had our uniform guy make it when we had the coats done," Kirbie said. "It's just a prototype. I wanted to see what you thought before we made them for the rest of your team."

"*My* team?" Alex asks.

"Your Knights." She smoothed her blond hair back with one hand. "It's sort of based on an old Ranger uniform. Misty came up with 'Knights' back at the lake house. We can change it if you want. Any of it." She looked at him hopefully.

Alex took the uniform top in his hands. He stared at it, unsure of what to say.

"What are the Knights supposed to do?"

"Think of them as a special branch of the Rangers. The people who can do stuff behind the scenes while the Rangers of Justice are the public face. Like the kinds of things we were just talking about. Tracking down Legion."

"This is . . . ," Alex said, but he didn't have the words to explain how he was feeling, the drumming in his chest.

"I've talked with all the Rangers about it, and they're on board if you and the others are. Photon would technically oversee everything, but you'd be team leader."

"He does seem to get along really well with Gage and the others."

"The Rangers have sworn to protect Sterling City. That leaves a lot of places in need of heroes. Lone Star's specifically concerned about this Guild of Daggers in New York. What do you say? After we track down Legion, I say we start investigating who they are and what they're up to."

"We?" Alex asked. "So you're a Knight too? I figured you'd all go back to just being Junior Rangers."

"Are you kidding, Alex? After all this, of course I'm with you. We can operate out of the old Cloak compound, or the new Justice Tower—whatever you prefer," Kirbie said, getting excited. "Whatever feels right for a home base."

Home.

"We could do good in this world," Kirbie said. Her eyes dropped to the ground. "Besides, we make a good team."

Alex smiled at this. His eyes went down to the ground, too. His face suddenly felt hot.

"So? What do you say?"

Alex rubbed his fingers over the gold sword on the chest of the uniform top. He looked back up at Kirbie, who stared at him in anticipation.

"I say let's do it. This is perfect."

She grinned. "We've got bright superhero futures ahead of us."

"I hope so," Alex said. "But if the rest of this uniform is made up of tights and spandex shorts, I'm changing my mind."

He flashed her a smile. She laughed.

"You guys!" Misty shouted from halfway down the block. "What are you doing? Come on!"

"Your Knights," Kirbie said, gesturing toward the others. She jogged to join them.

Alex stood by himself for a moment. The blue tint faded into his vision again, the world crackling around him. In that moment there was such a well of energy in him he was afraid his powers might cause him to explode. He exhaled slowly and smiled, then started down the steps. His teammates were waiting.